Cha
Day One

Book 1 of the Rotting Souls Series
Timothy Ray

Also by Timothy Ray

The New Age Saga:
The Acquisition of Swords
Phoenix Rising
Coalescence
Wrath of the Phoenix

New Age Novels:
Nightstalkers: Origins

Rotting Souls:
Charon's Blight: Day One
Charon's Blight: Day Two
Charon's Debt
Charon's Coffers
Charon's Vengeance
Rotting Souls: the Complete Series

Slipstream:
Focal Point
Fifth Column
Faith's Embrace
Hardwired

Legacy:
Sanguis

Charon's Blight: Day One
A Ray Publishing Book/ May 2017

Published by
Ray Publishing
Tucson, AZ

All rights reserved
Copyright © 2017 by Timothy Ray

Cover art by James Price

Timothy Ray

for my wife
the first person that believed
my most avid supporter and fan
I love you

Timothy Ray

They say time is the fire in which we burn.
Right now, Captain, my time is running out.
We leave so many things unfinished in our lives.

> Dr. Soran
> Star Trek: Generations

Timothy Ray

Chapter 1
Unanswered Text

Linda
Sacramento, CA
9:05 a.m.
September 8th, 2021

Ben: It's a wipe

    She looked down at her phone in frustration. It was the second time in it had buzzed in the last thirty seconds and she was resisting the urge to open it lest the person who'd sent it be let on that she'd seen it. She had never wanted to be involved in her wife's Doomsday Cult and had forgotten that she was on their mass text list. She'd spent years humoring her wife's obsession with this end of the world crap and had only accepted the phone because it was one less bill they would have to pay. She had never intended to actually respond if they called, she had better things to do with her life; like have her toenails yanked out slowly with a pair of rusty pliers.
    She was a schoolteacher and considered herself grounded in reality, unlike those fools her wife palled around with. The world was not going to end until the sun cooled and went supernova. In other words, not for a very long time. Mankind might cease to exist by then, but the world would still be there; it could survive anything they threw at it. There had been five extinction level events that they knew of and still the planet continued rotating without the slightest hitch in its step.
    Finally, she gave in, knowing that her wife had received a similar text and would likely be messaging her next. She powered on her lock screen to view the message and cursed; they were having another one of their damned drills. That meant her wife would be

racing over to pick her up with the intent of dragging her out of town on another fruitless fantasy ride.

She couldn't let that happen.

Staring at the camera, her screen unlocked, and she opened up iMessage with a slight grunt of anger. Her fingers quickly typed out a message telling her wife that she was too busy and that if she wanted to go alone, she'd see her after the drill was done. Her patience was running thin and her workload was overwhelmingly oppressive this week. She had exams to grade and counseling sessions scheduled. There was no possible way that she could just drop everything and run off; it just wasn't happening.

She had humored them long enough. It was her fault for letting it go on this long and she shook her head with frustration, intending to put a stop to it once her wife got back from her road trip. She clicked the power button and made a mental decision that this was the line in the sand; she would go no further. She tossed it aside and forced herself to look away as even more arrived, annoyingly causing the phone to vibrate across the smooth corner of her desk.

Sitting back in her chair, she looked at the students bending over their desks, their pencils writing furiously. Her hair was up in a bun, her wire-framed glasses resting on the tip of her nose as her blue eyes swept the classroom around her. Her white blouse lifted a bit as the cooler blew cold air upon her chest, cooling the sweat that had formed along the edge of her under-wire. Her knee-length black skirt had ridden up one of her slender thighs and she pulled it absent-mindedly back into place.

Her peripheral vision alerted her that she was being watched and her eyes shifted in that direction. A young boy named Randy had stopped working on his test and had his eyes glued to her cleavage. It would have been flattering if she found that kind of attention attractive, instead of only adding to her frustration. The frown upon her face met his gaze and he blushed; looking away.

"Eyes on your test Mr. Rattigon," she told him firmly, and some of the other students looked up at the sound of her voice. She swept her gaze across the room and they each hurriedly went back to writing. She could tolerate a harmless crush, but she didn't have to encourage it. If it continued, it would have to be addressed with either the principal in attendance or the boy's parents. But for now, he was a teenager with raging hormones and his ill-conceived fantasies were easily dismissed.

Her phone was vibrating again, reminding her of the real reason her hackles were up. Grinding her teeth, she thought back over the long escalation of events that brought her to this particular breaking point and what might be the end of her marriage.

If she hadn't foolishly bought that damned World of Warcraft game for her wife's birthday, her relationship with her wife would be healthier. She sure as shit wouldn't have the tendrils of an oncoming migraine slithering through the back of her skull threatening to make the back-half of her day miserable with little chance of reprieve.

Jackie had always loved those types of games, having played Everquest for years before they had even met. She had found it cute at first, it was kind of sexy in a nerdy kind of way, but after years of being together she was forced to wonder if her wife would ever grow up.

Not that she hadn't contributed to the problem, even past the purchase date. No, her mistake had been in choosing to sit in a chair by her wife's side and watching her play. It had drawn her in against her will. Jackie had insisted that she get a copy, seeing that she had so much advice and suggestions in how to improve her gameplay; clearly interested in playing the game herself.

Reluctantly, she had given in, not realizing how involved she'd end up getting with it. Even though she stayed detached from most of the social aspects, it did provide her a nice distraction from the everyday struggles in her life. They had played on adjacent computer desks and she chose to see it as just another way they got to spend time together. However, it hadn't taken her long to realize the lack of intimacy involved, even with them sitting side by side for hours at a time. That was the part of their marriage that had been lacking recently and she mourned the time they'd lost playing that stupid game.

Their friends began to distance themselves with the long periods of silence that followed, and they had gone out less and less. That she had lost years of her life, her marriage, time that she could never get back to a damn video game, seriously damaged her feelings towards her wife. She still loved her, but their relationship had suffered; she could no longer fool herself into believing otherwise.

Even with Jackie sitting three feet from her, it had been a terribly lonely experience, despite the thousands of avatars surrounding her at any given time. While her wife made friends with those she raided with, she hadn't been able to feel that same connection. She wanted people she could go hang out with, drink at a bar with, not talk to over a microphone while staring at a cartoonish representation of her characters. Who got into shit like that?

Even after they had met those people at the compounds in Arizona, she hadn't felt like she truly belonged. She had spent most of the time grading tests and preparing to go back to work; refusing to get involved in any of their survival games; it was a dreadful waste of time. The only good thing that came of it was the intimate time with her wife in the car and the amount of reading she got caught up on during the days she'd spent alone in their room.

Her anger rose as her phone began vibrating once more. Randy glanced at her with a questioning look, but she kept her face passive; her mouth set. He quickly returned to his test before she could say anything, and she clicked the button on the phone to stop it from going off. She briefly considered just turning the fucking thing off; if for no other reason than to create a fabricated silence to help slow her thundering heart.

A scream echoed throughout the hallway outside her classroom and every head in the room jerked up in response; pencils dropping, like they were a bunch of antelope alerted to a nearby lion prowling the grasslands.

The horrible wail continued as she drove herself to her feet, intent on finding out exactly what was going on and put a stop to it. She strode around the front of the desk and headed for the classroom door. "All of you stay in your seats while I step outside. You have fifteen minutes," she told them, looking at the mounted clock for dramatic effect. She saw from their anxious looks that it was a waste of time; half of them had already risen to their feet and were preparing to follow her out the door. She sighed as she threw it open; shaking her head with disdain. Striding through it quickly, she slammed it behind her as if to illustrate to her students that they were to stay within.

Taking another deep breath to calm herself, she turned in the direction of the screaming teenager, the wail so long that it was a wonder she hadn't passed out from a lack of oxygen. The young girl was standing over the body of their custodian, her books scattered across the floor, her book bag open and its contents spilled across the floor. Her mouth was open full tilt and she let go of yet another agonizing wail loud enough that they probably heard her out on the basketball courts, her terror so complete that a fresh pool of urine had formed at the girl's feet.

Greg was an aging man that had worked for the school district for more than twenty years and had shockingly white hair that contrasted violently with his tattered and filthy olive overalls. A mop bucket lay on the floor, the mop lying askew and forgotten at the elderly janitor's side. He was struggling to breathe, his hands clawing at his throat in a desperate attempt to get air.

She needed no more encouragement to act as she darted forward, her students forgotten as they opened the door and peered out of the room behind her. Others opening as well, but none of that registered; the whole world had disappeared with the exception of that screaming girl and the dying man at her feet. Stepping swiftly over the mop, she grabbed the girl and slapped her hard across the face, rocking the girl's head back and to the side with the force of the strike. She'd get into shit for it later, but she'd deal with it then. It had worked as intended. The scream cut off immediately and the teenager hovered there stunned, mouth hanging open, a hand reaching up to rub her cheek where she'd been hit.

She risked a glance at her dying coworker and saw the frightened eyes peering back; time was slipping away, and his life was nearing its end.

Reaching out with her right hand, she tilted the girl's head up until their eyes met. "Call 911," she commanded, and the girl nodded, her fragile and shaking hands fumbling in her pockets for her cellphone.

She let go of her and dropped to her knees; trying to frantically think of what to do. She tenderly reached beneath his neck and lifted, tilting his head back with her other hand to clear his airway. He gave a short gasp, but that was the only reward his body gave in exchange for her effort. Had a lung collapsed? Was there something lodged in his throat? She didn't have a medical degree; she was a math teacher for fucks sakes. She had taken her mandatory CPR classes, but the recent ones had cautioned against the exchanging of bodily fluids with mouth to mouth contact. She had been told that the choice was hers;

that if she wasn't comfortable with the risks, she would not be held accountable for not doing it.

Still, she had to do something; she couldn't just sit there and watch him die.

Her hands moved to his chest to start compressions; she had to keep his heart pumping. She met resistance and realized that his hand had reached out to take hers. His grip was strong, and no matter how hard she tried to pull free, he wouldn't let go. His breathing had started to slow, and she felt a tear form, then run down her cheek and off her chin.

People were surrounding them now, talking in hushed tones, and none of them were helping her. They were keeping a respectful distance; leaving the two of them alone in the circle of onlookers, as if the man's fate had already been decided. It was both terrifying and isolating; making her solely responsible for the man's passing. "What the fuck are you people staring at? Someone go get the school nurse! Do something other than stand there for God's sake."

Tearing her gaze away, she looked down at the custodian once more and temporarily lost control of the fear she'd been barely holding in check. She slapped the dying man across his cheek as his eyes broke from hers. "Don't you even think about giving up. Just hold on, help is on the way."

She stole a look at the young girl she had asked to call 911 and was heartened to see her speaking rapidly with an operator, nodding in return. She glanced back down and noticed that most of the color had begun to fade from his slackening face. His body was beginning to shake as if realizing its end was near. His eyes were still looking in her direction, but they no longer saw her; he was gone. His grip finally loosened, and her tears flowed anew.

A sob wrenched from her chest as grief encompassed her entire being; her soul torn asunder by her inability to save his life. Overcome with misery, she lowered his hand to the floor and put her hands over her face. She had never seen anyone die before; never been there when the life had just gone out of someone. She had been to funerals, but the people lying in those coffins had been but empty shells that only vaguely resembled those that had passed. It had been easy to believe the person she knew was already gone and not lying there in the casket before her.

This was entirely different.

She had seen the fear, had felt it when his life had slipped away. Others were rushing forward now that it was over; as if spurned into action with her sobs. She hated them for leaving her there exposed and alone for so long. A set of hands gripped her shoulders, but she shook them off and sobbed harder.

The body lying before her spasmed violently and Greg's dead hand flopped onto her skirt, making her scream at the sudden contact. There was a foul stench in the air as his bodily fluids began to seep free and she could hear a raspy breath where there shouldn't have been one; as if the final death rasp was late arriving to the party.

"He's not dead!" one of the kids screamed, a cellphone in his hands, recording.

How disrespectful! her mind tried to respond, but she found herself utterly speechless. Her eyes had fallen on her dead coworker; fixated on the corpse jerking at her knees. Her hands had slid from her face and were beginning to reach for him when his head jerked; eyes fixing on her once more. They were the eyes of the dead and the irises moved with the change of lighting; focusing solely on her.

Her soul ripped from her as she screamed in terror.

Greg surged forward faster than she could react, cold hands gripping her as she vainly tried to pull away. The person that had been trying to help her up had disappeared and she was alone once more in the horror show that had become her life. She had fallen on her knees and her skirt was preventing her from bringing her legs around to push backward. The angle allowed the moaning man to draw her closer. Screams erupted around her as she tried to work her legs free, twisting her wrist in an attempt to break the grip he had on her. She hadn't made any progress and her body tilted in the opposite direction; towards the rabid man drooling below; his mouth opened wide as if anticipating a bite of a juicy ribeye.

Randy strove into view and kicked the custodian, trying to distract him long enough for her to break free. Greg ignored it and her eyes widened as his teeth surged forward with a sudden jerk of his head. Pain flared from her left breast as her blouse gave way under the pressure of the dead man's teeth. His mouth clamped down harder than anything she had ever felt in her life and her head filled with agony as she felt the skin begin to tear away. Her mind started to darken, wanting to pass out from the pain, but she fought against it. If she did that then she'd surely die; her death forever immortalized on YouTube.

She had to get away from him, he was actually eating her! She could feel the tug of flesh and the grinding of his teeth, as well as the sickening noise of his throat working with whatever he was chewing free.

His head jerked to the side and she felt her skin tear loose, his teeth working on chewing her flesh right before her eyes. There was a loud gulp and he surged forward once more. Her voice reached a higher octave as she lunged backwards away from the searching teeth, trying to draw anyone forward to help get this monster off of her.

The shocked throng of students had taken a few steps back in fear and indecision; not sure of what they were seeing or if it were even real. Randy, the only person that had acted since the old man's terrifying resurrection was rooted in place, apparently unable to move. No one moved to assist her as she fell backward onto the floor, knees popping and fresh pain screaming its way up her legs, as if it could compete with the searing pain in her chest. Greg was fast upon her, blood dripping from the corners of his mouth, his eyes wide with insatiable hunger. Bile escaped her throat as she saw a portion of her left nipple caught in one of his back molars.

"Somebody get this fucking thing off of me!" she screamed, but no one moved.

The horror of what was happening was apparent on their faces and they seemed paralyzed by it; almost like it was a nightmare and they were sure that at any second they would wake up. There was blood gushing from her chest wound and her head was beginning to feel lighter, her pounding heart slowing as it began to run out of fluid to pump. She could faintly hear the sounds of escaping feet and she was probably imagining the quick patter of approaching ones.

"**Help me!**" she screamed. Then there was pressure on her chest and fresh pain in her throat as her plea was suddenly cut off. She felt warm liquid stream from her neck and her breathing ceased; her airway blocked. Her lungs yanked inward, trying to draw in air, but to no avail. Blood filled her stomach. She felt the urge to throw it up, but it had nowhere to go. Her vision had begun to fade, and her body was starting to feel numb. She barely felt it as teeth clamped down on her neck and pulled at her, jerking her neck upward just as she had done to Greg only minutes before.

Something must have torn free because her neck suddenly dropped against the blood covered tiles. She laid there, her head turned away from the monster ripping her apart; searching for help. Randy's eyes met hers once more and then he bent over; throwing up on his shoes. He wiped a hand across his mouth, gave her one last frightened glance, then fled; abandoning her to her fate.

She could hear people yelling, pushing towards her, but she no longer cared. Someone tried pulling the custodian off of her, but it was too late; it was over. Her lungs were still trying to pull in air as she struggled to take one last breath, her body rocking upward with the strength of her inward pull. Her body was slowly shutting down, her mind not far behind; almost eager for oblivion and an escape from the pain it was suffering. Death was coming and she wondered where the white light was or the loving people who were supposed to guide her on.

It had all been bullshit!

There was nothing to go to, she was just going to wink out forever.

She wasn't ready yet!

Fear surged through her as her heart thudded one final time, giving up the fight.

What the hell? she thought as her life slipped away.

Then she was gone.

A friend and fellow teacher were suddenly there and had begun performing CPR. She had been right about the mouth to mouth, because as the man's lips clamped down on hers, she spasmed and tore them off, chewing them like a large piece of gum. Then she reached up for more; her own hunger driving her forward.

In the ensuing panic, no one went back into her classroom to look at the phone vibrating across her desk—no one cared. They had more pressing matters to attend to. The phone continued its trajectory across the flat surface, where it would eventually fall into a trashcan beside the long desk; forever forgotten. The screen lit up once more and a newer text flashed across the screen.

Ben: you need to get the fuck out of there right now!

Jackie: I'm on my way to pick you up

Jackie: This is serious. It's not a drill. I'm just around the corner. Be ready.

Ironically, she did go out to greet her wife when she got to the school; as she had sworn not to do. Their last embrace left Jackie lying on the ground, her insides steaming on the concrete below. The stunned woman's agony was choked off as her wife gave her one final kiss, tearing half her face off with a strong wrench of her neck. As Jackie lay there dying on the school's front steps, she watched in horror as Linda continued on without her, leaving her to die alone.

A flurry of screams had drawn Linda's attention. As she worked the torn piece of flesh into her mouth, she began to shamble towards a bus of screaming kids. They had been waiting on a driver to get them out of there and a few tried to bolt out the emergency exit when she stumbled up the steps. The horrid display of blood that covered her face almost looked like a smile; school was still in session and she had one final lesson to teach.

Chapter 2
TEOTWAWKI

Todd
Tucson, AZ

*"Thunder, thunder, **thunder**—"*

His finger automatically slid to the phone case on his belt and silenced the ringtone before it could finish. He grimaced as the theme song for the Thundercats continued through his mind unabated. It had been nostalgic at first but hearing the same tune every time someone sent a text message—it got annoying after a while. He generally switched tones every couple of weeks, or whenever he started getting bored with the chosen theme; nothing really survived intense repetition.

His wife had loved the Hunger Games whistle he had been using the week before, but he got hit more than once for assigning the Imperial March the time before that. While it was fun to let technology give these personal touches to his phone, he would probably end up going back to the single note generics before too much longer. On nights when his wife really got a bug up her ass, having He-Man yell, *"I have the **power**!"* twenty times an hour drove him insane.

His hand rested on his phone case and he marveled at the fact that a century before his ancestors would have had a Colt holstered there instead. Times had changed, though not always for the better. People had this incessant need to stay in touch that was steadily growing out of control. You walked down the street or sat in a restaurant and all you saw were people with phones in hand, too busy looking there instead of the people with or around them. They even loved to do it when grocery shopping and there had been multiple times someone smacked him on the ankle with their cart because they were too busy finding out what Sally was having for lunch, or watching cat videos, to pay attention to where the frack they were going.

Sadly, he was forced to admit, at least to himself, that he felt naked without it as well. He made a concerted effort not to look at it when on a date with his wife, or when crossing the street for that matter, but that incessant need to check in was constantly there. Did they have support groups for that kind of addiction? They seemed to have one for everything else.

His phone started to go off again and his finger quickly silenced it. Whoever it was would just have to wait until he got to the back room. It was probably his wife. She knew to be patient when it came to his responses; he could not check his phone while on the sales floor. If he got caught, the manager would have his ass in the office, and he'd be signing a write up slip within the hour.

He was not in the mood for that, it'd already been a trying morning. He had walked into a flood of bitching from the overnight manager and it had spread to the morning assistant as well. The last thing he needed to do was give them a reason to take their misplaced aggression out on him. There was a zero-tolerance policy regarding use of cell phones in sight of customers; something that was easily avoided by showing a modicum of self-control and restraint. His lunch was in forty-five minutes and she could talk all she wanted to then.

He had very little else to do on his unpaid lunch hour.

The night crew had made a mess of things and he didn't understand how that translated into his responsibility to fix. He wasn't in charge of the department, or of anyone for that matter. He was about as low on the totem pole you could get at Wal-Mart without cleaning toilets all day. So why was he getting all the grief? It was just another example of why he hated his job. When you did everything you were told, when you left clear instructions for those that followed after—

He sighed. He was one of the veteran workers and was being held responsible for the rookies they'd hired. He could have argued, held his ground, but to what end? He'd had a long night and his strength had felt sapped from the instant he rolled out of bed that morning. His wife had spent most of the early morning hours bitching about work and his wired mind had refused to shut down. He couldn't blame her—entirely. He was doing a turnaround and he just wasn't one of those people that could go home, fall into bed, and be out before his head hit the pillow. He needed time to wind down before turning in. Even then, it'd be more drifting than actual sleep.

Stretching his back, he twisted from side to side as he worked the stiff muscles in his back and arms. They were resistant, refusing to loosen up. He gave his neck a good twist and heard a loud pop at the base of his skull. It felt good, but he knew that would only be brief as pressure was already starting to rebuild there. The irony was, the second he got off work his body would wake up and all that energy he wished he had while working would spring into being as if purposely held in reserve. He'd have too much of a headache to do anything with it. He'd end up in his recliner trying to watch a movie while the kids argued over game systems and who ate who's food. The headache would start to evolve into a migraine; he'd eat a pitiful attempt at a meal, maybe read a little, then try to turn in. His wife would come home shortly after and wake him up to talk about her night; the cycle repeating all over again.

God I'm getting old.

His phone went off again. Anger began to rise at the insistence of the person texting him. His wife and kids knew better than to bother him at work. He usually texted them on his breaks and they generally held most of their needs until then. They needed this paycheck and couldn't jeopardize it with idle chat. If it was a request for a gallon of milk and not an emergency, he was going to be royally pissed off.

Yes, he was forgetful, but he hated the constant reminders his wife was prone to giving. It made him feel like a child, or worse— senile. Besides, she knew the best time to send a text like that was close to punch out time, not midway through his morning.

He looked to the left as he passed the meat counter, yellow discount labels catching his eye. The steaks were marked down fifty percent as their due dates approached; he'd have to snag a couple and hide it in the cooler before someone else came along and snatched them up. He reached for a good-size package and his phone went off, yet again.

Attention was being drawn his way as customers gave him looks with raised eyebrows like they didn't have phones themselves and it was such an affront for him to own one. He growled and rushed to the double doors that led to the back room. He felt the gush of wind as they closed and couldn't help but grimace at the amount of freight waiting for him; eagerly taunting him with their presence. The docks were packed with pallets of overstock, items that the overnight crew claimed wouldn't go out, but experience told him half of it still would.

It was going to be a long morning.

He paused long enough to pull his green shirt down in the back where he felt exposed skin. The belt had been cinched tight, but the rush to get to the back had freed his work shirt and he hastily started poking it back in. His tan slacks didn't have much in the way of ventilation, a trickle of sweat tingled as it slowly slid down his inner thigh. His fingers ran absent-mindedly through his short brown hair, then settled on his goatee as he tried to remember why he had come back there. The sight of the mess beyond had stunned his mind into submission and despair.

The ringtone started playing again, snapping him back to reality like a shot in the gut. "All right!" he growled with annoyance, releasing the catch holding his phone in place and sliding it free. He hit the power button and looked at the messages littering his unlock screen.

His heart stopped.

Ben: It's a wipe
Ben: are you getting this?
Ben: dammit Todd check your fucking phone
Ben: IT'S A WIPE

It was a trigger. Even though he had trained for this he didn't move; frozen by indecision. He had never thought it would ever happen. All that training had been an exercise, not something he ever thought he'd actually use. He knew he needed to go, seconds mattered, but his muscles wouldn't respond to his commands.

His mind was warring with itself. *It had to be a drill. It's not possible. Ben wouldn't send it otherwise, right? There'd be a drill warning listed as to not cause a panic?*

The phrase "it's a wipe" harkened back to his World of Warcraft days. He had spent eight long years playing that online game and all-consuming was not an appropriate description of how much it swallowed up of his life. He joked with people now and then, claiming he was a recovering WoW addict and they laughed like they understood; they didn't. That urge to go back was always there, like something pulling at the back of his brain, refusing to let go. The second he gave in, the instant he double-clicked on that icon, he would be gone. He had worked hard at moving on with his life and that was not a game you could do with moderation. Once you were back in, your entire life revolved around it to the detriment of everything else.

He had been a hard-core raider; a member of a group that spent almost every night trying to kill virtual bosses for gear upgrades and achievements, and most importantly—bragging rights. Game progression had been a driving force in his life for a long time, and as former guild master of Déjà vu, he was usually the one that led their raids. "That's a wipe" was a term he used to signal that the fight was lost, that everyone was going to just stand there and die. When you had three hours to work on something, you didn't waste time on attempts that just weren't going to work. It was best to just let your character die and start over.

To hear that code phrase outside of the game sent a shiver of horror down his spine. It now held a very real and terrifying meaning for him. It was a signal from one of his group members that indicated that an apocalyptic event had begun.

TEOTWAWKI. "The end of the world as we know it" in Prepper speak.

His heart was thundering in his chest so hard that he was sure that his body was moving in tune with it. His breathing was coming in short gasps; the increased oxygen flooding his already numb brain. It felt like someone had injected him with a syringe of terror and he nearly lost his bladder.

Forgotten were the steaks and the scolding he'd received that morning. Gone were the angry words that had been forming in response to the persistent texts. His whole existence had winked out the instant he read those three simple words—it's a wipe.

Fear crept up on him and his hands were tingling. The gooseflesh had risen on his arms and there was a cold chill snaking down his spine. It **had** to be a drill. There had been nothing out of the ordinary on the radio earlier that morning and he had checked the news on the CenturyLink homepage before leaving. If the world had been ending, there would have been something other than Bieber's prison stint leading the news, right?

He let out a pent-up breath and cast his eyes to the side, trying to recall if there had been anything he had missed. Had Korea or Iran launched Nukes?

No way they were that stupid, he thought, shaking his head.

He was unable to focus his mind, the panic settling in, driving him rapidly towards chaos. The numbness spreading across his mind was paralyzing him from the neck down. Indecision flooded his thought processes. If he acted on this and it turned out to be a drill—he'd most certainly lose his job. He had been sick recently and racked up enough call-ins that another miss would mean immediate dismissal. That would make coming up with rent the following month impossible, and his family would end up on the street.

This just can't be happening.

His phone went off again.

Ben: This is not a drill. It's a wipe. Auth: 4HorseMenAE. You need to get moving RIGHT NOW.

"Fuck me," he groaned as his fingers typed K and hit send.

It caught the attention of the man that was stepping out of the meat cooler. Jeremy had paused with his hand upon the door and appeared to be awaiting an explanation, but Todd was at a loss for words. Jeremy was taller than he was, over six-feet, thin, wearing a white coat and nodding his head in a *"What's up?"* fashion; trying to coax something out of him.

He opened his mouth to respond, but when nothing came, slowly shut it again. What would he even say? He didn't know himself what was going on. There had been no details following the authentication code and he could offer nothing more than *"we need to get the fuck out of here"*. He didn't know the guy well enough for anything to be taken on faith. Jeremy wouldn't put his own job at risk just because he was told the sky was falling. He would need evidence—maybe the fucking meteor itself.

He also couldn't afford to make a scene, it would just hinder his chances to get out quickly; that was not something he could allow. He had a wife and four kids; they were depending on him to move fast, to be ready when they got there. He had to be free to leave the instant the van pulled into the parking lot. They needed to be on the road before anyone even noticed that they were gone.

As cold as that was, his family came first. There had been numerous arguments over the years about what to do when this moment came, their humanity causing a multitude of reasons why they had to do more than just run. He had told his wife repeatedly that they couldn't save everyone; that playing hero would get them all killed. But now that it was happening, he couldn't help but wonder, did that mean that he shouldn't try? What kind of person did that make him if he didn't?

It was too early to be facing these kinds of moral questions. He didn't have a clue what was going on, whether anyone was actually in any danger. Why start something over nothing? That's how he rationalized it as he waved off Jeremy's questioning look and shook his head. He turned quickly and strode back through the double doors.

"Dude? You sure everything's all right?" Jeremy asked, holding one of the doors open to holler at him as he walked away.

He twisted to look at his co-worker and winked. "It's the end of the world as we know it," he sang with a grim smile.

Jeremy laughed, "yeah, okay." The man chuckled, then ducked out of sight.

See? his mind insisted. He was making the right choice. Jeremy hadn't even considered that he might be telling the truth and he really didn't have the time to convince his co-worker otherwise.

Thoughts racing, he marched towards the break room and the office beyond. His phone was gripped tightly in his right hand, but he was mentally unable to look at it. It had told him what he needed to know and now it was time to act. The authentication code made this real and now he had to trust in his preparation and training to get them through this. For better or worse, he was now fully committed.

He nearly walked into a customer that had stepped in his way. She had a sales ad in her hands and was looking at the bacon section. *Screw the ad, better stock up on that bacon while you can,* he nearly blurted out. He swallowed to keep from actually saying it, biting his lower lip hard enough to sting. She hadn't excused herself and was actually giving him the dirty look, like he was in the wrong. It was just too much, and he quickened his pace, nearly jogging down the back aisle. His legs were aching to sprint, but he fought it. Once he began to run, he might not stop; the panic was that close to taking over.

"Do you ad match the Safeway brand?" the customer asked, but he ignored her as he ducked around the corner and into the break room.

He poked his head into the office and told the flustered assistant manager that there was a family emergency and that he had to go. He had his phone up and was waving it as he talked, no longer caring if they knew he'd been using it. Tyler swiveled in his chair, face flushed, preparing a heated response, but Todd didn't wait to hear it. If things really were going to hell then nothing mattered anymore, especially his future at Wal-Mart.

He briskly walked across the break room, sure that Tyler might actually get off his lazy ass and chase him down. He threw the door open violently, knocking a stack of empty milk crates askew that had been stacked up behind it. He didn't notice nor care. He ripped his badge off his neck and looked at the time clock.

"Fuck it," he muttered and threw his badge in the nearby trash can. He didn't get paid again for ten days and something in his gut told him the world didn't have that long.

As if to illustrate the point, his phone went off again.

Monica: OMW. Sam too

He and his wife lived an unorthodox lifestyle that got a lot of heat from people who just couldn't understand, nor approve. Being poly was not the social norm, and therefore taboo. Neither he or his wife gave a shit what other people thought, and they were both happier for it. She was telling him that she and his other wife Samantha were both on the move. That would give him very little time until Monica got there to pick him up. She must have gotten the kids from school and the gear ready in record time; now he was the one lagging. He looked at the clock on his phone and noted when she texted him. He had fifteen minutes to get everything they needed before he had to be out front and ready for pick up.

His free hand went to his box cutter; it was nowhere near an effective weapon. For a few seconds, he regretted working at the Neighborhood Market rather than a Super Center; regardless of how much quieter it was. At least the Super Center had a sporting goods section. This place was nothing more than a glorified grocery store. He had a couple of sharpies and a few pieces of candy for his sugar level; nothing of any real worth. His mind tried to think of what he could get that would make a difference on the road ahead. They did sell kitchen utensils—

He ran for the front doors and grabbed a shopping cart. Rushing back into the store, he cut a glance to the right to see how long the lines were at the registers and gave an audible sigh of relief. For now, the aisle was empty. It was a school day, and this was a slow period for them. The early birds had come and gone, the senior citizens hadn't yet begun their afternoon arrival. He wanted to be out of there before the first Van Tran bus arrived, or he'd have to leave without buying anything for the road.

Time was a rabid St. Bernard and it chased him down the aisles, nipping at his heels, trying to sink its teeth into his ass. He had to stay ahead of it; his life depended on it.

Chapter 3
Stash or Dash

Casey
Ft. Worth, TX

He had been on the move since the first text had come in. He had changed his clothes quickly, put on his survival gear, and grabbed his Bug Out Bag from the closet. After retrieving the box of shells from the top shelf, he had taken the rifle from its stand and promptly loaded his weapon. He slung it over his shoulder and grabbed his axe as he headed for the front door, but ended up pausing in the doorway, wondering if he had time to grab a few more things before leaving. Seconds counted in these situations and he wasn't sure if he had time.

"Fuck it," he grunted and ran back after his stash. He had a feeling his supplier would be out of business—well, forever.

"Come out to the coast, we'll get together, have a few laughs," he said in his best Bruce Willis voice as he grabbed a bag of pot from the cookie jar and put it in his pack. He also grabbed the empty jar of peanut butter down from atop the fridge and pulled free his money roll. He didn't know what the hell he'd need but it was better to have it and not need it than—

His internal clock was vibrating through his bones, warning him that time was slipping away. He grabbed a bottle of Jack and took a quick swig, then poured it all over the couch. Making sure that he had his bong and the rest of his drugs, he lit himself a cigarette and inhaled a long deep drag.

"Well Ben, if you're wrong, I'm totally fucked," he confessed, pausing briefly to reflect on the wisdom of what he was about to do; he was putting a lot of trust that the young boy was right and not fucking with him. He was going to be leaving the state and he had no idea for how long; most of his shit would probably be gone when he got back anyways—fucking looters.

"Aw fuck it," he muttered as he tossed his burning cigarette into the pool of alcohol. His couch went up in flames as darted out the front door. When he got to his car, he turned to look at the golden glow of his living room, both excited and full of regret at the same time. His trailer had plenty of fuel to keep it going til the entire thing burnt down; they were built that way.

"I'll kick your ass if this is a drill boy," he muttered, looking at the authentication code that flashed on his screen. He remembered an episode of the Walking Dead that he'd seen awhile back and flipped the inferno off just as Daryl had, a smile stretching across his face.

He threw the door open on his hatchback and turned the engine over.

Click.

"Fuck!" He pounded on the steering wheel then tried it again. It refused to turn over. "What the fuck?" he raged. Then he saw that it was in gear. "Goddammit," he swore and put it back in park, having forgotten that the parking brake had been acting up and he had been leaving it in gear to keep it in place.

He turned the key again and the engine roared to life. Hitting the gas, he left the burning house behind and fled down the dirt road towards the highway.

The kid was sending him updates as he drove, but he only spared it a few short glances; he got the gist. *Get the fuck out? I'm trying!*

The car was flying towards the main road as fast as he could manage. He silently congratulated himself on living on the outskirts of the city. According to the image on his phone, Dallas was heavily infected, and he needed to put as much distance as he could between it and him. He stamped on the accelerator, the hatchback bouncing with the increased speed and whining as he shifted quickly to a higher gear.

He had been high and full of shit when he had suggested that they prepare for this; there was no way he could have been right—no way. This had to be a prank. Even though he thought it, he didn't for a second believe it. His heart was pumping, and his hands were trembling; his fingertips tapping the steering wheel to a rapid beat as he struggled to calm down. He tried to brush his long brown hair out of his face and failed miserably. Full of shit or not; he was getting the fuck out of Dodge. He was nervous as hell and needed something to calm his nerves, but there was no way he was going to pull over now; it would have to wait.

He thought of his ex-girlfriend, but it was only a passing thought. She had bailed on him to move to the city and there was no hope of getting in there to get her out. That was her loss. They hadn't parted on good terms and Nikki wanted bigger and better things. Well, she got her wish, for all the good it would do her. She wanted to leave? Well, fuck her.

He hit the brakes as he came to the main road, dust kicking up behind him as the hatchback skidded and lifted off its left wheels. It plopped back down on the asphalt with a jolt as he hit the gas once more. Turning the steering wheel as quickly as possible, he pointed the nose of his hatchback west and prayed it hadn't begun to spread before him as well. If his luck held, he would be totally screwed; you couldn't make lemonade if life kept giving you spoiled lemons.

According to Ben the I-30 was clear and as of a few minutes ago, the 20 was as well. If things went well, he'd be the hell out of here before it got this far. Abilene was said to be clear, but traffic from Albuquerque worried him; it was a hub for connecting flights and anyone that'd flown in from Dallas was probably there ripping people apart even now.

Yet he knew that he had a long drive ahead, and there was no way he'd avoid it all; it'd cross his path eventually. The skin-tight rubber suit he wore chafed at his balls and he adjusted it as he drove. His right hand slid to the passenger seat and he stroked his bong absent-mindedly. Maybe he could make time?

"Fuck, I forgot the Fun Yuns!" he cursed, banging his hand on the wheel.

A car flung itself into his lane and it took both hands yanking his steering wheel to the right in order to swerve out of the way in time. He heard a scrape along the side of his car as it bucked violently from the impact.

The fucker had nearly run him off the road!

He slammed on his brakes out of habit and looked in his rear-view mirror at the crazy motorist that nearly taken his life. The jerk-off wasn't even stopping. Then it hit him, he wasn't going to either. "Asshole!" he yelled, extending his arm out the window and flipping the guy off. His heart was in his throat, he felt ready to puke; this was getting out of hand way too fast, especially considering how far he was from the contagion pushing him west.

"Fuck, fuck, fuck," he swore, pounding his hand on the steering wheel once more, the right side of his palm aching with the repeated violence inflicted upon it.

His phone was going off, but he was too shook-up to look at it.

He inhaled slowly, but nothing was helping. His nerves were lit up and the increased blood flow was making him light-headed.

The damned thing went off again; pissing him off even further. He nearly picked it up and threw it out the window. Man, he needed to take a hit off his bong before he drove his car off the road; he'd have a heart attack for sure if he kept up this pace. His nerves were shot from his close call, he was resisting the urge to check his text message, but the boy's insistence was proving to be a distraction he did not need right now. Admitting defeat, he finally chanced a glance at his flashing cell; his breath catching as his eyes scanned his lock screen and the messages that had been waiting for him.

Ben: pull off

Ben: goddammit Casey! Pull off!

Ben: HEY STONER CHECK YOUR PHONE AND PULL THE FUCK OFF!

He had just gotten on the I-30 and he saw a sign for Linkcrest ahead. Swearing, he pulled into the breakdown lane, his car idling as he came to a stop. Ben had said pull off. Did he mean the interstate or just off to the side? Why the hell hadn't he been more specific? This wasn't the time for half-assed instructions.

He looked in his rear-view mirror and didn't see shit; what the hell was Ben so worked up about? Then a glint of light caught his eye and he saw the flashing lights of emergency vehicles. They were approaching at high speed on both sides of the highway and his hands began to shake. He gripped the steering wheel tightly and tried to control himself, but the absolute terror that racked his body was overloading all his senses, urging him to hit the gas and flee.

More than ever he needed to take a hit, but those brilliant flashing lights instantly made him wary of that. He looked at the off ramp ahead and threw the car into drive. The approaching vehicles were going way too fast to trust they wouldn't to hit him as well. There was sporadic traffic on the highway, all looking to get over as far as they could, the guard rails impeding their efforts. He was the only one that appeared to be smart enough to pull off the interstate entirely.

He flew down the off ramp, drove through the red light, rolled to a stop at the top of the onramp, put it in neutral and yanked his parking brake into place. His eyes widened as the emergency vehicles swarmed past, some of them scraping the cars parked on the sides of the highway behind him. A squad car hit at a bad angle, twisted, and flipped into the air. It flew forty feet before finally coming to a rest just yards from where he would have been had he not stopped. It was hardly hanging onto its front passenger tire, the grill was being eaten by its engine, the roof was crumpled, and there was a splatter of blood on the spidered windshield from where someone had just cracked their skull open.

The other vehicles didn't stop, they just kept going; oblivious or uncaring that one of their comrades had just entered the afterlife. His hands were trembling even more as he realized that if he had stayed up there, there would have been no way he could have avoided getting crushed by the flying squad car, and that wouldn't have been all she wrote; whoever the fuck "she" was.

"Holy shit brother, you just saved my ass," he said softly as his eyes looked at the carnage to his left, the black and white Crown Vic erupting into flames like a stunt car in a Fast and the Furious movie.

Ben: bout fuckin time you listen asshole
Ben: You're clear for now, get going

"Yeah, fuck you too buddy," he said with a chuckle, hands shaking. If he ever made it to Arizona, he'd have to give that boy a huge wet kiss and a slap on the ass.

Shifting into first, he floored the accelerator and pounced back onto the freeway before the other cars could pull in front of him. This was already going to be a hell of a long day and he needed to make up some time. Thoughts of Albuquerque still lingered in the recesses of his mind, but after the shit he had just seen, it was far removed as his immediate concern.

Fuck, why hadn't he moved closer? Not like his podcast couldn't have been made in New Mexico—or hell, even the compound. Surely Rodger and his family wouldn't have minded a little extra company. But even as he thought it, he knew that it was a useless question, as he already knew the answer.

It all boiled down to just how much he had believed his own bullshit.

Even though he had spoken of it with a strong conviction, he had never really thought it'd happen. Who the hell would believe something out of a Romero film would actually walk the Earth? That shit was so fake. Zombies could never exist. It just couldn't happen.

No matter how hard he tried, he couldn't wrap his mind around any of it. Had something actually escaped from a lab like he'd initially theorized, or would it all turn out to be a hoax and all of this was over nothing? If that ended up being the case, he'd really feel like an ass; not to mention homeless as his shit was currently going up in flames.

"Fuck me."

Traffic was starting to increase, and he fought the urge to drive faster. That would only increase the chances of getting in an accident and he'd had enough of that already. The vehicles around him moved erratically as other drivers frantically tried to get some distance on Dallas and he wondered if they or him would ever make it out in time?

The word must have started to spread, and he did his best to stay ahead of the pack, lest he get caught up in a traffic jam and left staring out his windshield as the world tried to eat him alive.

Shit, how hadn't he got out ahead of this? He was far enough out! He turned on the radio and was stunned to find music blaring over his speakers. He had expected a warning from the authorities, news reports from the DJ's, something other than Alice in Chains. He sighed and turned it down; he'd wait to see if anything aired after the song was over; they couldn't be oblivious to what was going on. Obviously, the cops were upset over something!

Man in the Box was thundering softly from his speakers and he could relate as he sighed and stared at the road ahead; traffic had him boxed in pretty tight at the moment.

His phone beeped at him and a map had begun to download on his screen. Dallas had spread to Ft. Worth and he shook his head in shock. Damn, it was moving fast; which didn't mesh with what he was seeing. People were acting fucking crazy, but he hadn't seen any sign of an outbreak. It could have easily been a fire or other emergency driving the ambulances and squad cars west, right? There were no other signs that the world was ending and no broadcast indicating an outbreak of any kind. Where were the frantic newscasters, the breaks in scheduled programming? He was flipping stations as he drove, and realized he wasn't even hearing advertisements; just music. It was almost like the radio stations were on autopilot.

Someone had to know something! They couldn't just leave him in the dark like this!

His cell went off again, but he didn't need to look at it this time. Having kept his eyes peeled for more emergency vehicles, he had quickly noticed the National Guard caravan coming up hard on his ass. He didn't have an off ramp to race down this time so he got as close to the guard rail as he could and braced himself against the steering wheel. The wind from the passing trucks caused the car to rock and he almost threw up from motion sickness. He was surprised to find himself still in one piece as the last Humvee swept past. He'd been damn lucky they hadn't hit him.

Still, it had been close, way too close.

One of the soldiers gave him a passing glance and the fear in the man's eyes was enough to bring it home—this **was** happening.

"Fuck!" he cursed as he pulled back onto the interstate and continued on. It was the only thing he could do to keep from going insane. *What the fuck is going on?*

"School's out for summer!" Alice Cooper sang.

"No shit," he muttered, gunning the hatchback even harder as he headed west as fast as his piece of shit car could take him.

Chapter 4
Left Behind

Todd
Tucson, AZ

He considered buying more canned goods but there were already some in their Bug Out Bags, and the place they were heading was well stocked in the off chance something might actually happen. He didn't need to focus on any of the heavy stuff either; that had been taken care of. Instead he made sure to grab a four-pack of butcher knives and a rolling pin, though he couldn't imagine what he'd hit with it. It was just the sturdiest thing outside of a mop handle they had in the store. He then rushed over to the chemical aisle to load up on disinfectant and towels.

Finally, after grabbing various types of medications, he made his way back towards the grocery part of the store. Since most of their basic supplies were taken care of, he focused more on the novelty stuff; the things they might never have again. He snatched three party size bags of Cheetos for his wife and snatched the full case of David Sunflower Seeds from the bottom shelf of the nut section. Looking to his right, he stared at the beef jerky. Unable to help himself, he grabbed three of every kind and then pushed his already heaving cart to the soda aisle. Stocking up on Coke and Crush, he put the last bottle on the top and held it in place as he made his way towards the registers.

He found an empty line and began to unload before the cashier had time to sign in and start ringing him up. He got some worried glances from his co-workers, who saw how frenzied his unloading was and he mentally tried to slow himself down. Attention was not something he wanted right now. They were used to his briskness, but not the panicked *"run for your life!"* attitude he was displaying. He tended to be social and friendly with the cashiers and they were taking notice of the passive aggressiveness that greeted the questioning looks they sent in his direction.

After the last item was on the conveyer belt, he rushed the cart to the turn style that held the loaded bags and immediately began emptying them back into the cart. Nicole was his cashier and she'd been a conscious choice on his part, as she was the best bet for getting out of there quickly. Unlike some of the others, she was quiet and didn't like to talk up her customers while ringing them up. If he had gotten Cisco or Nikki, he'd be there all morning.

While he linked his fingers in the bags and hefted them into his cart, he tossed a quick glance her way and saw the honest eyes and friendly smirk. He felt her innocence and kind soul, and that's when it truly hit him; he was leaving her here to die. He was standing there bagging his groceries like it was any other day, about to rush out of work because a friend of his told him the world was ending, and he was doing so without warning a single soul about what was going on in the world. The inner conflict rose swiftly to the surface as he struggled to keep his Humanity at bay.

Would it really matter if he tried? Did he take a chance and try to warn her? He looked into those dark eyes again as his hands flew back and forth loading his groceries and tried to make a decision; to decide if silence was less costly to his soul. Playing out the conversation in his mind, he couldn't organize his thoughts into anything sensible that would make a difference if he did choose to speak up.

Hey, you need to get out of here, the world is ending! I belong to a group of Doomsday Preppers, and the day that we have trained and prepared for is actually here.

And **how** is the world ending?

I don't know. I just know that it is, and you need to go! You have to believe me!

Why must I do that? I don't know you outside of work and have no reason to listen to any thing you say.

Look, this nerdy teenage hacker says that it's happening, so it must be! He wouldn't lie about something like this.

Oh, in that case, by all means. Let's go. Before we do though, **where** exactly is this world ending event taking place?

Who the fuck cares? All that matters, is that you get the fuck out of here.

He sighed heavily and kept his mouth shut.

In all the scenarios that played through his mind, she remained at that register. Nothing short of taking her by force would get her to go with him and he wasn't about to do that. The obvious consequence for such an action would get his ass thrown in jail as the world around him went to shit. Not only was his family relying on him to get them to safety, he would be signing off on his own execution as well.

No matter what he told them, no matter how convincing he could be, in the end none of them would believe him. He knew how it sounded out loud, he'd rehearsed it plenty of times, and had also seen the looks on people's faces when he explained what he was doing on his yearly vacation trips. Nothing would be accomplished other than wasting his only chance to get out of there quickly by trying to be a hero. His family didn't need him to be the savior of others, just theirs'.

They came first. Above all else he needed to get them to safety. Everything else was secondary.

He worked on clearing his mind, doing his best not to dwell and move on. He tried to keep his face passive; nodding here and there with the flow of the short conversation. She hit the total button and he slid his card, not even bothering with his discount. That got a raised eyebrow and he realized that if he had wanted to maintain a sense of normalcy, he probably should have taken the time to do it. Anything else would draw attention.

"I left it at home," he told her weakly, hoping she didn't see the card sticking out of the right side of his open wallet.

He did his best not to look at the total, the jerky alone would have skyrocketed the price. He had enough money to cover it, their rent was in there waiting on a pending check, and he doubted he'd be back anytime soon to worry about the eviction process when it bounced. If this all turned into nothing, he'd contact Sean and ask to stay at the compounds for a while until they got a new place to live. They could hire movers to retrieve their things long before the locks got changed.

However, he knew that was just a pipe dream. Ben had never been wrong before and while there was a first time for everything, something in his soul told him that this was not one of those times.

Once the receipt began printing, he thanked her and rushed towards the entrance, ignoring the waving of the receipt he was leaving behind. He got stuck behind an old lady who was pushing her cart slower than a tortoise on ice and did his level-best not to make a snarky remark about it. He forcibly restrained an overwhelming urge to shove her out of the way and push past, he didn't have far to go, and it really wasn't worth making a scene over.

As she moved to go towards the exit, he rushed past her and went through the entrance doors instead. "Excuse me," he muttered as he rushed past a couple walking in. They stared daggers at his uncaring back, silently pissed that he'd gone out the wrong side.

Oh fucking well.

He was focusing so much on the ground that his heart stopped when the cart impacted a set of legs that had rushed into view; stopping him in his tracks. His daughter Michelle was standing there looking at him expectantly and his hands let go of the cart handle, letting her take it swiftly from his grasp.

When she was younger, he had been thankful she had her mother's good looks. Not so much now that she was the dating age. She had also inherited her mother's pale skin, which appeared burnt rather than tanned in the summer. Her short brown hair had been closely cropped in a style like her mother's, and with his wife's youthful looks, they often passed as sisters rather than mother and daughter. She was wearing a tight black rubber suit, which must have looked conspicuous to those approaching the store, even with the regular clothing she wore over it. She was already sweating, the added insulation a nightmare in the Arizona heat. Luckily, it was overcast, and the wind was starting to kick up. The suit ran from neck to ankles and was form fitting. It was also thick to prevent teeth from tearing the skin and tight to prevent anything from getting a grip on the wearer. It looked like a diving suit; which had to look odd in the middle of the Sonoran Desert, but he didn't care how ridiculous it looked as long as it got the job done.

He glared at the passersby that eyed her suspiciously, and they moved on; stealing glances over their shoulders as they entered the store.

Her seventeen-year-old hands ripped the cart from him and flung it towards his two sons, who were standing in front of the cargo door of their white Ford Windstar. The minivan wasn't stylish, but when you had six people to transport it more than got the job done. No one was cramped in a small ass back seat and he didn't have to listen to bellyaching over who touched who and how tight things were.

His oldest son was fourteen and tall for his age, his short dirty blonde hair was glaringly bright even in the muted sunlight. Nicholas's acne had sprouted with a vengeance and he was evidently trying to grow a moustache like his father. It wasn't working out too well. The younger son Caleb was trying to help his older brother unload, but Nick was taking the majority of the bags himself and pushing his brother out of the way.

Caleb was also blond, with his father's hazel eyes and a pair of glasses sitting on his nose. He was the only one other than his mother that needed them; the others grateful for his genes keeping them from being bullied at school. Caleb was also the only one with fear visibly evident upon on his face. The others were working hard to remain passive as they worked, but his eyes kept darting around nervously, his lips sticking out from his clenched jaw.

He wanted to tell his son to just get in the van and let Nicholas finish with the loading, but he knew how sensitive Caleb was and he'd take it as a slight. He didn't want to push him over the edge. *Avoid a scene,* he repeated in his mind; a mantra to keep him focused. The two boys were also wearing their black rubber suits and he briefly considered rushing to the bathroom to change into his. Judging by the looks they were getting by the passing customers; he didn't want to chance it.

Skye was doing her best to throw the grocery bags over the rear seat and on top of their stowed gear. She was trying to squeeze as much as she could back there but was running out of room. She was the youngest of the group, only nine years old, and had a more balanced mixture of both parents in her appearance. She had light brown hair, blue eyes, and her mother's face. She was rail thin like her mother and he had hoped that she would put on weight as she grew up. As she loaded the bags on top of the gear they'd brought, he began to wonder if she'd get that chance or if the end was looming closer than he realized.

Would they all perish while loading these damn groceries?

The cart was finally shoved away, the Wal-Mart bags packed to the roof of the back hatch; the last of which were thrown on the floor and nudged under the seats. Thirty-five minutes had passed, and it already felt like he was running out of time; that the overcast clouds would soon darken, and hellfire would begin to fall upon them all. His eyes cast towards the sky, as if expecting one of the Four Horsemen to suddenly appear with a scythe in hand to end their lives.

He was giving himself the willies.

Checking both sides of the road, he headed around the front of the van and towards the opening driver door. His phone went off again; a reminder that they needed to get moving.

Ben: I-19 n 10 clear atm

He looked up from his phone just in time to catch a bundle hurdling his way. His wife hadn't noticed what he was doing when she launched his suit into the air, and he almost dropped the phone while catching it. Cursing, he wondered why the hell she always felt the need to throw things at him? It was one of her favorite past-times. What was he going to do, change into the suit out here in the parking lot? They were getting enough attention as it was without him getting butt ass naked to boot. That would surely turn some heads.

He was of average weight, having spent a lot of time working out in the past couple of years, but he was nothing special to look at. There were bundles of protective pads lying on the floorboards of the van, not yet fastened over their suits. Once that happened, there would be no more curious glances; they'd become hardened worried stares. In this day and age of paranoia, it would definitely result in a call to the authorities.

"You didn't forget anything, did you?" he asked his wife as they passed each other in front of the van; barely touching hands as they did so.

"Put a call in to both our parents. Nothing so far," she responded, sounding worried. It was early yet, and she hadn't gone into full-blown panic mode. He wanted to be well on their way if that time came or they'd never get out of town. She loved her mother and sister so much that she'd risk it all to physically go to their houses and drag them along. If he let her get that far in her thinking, he'd never be able to convince her to keep going and would be constantly badgered to turn around.

No, if they were going to do this, they were going to do it full throttle and do what they could for the others along the way.

"Sam going to meet us over on Houghton?" he asked, trying not to worry before he had to. Sam had four kids with her other husband, and he could just imagine how hard it was to get them all moving; they weren't as well trained as his kids on how to respond when something like this happened.

"That's what she said," Monica returned, getting a couple of snickers from the kids in the back.

He didn't need to fish his keys out of his pockets; his wife had left the engine running. His hand had been digging in his pocket of its own volition and he jerked it back into his control. He opened the driver side door to the van and felt a rush of cold air from the maxed-out air-conditioning. That was to be expected from what the rest of his family was wearing, but his slacks were pretty thin, and he knew that it'd be a cold trip until he got his own suit on.

He watched his wife hop in and tried for a second to forget everything that was happening. Her short blond hair was cut in a style reminiscent of Gillian Anderson's in X-Files, which seemed quite fitting considering the current circumstances. Her suit was tight around her slender body, accentuating her features; especially the ass that he loved so much. She didn't look like she had ever given birth to four children. The fact that the first was cesarean dictated that the rest were as well; making it so her hips had never gone through that part of the process. It was something that he knew his wife was thankful for. Her youthful looks had garnered him more than a few jealous stares over the years; just reminding him of what he had and wanted to keep. She hadn't put the protective pads on either and her one-hundred-pound frame moved fluidly as she worked to get settled. Her seatbelt clicked and she glanced at him expectantly, obviously wondering why he was just standing there.

He jumped into the seat and rolled down the window as the cargo door slammed shut; the kids beginning to settle down in their accustomed places. His eyes scanned the skies. Was there some alien craft up there bearing down on them? Was there a nuke heading their way? If there were, he wouldn't see it through that cloud cover until it was too late. He chuckled and drew curious stares from his family. He doubted his eyes would catch something flying that fast even if the skies were clear.

He was frustrated; not knowing the nature of the danger was making it impossible for him to come up with a sufficient defense.

What if someone had launched a missile at Tucson? They'd be targeting either Davis-Monthan or Raytheon, both in their path out of town. Should he go north through Phoenix instead? Ben had said that I-10 was clear, but not which direction to head.

The indecision was paralyzing, and he didn't hear what his wife had been saying. "What?"

She sighed and glared at him; she hated repeating herself almost as much as he did. He looked in the rear-view mirror and saw that his children were all ready to go. He felt five pairs of eyes bore into him; wondering what was taking him so long to get moving. Someone had pulled up behind them, honking for him to move out of the way, an older woman giving them a hateful stare as she waited at the curb to unload her groceries.

It was past time to go, yet still he lingered. How could he explain to them that this was the moment where he left his previous life behind for whatever came next? The second the van moved there was no going back. He could still fix things with his boss, could still return the groceries he bought. Once they were on the road though, that was it. It was a heavy thing for him; he was the kind of person that hated change. He needed routine to make it from day to day. How did he just break from that mold and start anew?

A horn honked again, and he spared one last look at the two double doors of his work, then shifted into drive and pulled away. As he coasted around the corner into the side parking lot, his wife told him that she had texted Naima and Saint while she was pumping gas. He barely heard her over the yammering of his warring mind.

Unconsciously choosing to avoid the rubber necking at the front of the store, he swung around the back and headed for the parking lot exit and the street ahead. A flicker of movement caught his eye and his foot immediately applied the brake before his conscious mind realized what it was doing. A coworker of his was walking along the back of the store pulling a pallet-jack of RPCs; the black containers produce came in. He had nearly run him down; so mixed up in his own thoughts that he hadn't truly been paying attention. He needed to snap out of it.

Erik had begun to wave at him but had stopped mid-way; eyes narrowing. His face must have alerted his coworker that something was up. They had been hired on the same day, shared a locker for three years; and had spent their breaks smoking and bullshitting. How could he not say something? How could he just drive away? His own hand came up in a half-hearted wave; the smile he cracked feeling fake and weak. It did nothing to dissuade his friend that everything was all right.

The inner struggle continued as they rolled past, an insane idea of jumping out and forcing Erik into the van coming to the foreground of his thoughts. His foot was almost on the brake when he looked once more into his rear-view mirror and saw the four faces watching him. He sighed and put his foot back on the gas; no matter what happened his kids came first. He had to wake the fuck up and get on the ball if he was going to get them out of this; they needed him. He took another long look at his friend as he coasted to a stop at the edge of the parking lot. He mentally told Erik and his former life goodbye, then floored it and whipped onto Valencia.

He heard the sound of a clock ticking in his mind. His heart leapt to life, starting to pump adrenaline through his veins and clearing some of the numbness away. For better or worse, they were on their way. His wife was still talking to him and he hadn't heard a thing she'd said. He picked up on the name Naima though and he replied without thinking, "you know she's just going to ignore your texts," he told her, holding out his phone. "She never really liked you, try mine. I shouldn't be using it while driving anyways."

He had been friends with Naima since the eighth grade and twenty-four years later she had grown into being his best friend and Godmother to his children. The fact that she was his first girlfriend hadn't put her on easy terms with his wife, who had also gone to school with her and shared the same classes. The two talked occasionally, but the conversations were forced, and his wife did it more for his peace of mind than any actual need for it.

He hadn't spoken to her much over the last few years, as he had grown increasingly involved with his "cult", as she liked to call it. He had tried to explain that they weren't religious in any way, that they were just a group of people trying to create a safe place for their families to go in case the world came to an end. What was so crazy about that? Well, when he said it out loud like that—he could see why she was not so hot on it.

That didn't change the fact that after two decades she should have been more understanding and less judgmental. She used the term Doomsday Prepper; and although there was no other term to accurately describe what he had been doing, he hated it. It carried a lot of negative imagery and made what he was doing seem insane. He had watched that TV show and some of those people were just off their rockers.

Out of the corner of his eye he watched his wife send a text from his phone. He knew that Naima would probably ignore those as well. She wouldn't take them seriously. Not for the first time in his life; he wished that she would just listen to him for once. He was a Scorpio and she was a Libra; they were born to always disagree.

He gunned his way through traffic, the slow pace eating at his nerves. He wanted to get around all the slow asses and be on his way, but he refrained from doing anything overly drastic. The cops loved to patrol this part of the road. Getting pulled over, wearing what they were, their weapons visible at their sides, would cause a tremendous headache that he didn't want.

His left hand tentatively felt for his rifle, which was leaning between the seat and the door behind him. The corners of his lips tried to edge into a smile. At least he finally had something other than a dull butcher knife; which hadn't even been unpackaged yet and was probably lying buried in the back somewhere.

He eased his foot off the gas as the light turned red at Mission; forcing his way into the left lane. There would only be a few lights left before he got to the onramp to the interstate and he wasn't about to get caught in the middle; or worse, forced to go over to the other side. Making a U-turn in this traffic would suck.

His text notification went off again and he spared a glance at his wife; wondering if his best friend had actually answered for once. That would be a surprise. He couldn't make out what the screen said but he heard a quick gasp of breath in response to what she was reading. Her hand had begun to tremble. He reached out and grabbed it, squeezing it for support, trying to let her know that they were int his together, no matter what it said.

They were still stopped at the red light. He wanted to tear his phone from her and find out what had shaken her up so badly; it was a hard-fought battle and he needed to exude calm and patience for the sake of his children. "What did it say?" he managed; physically resisting the urge to act on his impulses.

Slowly she held the phone up so he could see the screen; unable to put to words what she had read.

Ben: GRIMES

Then his message screen closed, and an app began to load. It was something that Ben had designed for all their phones; an interactive map that could be manipulated and updated as they drove. It was to help them navigate the roadways on their way to the compounds; keeping them informed of obstacles in their path.

A map of the United States was loading, the pixels starting to fill-in with constant waves. He hit the brakes as he almost rear-ended a guy. He hadn't realized he had taken his foot off the pedal and the van had edged forward. His eyes jerked back to the phone and he felt despair start to flower within his heart. Arizona looked clear but there were red dots forming across the eastern and western seaboards. The mid-west had sporadic ones as well.

Crap, this was for real.

"He said Grimes," Monica whispered softly; not believing it even as she spoke. The fear in her eyes stirred the terror within. A chill ran up his spine and gooseflesh rose upon the length of his arms. She turned the phone around and looked down at the map through her glasses, eyes studying it feverishly.

"I know. It has to be a mistake," he replied, turning his gaze back to the road. The cars were beginning to pull forward as the light turned green. He inched the van along; eager to get moving. They had to get the hell out of Tucson before that shit got here as well. The thought of being trapped motivated him to chance a few close quick passes as he weaved his way through traffic.

"Grimes?" Nicholas asked from the backseat. "Really?" He almost sounded excited and he had to fight the momentary urge to reach around and slap his son. This was not a fucking game and was not to be taken lightly.

They had code-words that they had all memorized as part of their preparations and each one denoted a different type of crisis. If it said Tower, then they knew there had been a terrorist attack. If it said Mushrooms; the threat was nuclear. Algae denoted something biological. It was a long list, as Man had come up with plenty of ways to kill himself. Grimes had been his own contribution and had seemed the least likely to actually happen. There were twenty in all and each had been chosen because they weren't really used in everyday conversations; to keep the members of his group from acting without cause.

The inappropriate excitement his oldest son must have spread to the younger one and he had to work even harder to control his temper as Caleb blurted, "zombies? Cool!"

Gripping the steering wheel firmly, his knuckles turning white, he had to bite the inner side of his cheek to keep from losing it. He drove through the intersection and made the long left-turn onto the onramp for I-19.

"Cool?" he bit off, still trying to keep himself from pulling over and whipping his kid. He had never really been a violent man and he could count on one hand how many times he had spanked his children, but that didn't matter right now, because Caleb was about to get his ass beat.

Monica put a hand on his arm, and he shrugged it off. The last hour had been one of the longest in his life. He was dealing with so much stress that it was threatening to shut him down altogether. He didn't have the patience to explain to them that this was not something to cheer for.

"This is not one of your video games, Caleb," his wife told their son, scolding him before her husband could. "It's **not** cool. If this is really happening, then a lot of people are going to die. **We** could die."

"Yeah, you moron," Michelle sneered, slapping Caleb on the back of the head.

"Knock it off," he growled at them. "We had this discussion, didn't we? This is real life we're talking about here. I thought I had raised you better than this."

He couldn't have done more if he **had** pulled over and slapped them. He had always encouraged his children to speak their minds, but to also be mindful of how they spoke. He had tried to instill compassion and a strong sense of right and wrong. But just as any other parent must feel at some stage, he wondered if it had been enough. He was rarely harsh with them, but when he was, it was like an emotional hammer blow. Each of them lowered their eyes, not wanting to meet his gaze.

Well, almost all of them. Skye was looking to him, her eyes full of fear, a tear falling from one eye; begging him to say that everything was going to be okay. It mirrored his soul and broke his heart. Michelle reached over and gathered Skye to her, hushing her younger sister. He wished that he could pull over and comfort her as well, he needed it as much as she did. As he glanced at his wife, he saw his own thoughts staring back at him.

"You just wish you looked as good as Alice," Nicholas said over his shoulder at his older sister; egging her on.

She responded by slugging him in the shoulder, grinning wildly as Nicholas yelped, grabbing at the spot where she'd hit him. "What the fuck?" he exclaimed.

"Language," Monica scolded; no one was listening.

"This isn't a joke!" Michelle said, her maturity showing, her authority as the oldest instilling itself upon the others. "You need to grow up."

"Mom, she hit me," Nicholas whined.

Without looking back his wife replied, "keep it up and I'll hit you too."

He was already tuning it out, the familiar bickering somehow soothing in the face of everything that was going on. He was trying to convince himself that this was actually happening but couldn't wrap his mind around the impossibility of it. Even though they had planned for this; did any of them truly believe it would ever happen?

A biological attack?

It could happen. There was some scary shit out there.

A terrorist attack?

More likely. They'd had more than their share of those over the years.

An invasion of the US by Chinese forces coming up from Mexico?

Sure, that too. He'd seen Red Dawn as a kid.

But zombies?

ZOMBIES?

Something out of a Robert Kirkman television show?

No fucking way.

"Keep it up and I'll turn this van around—," he began automatically and had to stop himself. The rest of it had died in his throat as the realization hit that there was no going back. Their home was no longer behind them, but at the destination they were trying to reach. And unless a miracle happened, it would be that way for a very long time. He had to start getting used to the idea, no matter how much his mind rebelled against it.

He brought the van up to seventy and flew down the interstate; their journey just beginning and his mind questioning whether he had the strength to bring them through.

He didn't know the answer.

His thoughts turned to his friends and family who were oblivious to what had begun and wondered if any of them would live to see tomorrow. His heart yearned for him to reach out to them, to somehow get them on the road and follow him out of town. Had the others in his group responded? Were they already on their way? Did any of them feel as helpless and divided as he did? Most of them had a very long drive ahead and he sent a silent prayer to whoever was listening that they'd all make it in one piece.

"Double check to make sure Sam is on the move. We're going to be there in thirty-minutes, and I want to pull off, make sure she's with us, and then get right back on the interstate," he told Monica, who nodded as she picked his phone back up.

"Think Ros and Matt are on the road yet?" his wife asked. They were a part of his extended family and they were closer to them than the others in their group. While not a committed part of his life, Ros and Matt did share the same views on relationships and if it got a couple of stares from the judgmental types, so be it. It didn't matter anymore anyways, not if the world was ending as Ben suggested it was.

"I'm sure we'll find out soon enough," he returned. He'd check in with Ben when they got to the compound. He chose the word *when* rather than *if*. Nothing was going to stop him from getting his family to safety. He'd do whatever he had to no matter what the cost.

"I get to be Chris," Caleb told his older brother, but Nicholas refused to reply; he was still massaging his sore shoulder. Their shared interest in everything Resident Evil was only spurring the boys' excitement.

"Caleb," his mother warned, stopping the young boy from commenting further.

"Fuck that shit," his older daughter decided to chime in, being drawn into the conversation despite her earlier reservations. "Dad's Rick, Mom's Lori, and I'm Carol. You're just a wimpy version of Carl."

"Carl!" Nick exclaimed in a weak imitation of Rick's voice.

"Hey, that's not nice!" Caleb responded in disbelief. "If I'm anybody, I'm Daryl cuz he's the shit." That got all the kids laughing, including Skye, who was still wiping tears off her cheeks.

"Kids. Seriously, knock it off," his wife growled. Her hands were opening and closing on her lap and he was sure she was close to acting on her inner rage.

Zombies, his mind whispered again. *This just can't be happening.*

His foot lowered and the van surged forward. He passed a trucker and a blast of a horn rang out as he cut in front of the semi to get around a convertible that was cruising five miles below the speed limit while in the fast lane.

As they approached the turn off to his mother's house, his wife gave him an expectant look, but he let it pass without slowing. A question formed on her mouth, but he shook his head. "There's no time. Try calling them again," he said softly, his heart tearing from his chest as he tried to keep his eyes on the road. Los Niños park was passing on his right and he spared one last glance at his childhood playground; feeling that he would never see it again.

I've got to get them to safety, he told himself again, forcibly shoving it through his doubts and focusing on the task at hand.

Chapter 5
the Girl on Fire

Mark
Columbus, OH

Mark didn't have his cell on him.

There was a fire blazing as he ran to the rig to grab his gear. They had responded to the call-in record time and the hoses were already being run. Suiting up, his hands ran through the sleeves of his vest as he turned to face the blaze; not knowing that the world around him was starting to burn faster than the inferno roaring out of control before him.

Sweat was forming fast all over his body from the heat of the two-story house, and it was far worse than a sauna at his gym set on its highest setting. He grabbed a rag and wiped his large brow, his dark skin glistening in the morning sun. His helmet felt a bit raw on his freshly shaven head, and he turned his green eyes towards his crewmates as they frantically worked to get the chaos under control.

Taking a deep breath, he purposely strode forward to help the other firefighters in their attempt to tame fiery beast and bring it to heel. The rest of his team was working quickly; the hose already beginning to spray down the house. The flames had begun to lick the buildings around it and the man on the hose alternated from one building to the other, trying to soak it down and prevent it from spreading. They only had the one hose and it was borderline getting out of their control.

He waited, axe in hand. He knew from experience that if anyone was in that house, they were already dead, but stranger things had happened. There could be an isolated pocket that had not yet been caught up in the blaze and someone could be hiding in it; needing his assistance. With the violence of those flames he hoped that wasn't the case, because there wouldn't be anything that he could do about it; there would be no heroic rescue. The houses around them had been evacuated in case the fire spread and there was really nothing he could do but watch and wait.

A door burst outward and hung off its hinges at an askew angle. He didn't even flinch with the suddenness of the violent act. His training and experience instilled in him a calm that the rookies had not yet mastered. A flurry of flames burst from the interior of the house and began to march across the front lawn. He realized with horror that it was a human being trying to escape the inferno. He kept his fear in check as it made its way towards him, his heart going out to whoever it was as they were already dead, and just didn't know it yet. He hesitated to act, his hand tense on his axe as he considered stepping forward to put the poor bastard out of their misery. It was the humane thing to do; no one would blame him for it. There was no way they'd survive the violence being inflicted upon them.

Ten feet from the front door the figure dropped to its knees, hovered there and then fell forward; scorching the grass around it. The hose turned onto the body, but it was too late. The blackened corpse smoldered beneath the spray and fought for its life against the force of the water.

Doing his best not to puke from the smell of burnt flesh, he turned his head away and looked at his team. One of the rookies wasn't so lucky, he was puking his guts out near the back of the truck.

The others mirrored his expression of sorrowful resignation, all but his Captain. The man was standing there with his eyes on the scene calculating their next move, how best to conquer their enemy; nothing fazed their leader. He ordered the hose back on the house as the corner of the neighboring building began to spark with flame, knowing just as well as the rest of them that nothing could be done for the crispy corpse smoking nearby.

A scream ripped the air from his right, and he turned in that direction, gripping his axe tighter. He watched as a woman ran from the backyard of the flaming house, her clothes rippling with bright orange and yellow flames. Her hair was on fire and it rippled like Carrie at the prom. She was running straight for the paramedics who had pushed forward with blankets in an effort to smother the flames and save her life.

Yet, he couldn't move; the look on her face paralyzed him. He had expected to see pain and anguish there, not cold naked fury.

This bitch is rabid!

He moved to intercept her before the paramedics got there but he wasn't fast enough. She leapt with inhuman strength and tore into them; jaws wide. Her fingers were ripping at their flesh even before her barred teeth sank into the first paramedic's throat. Blood erupted into the air as if from some horrid scene out of the Evil Dead; the man's throat torn to shreds.

Stunned, the other paramedic backed up a few steps, attempting to get out of range of the claws reaching out to him. The man did the only thing he could; he brought his gear around and bashed the woman in the back of the head. There was a sickening crunch from the impact but all it did was draw a nasty snarl from the flaming beast. The dent in her head rippled in a sick slow-motion effect; it was unnatural. He could see the spit fly, the blood gush upward, and the flesh rend.

The paramedic stumbled back a step and brought it down again. She crumbled beneath the strength of the blow, falling on top of man she had been tearing apart. She jerked with violent spasms as her body finally got the message that it was dead; it could finally stop. The paramedic she had attacked was fumbling at his gushing throat and looking at them with pure terror in his eyes; his partner too stunned by what he'd just done to act and save his life.

Responding on instinct, he rushed forward to help the dying man.

"Get that bitch off him!" his Captain yelled from his rear, but no one seemed to be moving other than him. "Move, goddammit!" their leader roared, shoving one of the paralyzed firefighters forward.

He was surprised to find his axe flipping the dead woman off the fallen man; he hadn't realized he had crossed the lawn that quickly. He bent down at the paramedic's side and clamped a hand on his neck wound, doing his best to keep the blood inside the man's body instead all over the soaking grass surrounding him. He yelled for the stunned paramedic to help him, feeling the pulsing blood starting to slow; the fallen man was dying. The man's jugular had been ripped apart and he knew there was little chance to save his life, there really was no reason to even try. He looked into those fearful eyes and watched as the life left them. Shaking his head in despair, appalled at what had just happened, he barely noticed their chaplain rushing forward to read the last rites.

He let go of the man's neck, his hands covered in bits of flesh. He jerked himself upright and beheld the smoldering ruin of the woman that had attacked them. She **had** been on fire and it hadn't come from being in that house. Her back was a charred mess, but her front had barely been touched. She had most likely been blown free when she had tried to go out the back. The heat of the fire was intense, and the sweat was flowing but he saw no signs of trauma other than the blows to the head from the paramedic's gear. In all his years, he had never seen anything that gruesome.

Backing off, his mind began to work in overtime, memories flooding him. His comrades had everything under control and he quickly strode towards the rig. He reached in and retrieved his phone from his black leather jacket on the seat. He flipped it open; oblivious to the world around him and saw that he had five missed messages from that kid in the compound.

"No fucking way; this shit isn't happening."

Ben: Columbus is ground zero get the fuck out!

Someone else screamed and he tore his eyes from his phone and looked over his shoulder, the flight response in him triggering. He stuffed the phone in his jacket pocket, no longer worrying about protocol, and turned to the scene he'd just left.

Joey, one of the most reserved fun-loving men on their crew was now swinging an axe in a crowd of black and yellow. Another scream rent the air, but he couldn't find its source. The men backed up; not one of them paying attention to the fire blazing beyond. The flames had begun to spread to the neighboring houses, but the hose lay on the lawn forgotten, whipping around like a snake and spraying water everywhere it possibly could.

Stunned onlookers were on the street with their jaws hanging; frozen into inaction. The human mind refused to let go even though every instinct told you to flee.

"Back the fuck up!" his Captain hollered, rushing towards his men.

Joey was slumped over, his axe held limply at his side, blood dripping off the recently used blade. The paramedic that had just died lay there with his head split open. The other paramedic was sitting on the grass, his hand hastily trying to clean a bite wound on his arm; it was too massive to staunch.

That's when it hit him; this was real.

His Captain must have been thinking the same thing. He had pulled his pistol and before anyone could react, shot the young paramedic in the head. The man's head blew apart, brains and blood spraying a nearby fireman as it ejected with the force of the impact. Frank, an elder member of the crew, hovered there in shock, then bent over and began ejecting his breakfast all over his polished boots.

The rest of his team could only stand there and stare, some of them giving their leader a wide-eyed look of disbelief. For the first time in Mark's memory, his longtime friend and Captain showed something other than his usual calm exterior; tears were running down the man's face as he looked at the gun in his hand.

The ensuing silence was quickly broken by the burning house beyond. One of the roof supports had given way and was vibrating the ground as the building began to cave in. None of the assembled men paid any attention; they had other more pressing issues to tend to than the job they'd come there to do. They couldn't believe what their eyes were telling them and hesitantly, they stepped towards their leader.

Regaining his composure, the Captain holstered his firearm and wiped the tears from his face. "Stow that shit and back the fuck off them, now!" he yelled, pointing at the downed paramedics.

Years of training snapped through the fog that had enveloped them and they began to move, avoiding their Captain as they retreated from the lawn. Phones were being held by the locals and he knew that they were videoing everything that was happening. Horror had spread across all of their faces and he doubted they'd wait long before posting it online. No matter what, their Captain was in a world of shit and Mark seemed to be the only one that realized what his friend had done and why.

"Holy fuck," he whispered out loud, still unable to move.

"Hey, where do you guys think you're going? We saw that shit! It was murder. Someone get that son of a bitch!" a man garbed in flannel pajamas bellowed as he stepped from the crowd and pointed in their direction.

The rest of his team turned and stood in front of their Captain, protecting him from the sight of the onlookers looking to rush them.

None of them knew for sure what was going on, but they weren't about to give over one of their own to a frenzied mob.

His Captain pushed his way to the front of his men but whatever he was about to say was lost by another scream from the rear of the crowd. A few houses down there was a man on the ground getting attacked by a deranged woman in curlers; a face of fury not unlike that of the flaming woman that had just rushed them.

That settled it; he had to get the hell out of there. His wife had to have gotten the message and was probably on her way to the station at that very second. His family needed him, and he had to get them as far away from this shit as possible.

Axe in hand, he walked with swift purpose towards the rig and climbed into the driver seat. His Captain was already climbing in next to him and the others quickly hopped in the back, silence reigning as he hit the gas and raced for the station, barely missing a cop car flying his way.

Chapter 6
Broken Bodies

Rosilynn
Las Vegas, NV

It was either great fortune or some sadistic sense of destiny that found the two of them in bed together when their phones went off simultaneously. They were in the heat of the moment and neither one of them wanted to stop and check them. There was nothing like having the best sex of your life interrupted by an alert from CNN about sixteen things people found when renovating their homes; the sound was staying off.

Rosilynn was of average height, with long straight brown hair, which bounced softly against her back as she worked herself through another intense orgasm. Matt's hands were on her hips and she brought one of them up past her bouncing breast to her face, hugging it to her; letting his fingers stroke her cheek. Her thin curves twisted backward as his hand slid along her throat. She threw her head back and groaned. Her brown eyes glowed with ecstasy and the sweat covering her body cooled under the air-conditioning, almost dried out before it even formed. It might have felt cold when they got started, but now it was like being curled up in a damn oven.

The white sheets were thrown back and as she fell upon him, her long legs stroked his strong muscular form, their toes playing with one another as she tried to catch her breath. He grunted playfully at her added weight and she smacked him lightly on the chest for it, then flopped onto her side and curled up with a hand draped over his chest, listening to the thundering of his heart; unwilling to withdraw contact just yet.

Matt had a square jaw, light brown hair, and was currently clean shaven. He was six-foot-three and his feet were barely able to keep from dangling off the end of the bed as he wiggled his toes and gave her a dazed look of satisfaction. He had a pleased smile on his face and his green eyes were dreamy; they were what drew her in when they met, and they still made her heart flutter when the mood was right. She ran a hand over his abs, her fingers tracing along his skin as his smile grew even larger. Sliding her hand softly across his stomach, her fingers lightly teasing his flesh as she reached down and grasped his manhood.

"You can't be wanting to go again so soon," he murmured, his usual brisk voice almost purring. His left hand was stroking her hair, his breathing labored but starting to slow.

She let her hand continue on, an amused smile spreading her flushed cheeks as she flicked her tongue along her lower teeth; her loving eyes fixing on his with delight. "Not at all, just enjoying what's mine," she whispered in his ear, biting him softly on the lobe.

Both phones lit up simultaneously, the glow bright and hard to miss; she should have turned them over. "That's odd, both of them going off at the same time. It can't be my work," she told him, her eyebrows drawing together with confusion.

She was a nurse at a nearby hospital and was off for the next two days. She had just finished a seventy-two-hour rotation and was badly in need of rest. Or fun exercise, whichever came first. Her husband worked security at one of the casinos on the strip and he had somehow managed to wrangle the day off as well; it **had** been perfect. Her hand fumbled for her phone and she brought it to her hip, letting it rest there for a moment.

"Don't check it," Matt whispered. "Whoever it is can wait." He was stiffening in her right hand and his eyes were beginning to show the hunger growing inside him. He reached over to push a lock of hair from over her eyes as he leaned over to kiss the crook of her neck.

A shiver of pleasure rushed through her and she almost tossed her phone back on the nightstand. He was right, it could probably wait. Then again, simultaneous texts usually indicated family was trying to get ahold of them. "It could be your mother. Doesn't she have bi-pass surgery coming up?"

"That's not until the fifteenth. Come on, you started it. If you didn't want to go again, you should have behaved and kept your hands to yourself," he teased, his tongue slowly working its way up towards her ear.

Her insides were beginning to burn with need and despite the clenching between her thighs signaling how overworked they were, she couldn't help but want him again. Yet, her hand had already lifted her phone, her eyes searching the texts pulsing on the unlock screen.

Her world shattered.

Sitting there with that glowing screen and its message glaring at her, time stopped. Her heart hammered out the seconds, but her mind had simply shutdown. She was unable to comprehend if she was really seeing it or if reality had finally slipped away and she was in some kind of sadistic nightmare.

"Rosilynn, what is it?" her husband asked, growing concerned by the look on her face.

"Check your phone," she managed, her mind trying to race and keep up with what she was seeing. There were things she had to start doing, her mind knew that, yet she was paralyzed where she was. The passion in her was gone with those three little words; words that destroyed her life forever.

Ben: It's a wipe.

As he turned over to his night table, her body began to move on its own. She crawled out of the bed and went to the bathroom. As the door closed, she could hear Matt's curses following after her. He was rummaging through their closet by the sounds that resonated across the tiles and as she reached for the toilet paper, she ran through a list of things they would need to do before leaving. She flushed, then strode from the bathroom to find her black suit lying on the crumpled white sheets of her bed. She sat down, fingered the texture of the suit, and then went about sliding it on. "How much time do you think we have?"

"I know as much as you do," Matt responded, working quickly to gather their things. He strode from the room in his boxers and she heard the television fire up in the living room. She knew that he was gathering some food to take with them, and her hand found the remote on her nightstand; flipping the power on.

As it came to life, she worked on putting her arms through her suit and zipping up the front. The pads were thrown on the bed and she began fastening them as the program that was on suddenly cut off.

She was told that they were sorry, that As the World Turns was being interrupted for an unscheduled broadcast. There was a news update for the city of Las Vegas. A breaking news screen flashed before her and she fought to keep moving as the video cut to a news anchor at the studio. There was no introduction, no graphics, just a scared older man with a piece of paper in front of him.

What the hell had they missed?

"Good morning. As of this morning, the city of Las Vegas is in a heightened state of alert. Homeland Security has changed the alert status to Severe. We are being told that an attack on the United States of America is imminent. Department of Homeland Security has been unreachable for comment and—," he paused in his broadcast as someone handed him another paper.

His brow drew together as he took a moment to read it, the confusion unmistakable as he blinked rapidly and tried to comprehend what he was seeing. Without reservation or paraphrasing, he began reading it out loud over live television. "You are hereby ordered by the United States Government under executive order from the President of the United States to cease broadcasting and return to your scheduled programming. Further instructions will follow. What the hell is this?" he asked the man off screen.

There was someone talking off camera, but the newscaster wasn't listening to them. "They have no right—," he began, trying to make sense of the paper in front of him. He held a finger to his ear, then stared straight into the camera. "We are receiving reports that a biological weapon has been released by terrorists on Las Vegas Boulevard. For that report, we now go to Angela who's reporting live from the Luxor Hotel," he said, but the video did not switch, it stayed trained on the news anchor, who looked anxious to hear from their reporter as much as the viewers. "Did we switch? Angela? No, I can't hear anything."

Someone was talking off screen, then you could hear a large bang and a rush of feet. Just before the screen went black, she thought she heard the sound of gunfire.

"Oh my God," she whispered, fastening the last of the pads over her suit. She couldn't believe what she was seeing. Had the government just murdered that news crew? If the text had scared her shitless, the thought of what that meant if it were true terrified her to her core.

Matt rushed back into the room, his own suit on and ready to go. He headed for the closet and their gun safe. "Did you see?" he asked needlessly; he'd had to have caught the Stand By logo on the screen when he had come into their room.

"A terrorist attack?" she asked, stunned at the news.

How do these things keep happening? Las Vegas Boulevard?

That wasn't far from where they lived; fifteen minutes at most.

Following him to the closet, she grabbed the holster he handed her, and began strapping it on. He tossed her a respirator just as she got both arms through her loaded Bug Out Bag. The rifle came next. Slinging that over her shoulder, she turned to the headboard of their bed and slid the Japanese sword from its stand. She held the Katana tightly as she moved towards their bedroom door, not bothering to strap the sheath around her waist. They'd be in the car within the next minute or so and she'd just have to take it back off again.

Ben: Las Vegas is ground zero GTFO
Ben: Auth: 4HorseMenAE
Ben: GRIMES

"Wait, what?" she asked with shock, standing there ready to go, sword in hand; the phone held up in disbelief. "I thought this was a bio-weapon." There was no question this shit was real. If the newscast wasn't proof enough, that authentication code was. It would only be sent out if it was verified and unstoppable.

Matt was moving through the door in the direction of the garage. "We have to trust that Ben knows what he's talking about. He's got the whole world at his fingertips and a hacker brain that would have gotten him a job at the NSA. If he says it's gone to shit, take him at his word," her husband replied, motioning for her to get in the passenger side.

"Why are you driving?" she asked out of reflex.

"You really going to give me that feminist bullshit right now? Seriously? Why the hell does it matter who drives as long as we get the fuck out of here?" Matt snarked, hopping in the car and removing himself from the debate.

"You're a guy, of course you'd say that," she growled under her breath as she jumped in beside him and stared out the back window; the garage door could not lift fast enough. Her eyes drifted to their empty backseat and remembered how much it had bothered her that they hadn't been able to conceive yet. The fertility doctor said Matt's sperm count was low, but that hadn't kept them from trying. It was one reason she wanted to spend the day in bed; it was a perfect time in her cycle.

Maybe it was just as well. It would be easier to move when it was just the two of them; less to protect.

She couldn't imagine how hard it would be if Todd and his family were here instead.

Shit, she hoped they were getting out of Tucson all right.

She thought of breaking protocol and calling them, to make sure they were on their way, but fought the urge back down as they began plunging backwards down the driveway. Maybe she'd chance it after they were further along, but for right now, she needed to focus on getting her own ass on the road and trust they were doing the same.

All along the block other people were rushing to get into their cars; hastily packed supplies tumbling from their hands as they raced to get out of Vegas. The news was out.

As he was pulling out a white Bronco roared by, nearly clipping their back bumper. It missed them, but it nailed their neighbor Karen; throwing the older woman back onto her car like she was a pillow tossed on a bed. She impacted the rear window; shattering it with her crumpled body, her head falling lifeless as her blank eyes glared at them in silent accusation.

"Karen!" she instinctively yelled, hand flying to the door handle. She was a nurse, it was her duty to help those in need and her first impulse was to respond.

Matt reached over and stayed her arm. "We don't have time for that. A lot more people are out there getting hurt and you can't save them all. Got to focus on us first, babe," he told her firmly.

"How can you say that? It's Karen! We've known her for years!" she snapped, struggling to free herself. Her eyes stared at her broken friend, knowing that every second wasted was lessening the chance the woman would survive.

Then her blood chilled and her heart stopped.

The woman's body was jerking in violent thrusts; her eyes and mouth changing from a look of agony to one of fury in a microsecond. Her hands reached out and gripped the car she was lying on, then pushed herself up swiftly, as if having never been injured at all. Yet, her back must have been broken because her legs hung there limply and did not support her weight as she struggled to free herself from the caved in windshield.

Driven by some insane violence, Karen dove off the back of the car and fell with a sickening crunch on the asphalt below. Her face lifted and her eyes were wide. They found hers and Rosilynn felt a scream rip out of her. Those were not the eyes of the woman she had known. Furiously, the woman began to claw her way towards them, her nails snapping as they dug into the unyielding asphalt; her broken body dragging along behind her.

Matt backed up, making sure to turn in that direction and cutting off her view. The car bucked and she let out another quick yelp; unable to help herself. He had purposely run their neighbor over. "Still think Ben's wrong?" he snapped loudly, sounding entirely too smug.

She loved the man, but sometimes she wanted to sock him in the jaw.

She turned her head to look behind them as they pulled away, unable to resist no matter how grisly it had to be. Even though the entire left half of her fallen neighbor had been crushed by their car, the right was still intact. Karen's head swiveled at an unnatural angle; following their retreat. Her right arm shot out to drag the crushed body forward a couple of inches, not knowing that it'd been ground to mush and could not assist in her efforts. The strength of the undead woman proved to be the winner though, as flesh was torn away and was left behind as she reached out with one hand and began pulling herself forward once more. Untethered, the half-body pulled itself even faster, defying all laws of nature.

There was no way she was still alive; no way.

Her mind logged every detail; promising to play it back to her at any moment it chose. Her stomach was turning, and she felt an instant need to vomit. Fighting it back down through practiced will, she put on her seatbelt; her eyes darting along the landscape to find the next source of danger.

They were approaching a light when she heard an ambulance coming up fast on their rear. Matt pulled to the side to let it pass but it wasn't enough as the emergency vehicle struck the corner of their bumper in its passing. The force of the impact drove them over the sidewalk and her husband cursed as he tried to bring the car to a stop.

"Damn it!" he growled, the steering wheel jerking free of his hands. Someone else had hit them as well, driving them into another car. She braced herself as her head nearly slammed into the dash.

Looking up through the cracked windshield she watched in horror as the fleeing ambulance entered the intersection and got plowed by a semi that appeared out of nowhere on their right. Metal screamed from the agonizing impact as the ambulance was thrown clear of the intersection and into oncoming traffic. The semi did not slow despite the damage it had suffered, and the multiple wheels along the back bounced over the broken metal and spewing gas. The driver had tried to keep it on the road, but physics took over and it veered into a Honda Civic on its left.

For the briefest of moments, she could see the stunned look of an elderly lady as she threw her hands up to brace herself. Thankfully, it was over quickly. The semi tore the car apart before bouncing violently twice, then fell on its side.

Shaken, she noticed that their car had stalled.

"Ros, we need to get out of here!" her husband yelled, grabbing their gear and his weapons.

Trained to act in a crisis, she instantly jumped out and did the same. Grabbing her sword, she strapped it to her left hip and made sure the knot was tight. There was mass panic in the street and even though she had been trained to notice every detail, the erupted world around her was too much for her mind to process. A broken body here, a dying woman there, gas spewing in fountains, the power lines sparking loosely on the ground. Her eyes couldn't follow how many people were already dead or dying; nor how many people were rushing to leave them like that.

It horrified her.

Ben: incoming from the north

As much as she appreciated his input, she had picked up on the increased volume of screams coming from the chaos before them. The strip was to the east, which meant they needed to get south to the

215 and try to loop around it. The casinos were the absolute last place she wanted to be right now.

Matt was standing there with his gun drawn; watching their rear. She turned to look at the scene of the collision and was confronted with a large mass of bodies pushing their way. People had stopped fleeing in that direction and were turning to run back at them in panic. She felt it in the air, this was about to get really ugly.

The elderly woman she had seen in that car had somehow crawled through her shattered windshield, half her face torn away, white hair smeared with blood. The lower half of her body had been left behind and her insides drug across the hood as she clawed her way forth. Perched on the edge of the crumpled vehicle, she snagged someone that had rushed too close and tore at him with her clawed hands. Her mouth was trying to gnaw at him but her broken dentures must have been left behind because she was not breaking skin. Her nails were more than enough though, as they tore the flesh from his bone, making blood spray out of his neck in some fake horror movie display. Granny Zombie unnerved her more than the mashed body of her neighbor had, and her thighs trembled slightly as her bladder threatened to let loose. Fear was fighting to break free and she purposely turned her back on the disgusting display, looking to her husband instead to calm and refocus her mind.

Luckily for him, he had missed the grisly act of violence. "Ros! We need to move," he repeated harshly. His eyes were focused elsewhere, and she turned to follow his gaze wondering what could have been more important than the massive car wreck and chaos before them. She got her answer as her eyes fell on the gasoline flowing towards one of the loose power cables.

"Shit on a stick!" she cursed. Adrenaline began to energize her body, waking her fully, making her pitch forward and run in the opposite direction. She trusted that her husband was by her side and did not waste the time to look. She pumped her legs harder, trying desperately to gain speed in the heavy gear she wore; it was protective but restrictive as hell. She wouldn't last long going full out like this, despite her conditioning.

Her world erupted in a fiery burst of heat and flame. The explosion made her ears ring and the concussion threw her from her feet. She landed on the pavement, her suit absorbing some of the impact, but not all. Her head smashed into the concrete sidewalk and stars filled her vision. Her respirator had been knocked askew, the mask covered in soot; too damaged to be of any further use. Her arm felt numb and she prayed she hadn't broken it. Something was wrong with her leg, there was pressure where there shouldn't be; maybe Matt fell on her?

"Matt," she groaned, trying to twist, but unable to move the lower half of her body. The pressure came again, only not in the same spot. The void of unconsciousness was threatening to overtake her, and she was about ready to just give into it.

"Matt," she moaned again but got no response. She tried to shake herself free, believing him to be unconscious, when she felt the pressure of nails digging at her suit. They were trying to scrape their way through the tight rubber and were thankfully failing for the moment. The suit was designed to be resistant to just that sort of attack. The pressure she had been feeling must have come from teeth because something continued to apply pressure further up her leg. She tried to scream but her voice had left her. The nails intensified, working their way up her body. Then her vision darkened, and she passed into the welcoming blackness that awaited her.

Chapter 7
Origins

Four years earlier

"Anyone for an achievement run through Naxx?" Linda asked over vent; a computer program that allowed the gamers to talk online while gaming. They were all sitting in a chat room designated for raids and even though he had heard her; he pretended not to. She was never really involved with their conversations and after a raid she'd try to get them to help her clear out her achievement logs. When that didn't work, she'd log right out and be gone for the night. Even now, she was ignoring their current conversation entirely.

"Zombies? Really? You're going there?" his wife asked, also ignoring Linda's question. She had keyed up her microphone as she leaned forward to inspect something on her screen. She had gotten a new piece of gear tonight and appeared to be checking out the stat changes. She had spoken into the mic attached to her large headphones so that his speakers didn't provide feedback from the conversations. He had tried a pair of headphones for a while but hated how claustrophobic they made him feel. Now his son had a pair to use with his Xbox, which was a double-edged sword. They no longer heard the other side of his conversations, but he spoke loud enough to be heard across the entire house.

Monica glanced his way, smiled, then rolled her eyes.

Casey was having another one of his nights.

No one had answered Linda, so as predicted, she promptly logged off and went offline. He could almost hear the slam of the door as she left the chat room. Her wife was still on though, but she was quiet, probably arguing on the other side of the connection. He was suddenly glad that she had her push to talk enabled; an open mic would give him an earful that he really wanted to avoid tonight.

"I think Casey's had too much to drink," he said over his mic, joining in. He knew that his friend from Texas loved to play drunk,

Casey insisting it made him play better. The logic behind that was glaringly stupid, but he knew there was no point in arguing about it. If he chose to make a stand on the issue, he'd lose a raider, and he had spent too much time on their current raid team to just piss away a good DPS now.

You could almost hear the bubbles of whatever Casey was inhaling as he queued up his mic from the living room of the small trailer he lived in. "No shit zombies." As he said it, you could hear him holding his breath, causing his voice to heighten in tone. He let it out forcefully as he talked once more. "Like that shit will never happen. The government loves to play with bugs. Tell me they don't have someone already looking into that shit."

"Hey guys, I have to go," Jackie said over his speakers. He had been expecting it; it was one of the cardinal rules, keep the wife happy, keep your life happy.

"They don't have someone looking into that shit," piped up Rodger, one of his older friends from Ohio. "Good night Jackie."

"Okay, good luck Jackie," he responded on the heels of Rodger and saw a LOL in chat before she logged off as well. He did wish her luck, he was glad that he wasn't married to Linda; they never would have lasted very long. She had impatience with anything male just seeping off every word she uttered.

You could hear the choked-up laughter Casey was trying to suppress as he queued back up, "fucking smartass."

Mark was laughing in officer chat. He had refused to purchase a mic, or at least that's what he had told them. He seldom did much typing other than short sentences or replies, and though a part of the team, was an unknown quantity socially. Todd wasn't sure if it was because he was shy or that he wasn't paying attention half the time.

The problem with online conversations stemmed from issues like that. What was the person really doing or saying on the other end? He said his name was Mark, but did he prefer not to get on vent because they'd learn he was really a Martha? Did that even matter?

People distrusted the internet with good reason. He knew that. If they wanted their privacy, who was he to intrude? It was their dime to do with what they choose. Mark was obviously one of those and he hadn't pushed. He had learned from past experiences that sometimes the fog of unknowing was a blessing rather than a curse. He shivered as he thought back to a woman that once said she played naked, sitting on a towel to soak everything up. It was a disturbing image he really didn't need.

"You realize that you're smoking that shit with a cop literally in the room with you?" came Joseph's voice and his wife chuckled. Their cop friend from Arkansas loved to give Casey shit about his drug habit every chance he got.

They knew it was an empty threat, but the bubbles suddenly stopped, and you could hear Casey's reply get choked off in a burst of static. "I'm pouring myself a beer, officer," he finally replied; his voice sounding like he had been coughing too hard.

"Bullshit," he fake-sneezed into his mic and his wife broke into laughter. One of the kids looked at them from the couch, but quickly turned back to their Xbox game. Nothing could distract them from that thing for long.

Vent broke out into laughter, gaining him another glare from his kids, but Casey would not be deterred. He had a line of thought and he was going to get it out no matter what they said to distract him. "You know they are looking into it. Along with every other possible thing ever created by Hollywood. If it can be turned into a weapon; they've researched it," he told them confidently.

He sighed as the laughter calmed down. If they let Casey go on too much longer, they'd be here all night and he wanted to get some heroics run before bed. "Log your healer," he told his wife and got a frown in return. She hated being a healer when he was tanking a dungeon. He tended to yell at her when his health got low and got really pissed if he died. She grumbled something but he couldn't make it out. Yet the log screen flashed on her screen and he couldn't chuckling, only softly so she didn't hear and throw something at him.

"You give me any shit and you're on the couch tonight buddy," she told him sternly, and he didn't doubt for an instant that she would do it.

"Paranoid much?" Paul asked, one of their other friends from Utah. "If you want to talk about something realistic, Christine is having one of her friends over tonight and we're going to have a little fun."

Monica groaned. "Paul, I don't want to hear about your sex life."

"Your own lacking there, honey? Come over, I'll fix that," the older man said, then laughed.

"Hey now," he chimed in, his voice losing the humor he had been nursing.

"All right, all right," Paul said, "just trying to lighten the mood a bit. Things are getting a bit heavy."

"He's not as paranoid as you make him sound," replied Matt.

That stopped him in the middle of his snarky reply to Paul. Had someone just backed up Casey's non-sensical rant?

"Wait, what?" Matt and Ros were the only part of the group that he and his wife had met in real life over the last couple of years. They lived in Vegas, which was just seven hours away and had met up with them a few times for drinks at the casinos. The first time it had been innocent. The others?

Well, you only live once right?

From time to time he dreamt of those nights and would occasionally push for them to take another trip up north. They were good people. Ros was a nurse and hadn't been online tonight because she had been called into work. They had filled her spot with another member of the guild, who had luckily been waiting for a dungeon queue, so it had all worked out in the end.

"I'm ex-military and I know for a fact that they are creating some freaky shit out there," Matt continued, cutting off Casey's mic as it lit up.

"Like what?" Ben asked. He had been the guildie that filled in for Ros and just happened to be Rodger's son. A bit young but a good fill-in player in a pinch. Beat getting a pug, he fucking hated pugs.

Matt's voice came over his speakers once more, filling his house as his mic increased in volume. He had to quickly turn it down. "If I told you that, I wouldn't have to kill you, someone would do it for me. Then they'd come after me next." There was a pause, then he laughed.

The mic cut off and vent was silent for a few seconds.

"I'm not paranoid," Casey finally managed. This time it sounded like he had inhaled something before queuing because his voice was coming out in a familiar rush.

It made Joe laugh in chat and he smiled.

"There's a lot of nasty shit in the world. If you don't control it, it controls you. We'd never let someone else create it first, we always have to lead the pack. The military applications alone would get them to pour money into the research for it. Reanimate slain soldiers or cause an outbreak in another country? They could just sit back and let the zombies do all the work for us! They have to be brainstorming and testing that shit somewhere. There is nothing we can do to survive something like that. No fucking way. If it got out, we'd be fucked," Casey finished, the sound of a bag of chips echoing across the speakers.

"So, what? You think we should just go hide in a bunker in Bumfuckegypt and wait for something to happen?" his wife asked jokingly.

"Hell no," Casey responded quickly. "But would it really hurt to have a plan?"

Chapter 8
Pit Stop

Todd
Outside Benson, AZ

Reflecting on that conversation four years before, he stroked his goatee, his eyes fixed on the gas station in front of him but not really seeing a thing as he perused his memories. No one in their group had taken Casey seriously that night, who would? Government scientists secluded in some remote part of the country cooking up superbugs, which then got out and killed the whole world?

It was straight out of a Stephen King novel.

He loved reading the Stand, but he had always felt that it had lacked a certain touch of realism; beyond the whole Mother Abigail/Flagg thing. The military was largely ineffective and did little but police the infection. He knew that if it did happen in real life, the military would play a much larger role then portrayed by Hollywood. But as a part-time want-to-be author, he knew that you crafted a story around the characters, trying to put them in harm's way, but always leaving them a way out. Hard to do if you had multiple nukes going off or an effective military response.

That would be a shorter story and wouldn't sell worth a damn.

A year after that fateful night on vent, there had been a terrorist attack at a football game in Boston. An anarchist hacker by the name of Kayha had orchestrated and financed a group of terrorists, procuring a dirty bomb for them and by-passing security so they could place it under the bleachers of Gillette Stadium. It was the largest attack perpetrated on American soil and the death toll had long past dwarfed that of the Twin Towers in 2001. The ensuing manhunt had not only netted the few remaining terrorists, but live footage had been broadcast when they took down the woman responsible; an event that had more viewers than OJ's bronco chase.

As it did after 9/11, the world had changed once more. They were no longer discussing zombies, as the climate of fear brought on by terrorism rose to new heights. They realized how naïve they had been about their place in the world and the safety of their families. Once more the government cracked down, taking more of their rights away, with little more than a peep from the citizens they stripped them from. They spied on their own people in the name of national security, and Casey's rants no longer seemed paranoid at all. After many discussions over vent, they'd eventually arrived at the conclusion that maybe he was right; they needed to have a plan if they were going to survive.

Right now, they were pulled over at a gas station on the other side of Benson; twenty minutes outside Wilcox. None of them had used the bathroom before leaving home and it would be their last stop for a while. After this, the only available restrooms would be in the towns they would pass through and he wanted to stay on the outskirts of those the best he could.

He had swept the area with his wife and then gone into the bathroom to change. His work clothes were packed away in the van now and he wore the same tight rubber suit that the rest of his family had on. Much to his dissatisfaction, it kept wedging itself between his ass cheeks despite his attempts to pull it back out. The material clung to him so tightly that he was beginning to feel claustrophobic. He had just finished strapping on the protective pads and the extra layer of clothing was causing his body heat to rise. He had three pads on each arm and leg and wore a heavy bulletproof vest strapped to his chest. He hadn't taken into consideration how hot it would feel to be wearing all this gear when he helped design it. It had been tailored to protect them, not to be comfortable in. His crotch was sweating; making his inner thighs chafe. He was also wearing cargo shorts over the body suit. Without them he'd have no pockets to stow any of the essentials they'd need if they had to make a run for it. He had to keep ammo somewhere.

Sweat ran down his neck and his hand wiped at it absently-mindedly. It was September, so this was not one-hundred and ten-degree weather, but ninety was still enough to make him feel like a turkey in an oven. Still, he didn't want to take a chance with his safety or that of his family's. He'd just keep the air conditioning on high the rest of the trip. A little sweat was worth it if it got them where they were going.

"I'm glad you guys got on the road," he told Sam as she walked back from the bathroom with one of her daughters in tow. She had four kids as well and her maroon Dodge mini-van was parked at the pump behind him; kids jumping in and out of the cargo door like they were hyped up on caffeine.

She came over and gave him a hug, then a quick kiss on the cheek. "Me too. I hope that you're right about this. If not, Ruben is going to be pissed."

"Like that's something new. He gets that way when you unexpectedly leave to put gas in your car. Where is that asshole anyway?" he asked curiously, taking a cigarette from his pack while moving around to the front of his van. "Is he following behind?"

She shook her head. "He didn't believe me; thinks I'm just making up an excuse to run away with you for the weekend. He's at his girlfriend's house and plans on staying there. I tried to talk him out of it, but he's ignoring my texts; probably turned his phone off."

He had never liked the man anyways. Even though they were all in a poly relationship, Ruben was one of those that felt that he should get to play around while the woman only attended to him. He treated his wife like it was the 1950's, expecting dinner on the table and everyone to sit and watch whatever he wanted to afterwards, like Leave it to Beaver. He preferred Sam to stand next to his chair with an apron on and slippers in hand; it was chauvinistic and archaic.

"We can't afford to go back and change his mind," he returned, lighting his cigarette. "We barely even have time enough for this. The phone shows this shit is spreading fast."

Sam nodded slowly, frowning as she looked at her van behind them. "I know that. You don't have to tell me. The kids though, they won't understand."

Her daughter Tammy was sitting in the passenger seat of the van and it looked like she was trying to scold Zeke, who was standing on the side panel of the vehicle, bouncing it up and down. He couldn't see Alan or Bea, but he knew that they were probably in the very back glued to their tablets.

"I'm just glad you're here. Thank you for believing me," he answered, put an arm around her waist and pulled her to him, giving her a warm embrace. "If you need anything, anything at all, you should probably get it now. I know you love your Doritos, so best go grab what you can."

She laughed and shook her head. "I'll be fine. The last thing I can think of right now is food."

Right?

He pulled his cell out and grumbled at the bars he got while in Texas Canyon. The mountain road was lined with large boulders that were greater in size than the semis passing between them. The whole mountain was nothing but rock, making him think of a movie he had seen as a kid. It had large monster that had pretended to be a mountain. He could see it clearly but couldn't think of what the damn movie was. It had a long white dog covered in fur—

"What the hell was the name of that movie?" he asked; drawing a couple of stares from the children behind him.

"What movie?" Sam asked, trying to be helpful.

He sighed. "Probably doesn't matter. We'll never see it again anyways." He saw the downcast movement of her eyes and recognized the despair that had been in his voice. "Had a long white dog in it and a man made of rocks?"

"Neverending Story!" Skye squealed from the back of the van.

"Huh," he said shaking his head. Imagine that, his youngest knew instantly what he was referring to. They had those old movies on DVD now and he didn't realize she had watched them. He had them for nostalgic reasons and hadn't seen them himself in a very long time.

The two younger children kept on talking but he didn't hear them. He was gripping his phone tight enough to leave impressions on his palms. He hated being out of touch at a time like this. He had texted his parents and sister, but they hadn't responded yet. He had also tried calling but kept getting their voicemails.

Surprisingly, he had gotten a text back from Naima. As expected, she wasn't taking him seriously. He was doing a horrible job convincing her that she needed to get as far away from Phoenix as soon as possible. Queen Creek may be far from the city center, seemingly isolated, but it wasn't enough. There had been an updated image from Ben fifteen minutes before and a small dot had appeared in Flagstaff. It was spreading to Arizona and they were running out of time.

Todd: I'm not fucking around, get moving now

Naima: I need to put my daughter down, then I'm taking a nap

Todd: I'm not making this up. Get Mike and your daughter in your car and meet me east of Safford. This is real. Please. Get out now.

Naima: lol funny. Prank on Naima day is it? GTG daughter calling. TTYL

Frustrated, he tried to think of something to say back. He dialed her number, but it went straight to voicemail. "Fuck," he cursed and ended the call; not bothering to leave a message.

"Is she still ignoring you?" Sam asked, watching as Monica started approaching from the restrooms.

"Worse, she doesn't believe me," he groaned, trying to call again, getting the same result.

Only one person outside of their group was paying his words any heed and it wasn't anyone he'd known for more than a year; their friendship a recent development. He called her Saint, a nickname he and his smoking buddies had come up with after a night of her lecturing about right and wrong; swearing she had never done anything unorthodox before in her life. Her real name was Sabrina and from the way she talked and acted, he didn't believe for a second she was as innocent as she played off. They'd had a lot of conversations when he'd been stuck on overnights and they had bonded on their cigarette breaks, still keeping in touch even if only in passing. The smoking crowd had been small, as there were fewer smokers these days; everyone worried over every little thing they put in their body.

He chuckled softly and ignored Caleb's questioning look. *Well, they'd be a healthier food choice for the zombies as well. Might as well keep on smoking.*

He lit another cigarette as checked his messages.

Sabrina was on her way but was stuck in traffic. She was just now leaving and that would put her at least an hour behind them. He remembered getting ribbed from the wife about their sudden friendship, but nothing was going on, no matter how many times his wife asked. He could almost hear her retort, *"just how many women do you need?"*

Sabrina respected the sanctity of marriage so much that if she caught him looking at any other woman, she'd hit him, and she didn't pull her punches. It was just another reason he always called her Saint. If there **had** been flirting between them, it had been harmless; they were truly only just friends.

His thumbs fingered the two rings he wore, and he smiled at the women who were chit-chatting in front of him. Between them and Ros, he had more than enough to keep him busy the rest of his life. He seriously didn't need anyone else. Every guy that knew of their lifestyle had talked about how great it must be. He didn't have the heart to tell them that they should try to keep three women happy and see how awesome it really was. Managing one marriage was a challenge, but two? And scheduling—he didn't even want to think on that.

Since Sabrina was stopped at a red light, she was typing a mile a minute, and he knew from her frantic questions that she knew no more than he did. He was using a phone on a dedicated network and he had hoped that since she was using one of the traditional carriers, that she might have heard news that hadn't spread to his own just yet. But there had been no updates from her cellphone provider and the news websites were surprisingly quiet. Even the ESPN website had stopped updating their box scores. It was surprising, because whenever there was a storm warning or a kid missing, the phones would send out an alert, waking him up at all hours of the night. So far, nothing had come through.

Ben wasn't sending her updates as she wasn't a registered member of their group. These phones were top of the line with their own satellite network, and not as easily replaced should one get lost or broken. They were firewalled by Ben, their resident hacker, and sent constant GPS updates so the young boy could keep track of them. He had wondered how much he had been sacrificing, privacy wise, when they got them. Whatever it was, it was about to pay off.

"Any luck?" Nick asked from behind him. His son was leaning out the opened cargo door and peering at them with concern. Nick was the closest of the four to his grandparents and he knew that the boy had been obsessively trying to reach them on his cell. Caleb and Skye were also preoccupied with theirs phones and the three of them looked funny, frantically tapping like that; they were almost in sync. They were as perturbed as he was at being out of touch.

He sighed heavily, "nothing so far."

His eyes kept roaming the countryside, constantly checking to make sure there wasn't anything out of the ordinary coming their way. They had swept the surrounding area before using the bathroom, but had they been thorough enough? Was it just a waste of time? The map said Flagstaff. Surely, they were still okay. He felt confident that no one could approach without his seeing it from up on this hill; but that didn't mean that they could take their time. They needed to hurry.

"Maybe they're at work," Nick offered.

"Your grandmother is probably sleeping, she stays up late. Your grandfather is hopefully at work and can't hear his phone. Don't start panicking when we don't really know what's going on. They are fine. See?" he asked his son as he pointed at the new update on their map. "It's still in Flagstaff. Hasn't gone anywhere near Phoenix yet. By the way, Naima thinks I'm joking around," he said in a pissy voice, eyes on the gas station beyond. The Coke machine caught his eye and he suddenly wondered if it was the last time he'd ever see one.

Nick grumbled something inaudible and disappeared from view, the mini-van rocking behind him. From within, he heard Caleb remark that he had tried calling Monica's mother, but that it was no longer going to voicemail.

That's odd, he thought. He had never known her cell to just ring off the hook. He dialed his mother's once more and got the "all circuits were busy" response from the operator.

What the hell?

He opened the app on his phone again to double check the map, but so far nothing had changed south of Flagstaff. Everything appeared to be all right back in Tucson, but that didn't mean there wasn't something they weren't picking up on. They could double back, but it was forty minutes to his mother's house now; that ship had sailed when he had passed their exit on their way out of town.

"Sam, try Ruben again."

Sam glanced at him curiously, then lifted her phone. She was middle-aged, and the crow's feet around her eye's deepened as she squinted at her screen. She constantly dyed her hair, the long purple strands constantly falling in her face, her free hand always free and waving them back behind her ears. She was average in size, with a large chest and round hips. She was wearing a Star Wars shirt with the Imperial symbol on the front, a blue flannel, and black jeans. It was her customary dress and he cursed himself for not getting her a suit made when he'd last been at the compounds; she looked naked compared to the rest of them.

Not waiting to hear if she was able to get through to her husband, he walked to the driver side and opened the door; climbing in. The three kids in the back were continuing to make phone calls but he could tell that none of them were successful by their furrowed brows and frantic tapping.

He turned on the radio and got static. That shouldn't be happening yet; they weren't out of range of the Tucson stations. KIIM FM always came through until they got into Wilcox. Then it'd fade and they'd start to pick up 99.1 out of Safford. He hit the preset button and turned it to KRQ.

Static.

"Dad, what's going on?" Caleb asked, but he ignored it.

He hit the search button and watched the tuner go to work. It flew through all the stations twice before he stopped it. There was nothing broadcasting out there. Even the AM stations were gone. He brought his phone up and opened the browser. He knew that he should be getting internet service, but nothing was loading. He heard his daughter making her usual sounds of annoyance when her service was down and felt the dread deepen further.

The feeling of being cutoff was feeding his fear. It had started with the lack of news coverage, then the radio stations, and now the phones were going down. Had it begun already? Was it too late? He wasn't the only one feeling angst over it, his children were looking as if told they needed to jump out of an airplane without a chute. They had grown up in an age where everyone was connected all the time, reachable with a push of a button. They didn't know what life was like without their cellphones or internet browsers.

He did, yet it was an alien feeling to him now and it made him nauseated.

Maybe he should find some twine and empty cans, that may still work.

"The Sprint network is down," he heard Sam say, as if mirroring his inner turmoil. She came around the side of the van, her brow furrowed; clearly concerned.

A notification went off as the app on his phone updated. Now there was a red dot in Phoenix and the one over Flagstaff had grown larger. The outbreak was coming their way; they were blind and not moving. If it continued on its current pace it could cut them off in Safford. While there were back up routes, they were few and would take hours longer to get there. The map **had** updated though, that meant that at least Ben was still capable of getting through to them. That meant their service hadn't been interrupted, but Verizon and Sprint networks had been. What did that mean?

He looked at the growing dots in Vegas, California, and Dallas; feeling a sinking feeling in his stomach. His friends were in the middle of that. How would they get out of there in time?

He wanted to dial Casey and find out what was going on but knew that he couldn't. They had strict rules to follow; ones that they had all agreed to when they had begun this group of theirs. For now, he had to just grit his teeth and bear it. They needed to focus on what they were doing and get to the compounds safely before they got trapped between outbreaks. Ben was the center point keeping everyone moving and they needed to trust him to do just that. He had a bird's eye view of things through his networking and hacker skills, he would know when best when someone could be reached. If he did chance a call, and that person was in a position where a noise could give them away; he'd be ringing the dinner bell.

His fingers absently turned the radio back on, but he lowered the volume. He had thought of the emergency broadcast system, wondering if he might have already missed it, and pushed the button so it tuned into one of the preset stations. As he expected, there was still nothing airing, but that could change at any time and they could get the warning from the government on what to do. That was what you did at times like this, right? But where was it? Why hadn't they been told anything? They had spent decades doing those damn emergency broadcast tests. Where were they now?

"What station is that?" Sam inquired, Monica coming around the passenger side and climbing in beside him.

"I have it on 93.7, but it doesn't matter, they're all like that," he answered through the window. "Maybe you should go get the kids strapped in, we need to get moving.

She nodded, then gave his shoulder a slight squeeze. As she headed towards her van, he watched her through the rear-view mirror for a second, smirking as she began hollering at the kids while disconnecting the gas pump from the side of her van. He had insisted that they get fuel while they could, just in case. Who knew what route they would have to take to get to the compounds? Best be prepared for anything.

His phone began to vibrate. He had turned the ringer off, knowing that sound was an unwanted friend in their situation, so it made him jerk with surprise. He pulled it out of his pouch and hit the power button.

> **Ben:** Quick status update. Todd n Monica, Casey, Mark n Roxanne,
> Joseph enroute. Linda n Jackie, status unknown. Ros n Matt responsive
> but not moving. Paul n Christine unresponsive.
> **Ben:** Someone tried to hack our system
> **Ben:** holding them off
> **Ben:** If I get cut off everyone keep moving n be safe

Responsive and not moving? What the hell was going on in Vegas? He knew they lived near the Strip, one of the last places on Earth he'd want to be right now, but they should have had a head start to get out of Dodge. Paul and Christine, he had expected, they were tourist, but Jackie should have gotten Linda out of Sacramento and been halfway towards Nevada by now. Something was wrong. At least Casey, Mark's family, and Joseph were on the way, that much was going right, but they also had the longest way to travel and their circumstances could change in an instant.

And who the fuck was hacking our system? Who even knew about us to know where to look?

"Dad?" called Caleb, interrupting his train of thought. He ignored him, trying to work things out and picture in his head every single person that might know the Compounds existed. It should be few and far between, that **was** the point, after all; to stay hidden and off the grid.

Michelle was finally exiting the restroom and was walking briskly towards the van. "What took you so long?" he asked, as she got in and shut the door. "I was getting worried."

"You unzip and piss, it's a little more complicated for us girls. We have to take these things almost completely off," Michelle replied, pulling on the rubber as if to demonstrate.

"We have to take it off to sit!" Nick piped up from the back; which got him a dirty look in exchange.

Their suits were designed for safety, but he made a mental note to point out to Sean that they could have at least made it easier to go to the bathroom. You couldn't always take everything off to pee. And let's face it, that's when you were most vulnerable. Comfort just hadn't been in the design. Then again, if it were really pressing, he guessed they could just go in them and clean it up later. No use worrying how sticky or smelly you were when being chased by undead cannibals.

Monica looked at her phone as he turned the van over and began to back up, waving his hand at Sam and watching her lights come on in response. She was ready to go.

"Oh shit," Monica said, reading her text.

"Yeah, we need to get moving," he said, not for the first time.

"I realize that," she responded hotly. "Saying it repeatedly isn't going to make it happen any faster!"

"Dad!" Caleb yelled at him.

"We do not raise our voices in the van," he told the boy sternly, making his son wince. Monica's quick temper was starting to grate on him, making his voice harsher than usual when talking to his son. The boy was just scared, and he needed to keep that in mind whenever dealing with the kids' angst. "What is it?"

Glancing in the mirror he could see the worry in his son's face, and he checked his other mirrors to make sure there wasn't something coming at him he didn't see, but there was nothing but an empty freeway. It was still early yet. When the shit really hit the fan, it'd probably be bogged down with people fleeing the larger cities and he definitely wanted to stay ahead of that. He got on the interstate and began to accelerate towards ninety, Sam's van following close behind.

"My phone says no service," Caleb replied softer, waving his phone in the air for effect.

He had already guessed as much and didn't really need to be told, but what was the point of creating an issue over it? His kids seemed to think the harder they pushed, the better the response they'd get, but mostly all it did was rile him up.

Controlling his anger, he only shook his head and said, "probably just the area we're in." Even after the words came out of his mouth, his own mind was rejecting it. They had come this way too many times over the years for him to believe that the service loss was due to where they were; especially with what was going on in the world today.

He tried to stay calm, but his nerves were starting to fray. Did all the phone carriers get shut down on purpose, not simply overloaded by people trying to call home? He thought back to the Stand and that scene in the movie where Kathy Bates is in the studio, broadcasting until the marines gunned her down. Had the military already anticipated that? Had they moved on the radio and television stations as soon as this shit began? Was that why it was so frackin' quiet? He wondered, if he had a TV before him, would any of the channels be broadcasting? All communications appeared to be offline. Was that to stave off panic? Because he didn't know about the rest of the country, but it was feeding his. Maybe someone other than the government had hacked them and shut them off?

The cut off feeling was getting worse and it was useless for him to try and speculate without anything to go on. He was only winding himself even more.

"Our phones are still up," Monica told him, showing an image update on her screen.

"But for how long?" he returned. Ben said that someone was trying to hack their system. Were they the same people that had shut everything else down? The timing was oddly coincidental not to be connected. She was texting Ben, but it was useless; he wouldn't answer. He had enough to deal with at the moment, and if they all flooded him with texts, he might make a mistake at the wrong time. No, it was best to leave him alone and focus on what came next.

He accelerated to a speed that felt uncomfortable but manageable. He doubted the highway patrol was issuing tickets right now. Their vans sped towards the rising sun, Sam having accelerated to keep pace with him. She had lived in Los Angeles for a time, he knew she could handle it. However, she had never been to the compounds before and he needed to keep in mind to make sure she stayed with him.

In fifteen minutes, they'd be in Wilcox and soon after that, the turn off for Safford. He had never driven this fast down this highway before and he prayed that the road was clear ahead. He had been relying on Ben's advice and now that may be gone as well. They were on their own. Gripping the steering wheel tightly, he vowed to make the best of it.

Chapter 9
Roadblock

Casey
Roswell, NM

    He had spent every minute of his drive with Albuquerque eating at the edges of his mind. He had read the texts about the others being on the road and their system getting hacked, and his stress levels had risen thinking Ben wouldn't be there to guide him once he got into New Mexico. Funny shit was, he had built up all this angst over traveling south of Albuquerque and it ended up being Roswell that gave him the most problems.

    The radio had quit playing music shortly after he got past Abilene. He had grown tired of listening to the hiss of static and had shut the damned thing off. There had been sporadic traffic on the interstate, though none of it seemed focused on one direction. It appeared everyone felt that they needed to go **somewhere**, just couldn't agree where.

    He had anticipated there being more people on the road than this. Were they all barricading themselves in their houses to wait it out? Maybe that was the smarter thing to do, rather than torching the place. Yet, they didn't have a place to go and he did. Now he had to only get there in one piece.

    So far, he'd been lucky enough not to run into any trouble, just the occasional emergency vehicle forcing its way passed. He had taken it slow at first, worrying he'd get pulled over, but he hadn't seen a highway patrolman in a very long time. They apparently had their hands full.

    He suddenly laughed, his voice coming out in a scratchy dry pitch. He needed to drink more. He reached for the bottle of water on the seat next to him and his eyes fell on the bag of weed. Maybe he should have brought more of his stash with him. It wasn't bloody likely he'd get locked up for drug possession.

He sighed and pushed past it. It didn't really matter. He had a secret grove at the compound he was quite sure Todd didn't know about; he'd flip out if he did.

The sign for Roswell appeared and he let up on the gas. Relieved at the sound of his phone vibrating, he let a smile break, and once he was sure that an asshole wouldn't hit him for checking it, he glanced at the screen.

Ben: roadblock ahead

"Aw shit," he swore loudly. There was no way to bi-pass Roswell without turning around and losing half the day backtracking. Even then, he couldn't guarantee he wouldn't just run into another one. The junction was directly in the center of the city and all of the upcoming exits would just take him through side streets and neighborhoods; places he did not want to be if he could help it.

His fingers had begun to tremble, and he gripped the wheel tighter, trying to work through it. His nerves were completely destroyed by the constant danger he'd been in. He needed a second to calm down but didn't see how that could happen until he crossed over into Arizona.

A sign for Red Bridge Rd flew past and he knew that he was fast approaching where the roadblock had to be. Sure enough, the sparse traffic started to slow and become more compact; the congestion increasing as traffic slowed to a crawl.

He cursed and banged his fist against the wheel in frustration. *What's with this shit?*

He saw panicked drivers on either side, most of which looked like fellow Texans fleeing the big cities. He wondered where they were all going that they thought was safe? He doubted they even knew themselves. As long as they were moving away from their perceived danger, they'd go wherever the road led them. At least he had a plan; even though it was majorly getting fucked with at the moment.

A few cars sped by him going the opposite direction, so traffic had to be getting through, right? Or were they turning people around up there? Wouldn't Ben have warned him before he came this way? Was that not part of what he was supposed to be doing, guiding them? Checking his phone, he didn't see any messages that he might have missed. He was beginning to think that instead of that kiss, he'd give that boy a swift kick in the ass.

Time had passed and the roadblock was beginning to come into view an inch at a time. There were school busses parked on either side of the freeway, forcing traffic into a single lane. Four men stood on top of each bus, heavily armed and pointing their weapons at the traffic below. It didn't look like they were turning people around, but it definitely looked like they were inspecting every vehicle that approached. He hadn't planned on this when he chose this route three years earlier and didn't know why he hadn't foreseen something like this.

Lifting his phone, he decided to break protocol and send Ben a text, asking if people were getting through the city. If he knew about the roadblock, then he also had to know something about what he was facing.

Ben: Some are, yes
Ben: For God sakes play it cool

Swearing once more, he decided the wet kiss would turn into a punch in the mouth **and** a kick in the ass. Play it cool? He was nothing but cool. The King of Cool.

Ben: take a hit or something

He had to laugh out loud at that. The boy knew him better than his ex-girlfriend did. They were at a crawl at the moment, would it hurt? He sighed and restrained himself. Even though he had the windows down to air out the car, he doubted these small-town hombres would appreciate a cloud of marijuana smoke hitting them in the face when he rolled up. He forced himself to relax and wait his turn.

A redneck in black pants, shirt, and cowboy hat stood at the base of the bus on the left; waving him forward. He had a shotgun propped on his hip and a cigarette dangled from the corner of his mouth; the Marlboro Man come to life. The men overhead were holding their guns pointed in his direction and he had to fight pissing his pants. His hand wanted to reach for the rifle in the back seat, but he didn't dare; not with all those men anxiously waiting for him to make a move.

Relax Ben had told him. *I'm trying*.

The smell from what he smoked at the last rest stop must have lingered because the man leaning forward instantly pulled back. He could hear the men cock their guns and his heart thundered in his chest. *Shit*.

"Have you been bit?" the man asked, waving a hand in front of his nose, as if forgetting a cigarette was burning just beneath it. He was keeping his distance; the shotgun now held with both hands for quick use. The man's eyes studied his face, looking for signs of deception.

"Once by my ex. Nearly took a nipple off. If you're offering, I'm afraid to say you're just not my type," he responded, trying not to squirm under the man's gaze and using humor to ease tension; it didn't work.

"A smart-ass pot-head, never saw that coming. Why don't you step out here a second?" the man commanded, reaching for the door handle.

He had restrained himself from reaching for his gun before; but now he was reconsidering it. If he was going down, he wasn't going to do it without a fight. The door opened and the decision was made for him. He forced his hand to his side and reluctantly climbed out of his hatchback. He was made to turn around and his suit was thoroughly checked for bite marks and blood. When the man started to check his hips, he let his anger slip. "You could at least buy me a drink first."

"How is it that a shit bag like you is wearing equipment like this?" the man asked. "You some kind of military wannabe? There's no way they'd take a junkie like you."

"I'm sure that after today they won't be so picky," he returned. "In case you hadn't noticed, the world seems to be going to hell in a handbasket. Do you touch your cow utters this way? Feels kind of harsh."

"Keep up it up asshole, you'll find out what hell really is," the man growled.

He remained silent, pissed at the treatment and wanting to tell the guy where to go. Then he felt a hand pat his upper thigh. "Hey, just a bit close there, Cowboy," he sneered. "Does your brand of hell include a colonoscopy? Never did like that sort of thing and I've got to tell you, I had burritos for breakfast and that can make things really messy down there."

His nerves were a wreck, but at least he sounded stronger than the way he was feeling.

"Your mouth is about to get you shot. You are not welcome here, stoner," the man in black growled in response; sounding disappointed that he hadn't found anything other than a wise-crack for his efforts.

"That's alright, I'm just passing through, Agent Kay," he said, unable to help himself. It had occurred to him how ironic it was getting the pat down from a man in black clothing in Roswell, New Mexico.

Man, I crack myself up.

The cowboy wasn't smiling, making him laugh harder; the stoic look of Kay represented even more by the man's firmly set mouth. "You will be escorted to the other side of town. Do not deviate. Do not stop." This sounded like a rehearsed line and he was less bothered by that, then the way the man kept looking away to the waiting cars to the rear. Something was catching his attention. The obvious distaste the man had shown was gone; it had been replaced with concern and fear. Well who knew? The man might have some feelings in there after all.

With the cowboy's divided attention and his permission to move on, he swiftly got back into his car. He turned the engine over and gave it some gas; preparing to leave. The man was absent-mindedly waving him on; dismissing him. He chanced a glance in his rear-view but didn't see anything other than drivers waiting their turn. He inched forward and a blue Dodge Dakota jerked onto the road in front of him. Three men with high powered rifles were in the back; guns pointed straight at him, daring him to make a break for it.

Holy shit, these guys are armed to the teeth. Well, except for the kid in the passenger seat of the truck that was pretending to shoot him with a flashing ray gun. Fat lot of good it would do against a zombie.

Sighing, he followed the smirking kid in the truck and pulled forward.

A rifle went off.

He jerked and grabbed his chest; thinking he got shot. Satisfied that he was still in one piece and realizing that his leg had grown a bit wet; he turned to look behind him. The men on the top of the buses were firing into the cars approaching the town and a sinking feeling filled his gut; it had finally caught up to him! The Dakota sped up and he followed suit. The sooner he got through this town and back on his way the better. He hadn't seen anything first hand yet, but he wasn't raring to either.

The gunshots were echoing around him as he gunned it; trying to put some distance on them. A flurry of shots erupted immediately after and he pursed his lips, fighting the urge to speed around the truck and floor it; the shit was starting to hit the fan.

He shivered at the thought of how close he had come to being trapped back at that roadblock. His luck was holding; barely. He would need it to stay with him if he was going to get to the compound in one piece.

How was it traveling so fast? He had expected it to come from the larger city to the northwest, not the half of Texas he had put between himself and Dallas.

Within minutes the chaos had dropped away and he could see the other roadblock coming into view. This one was larger than the one he'd left; they must have had the same misgivings about the turn off to the larger city that he did.

Some people had to be making that wrong turn at Albuquerque.

As crazy as things were, his funny bone had remained intact and he cracked up again. The boy was still shooting that damn fake gun at him too. He was literally living in another dimension and time.

Welcome, to the Twilight Zone. Jordan Peele eat your heart out.

A truck pulled forward, creating a gap for him to pass through. The Dakota pulled to the left and the men were yelling at their comrades on top of the busses; pointing back the way they came. He could hear them arguing against letting anyone else through. He had passed several cars on his short trip across town and he wondered how many were already turning back. There was a heated discussion between a guy atop a tour bus and the three men in the truck. The driver was yelling into a walkie and gunned his engine to let the other men know he was about to pull away.

Shit, it **was** serious.

One of the men was waving at him impatiently to keep moving and he wasn't about to argue. He passed through the barricade as fast and safely as he could, then floored it; the hatchback lurching forward. His nerves were making him jittery and he needed a hit, bad.

Getting up to ninety, he quickly put Roswell behind him. As bad as it sounded, he wasn't worried about their lives; only his. They could cover each other's asses; he was out here alone. Socorro was ahead and he hoped that they didn't have enough people to barricade a road. He did **not** want to go through that again. The thought of traffic fleeing south from Albuquerque was enough stress on his system; he wasn't sure he could take much more.

Not too much further, he told himself in an attempt to slow his breathing.

Going through this alone was harder than he realized. He had always lived a solitary life and never regretted that until now. When he considered what might happen if the world went to shit, he saw that as a benefit not a hindrance. He didn't realize how alone and vulnerable it would make him feel; how isolated.

He heard the motorcycles before they came into view. A large biker gang was driving towards him and his heartrate quickened. He slowed to a crawl and tried not to swerve, hands gripping the wheel tightly. The bikers passed on either side and he did his best not to hit one of them. They wore black jackets with Hell's Angels patches on the back and one of them pounded on the hood of his car as they drove by. He was too scared to say shit in response, keeping his eyes ahead and ignoring them the best he could.

Well, they'd need some kind of divine protection if they were heading into Roswell.

Hell, he could use some too.

As if answering his prayer for a guardian angel, his phone went off.

Ben: Roswell being overrun but Socorro looks clear and empty

Ben: How does a stoner like you get so lucky?

"I don't know," he responded, laughing as he read it. He hadn't done anything to earn it; not the way he lived. Someone **did** seem to be watching over him though, but unlike the masses of people that were probably streaming into churches, he knew that it wasn't the Lord taking time out of His busy schedule to save his sorry ass.

Oh no.

It was a twenty-year-old hacker sitting in front of a computer munching a hot pocket.

He sighed with the hilarity that represented. Today, he'd take the hacker over any kind of divine intervention. The way the world was going to shit, he wouldn't trust any sort of help from above.

Then his radio came to life and someone finally started talking.

Chapter 10
Starbucks

Rosilynn
Las Vegas, NV

"Ros, honey, you need to wake up," a voice said softly in the background of her dreams. She was in bed with her husband, their bodies intertwined. They were no longer two separate beings but one, enjoined together forever. Pleasure coursed through her and she groaned uncontrollably. The voice called to her again, but she didn't want to give this up just yet.

A phone buzzed and she broke from kissing her husband to look at her nightstand.

Granny Zombie was planted there, blood pooled beneath her severed waist. As she began to scream, the wretched creature lunged forward and tore into her.

She burst from her nightmare screaming and felt a hand clamp down on her mouth, cutting off her air supply. She struggled under the weight of the attack; but the force of the grip was too strong. She beat at the hands with her fists, but it wasn't enough to break herself free. She tried to scream again but without any air it was a futile exercise. She was starting to become light-headed, her limbs tingling as she grew closer to passing out once more.

"Listen to me," a harsh voice breathed in her ear. "It's just me. You have to stop screaming or we're going to die. Do you understand?" the familiar voice in the dark asked her.

She nodded. Her lungs were on fire and she knew she had to comply.

"Okay, I'm going to take my hand away from your mouth. Please Rosilynn, don't scream."

The hand was gone, and air flooded her lungs. It caused her back to lift to get as much in as possible; her breathing rapid and uncontrollable. Her eyes were open, she was sure of it, but she couldn't see a damn thing. Where the hell was she?

An image of that old lady tearing into her fluttered through her mind again. Her body began to retract itself despite the ache in her joints and the soreness of her muscles. Her head was pounding, and she tentatively reached out with her gloved hand, searching for whoever had been strangling her. "What the fuck is going on? Who are you?"

A hand touched her tenderly, then he was there, his body wrapped around her, enveloping her. She knew from the way she was being held that it was her husband trying to give her comfort. She was a strong independent woman who liked to work out in the gym by her husband's side. She liked to take runs in the morning to keep in shape; to challenge him to do something she couldn't do. But in this moment of vulnerability, she let herself go; letting him be the strong one for once. She gave herself over and felt the tears crushing their way out of her.

Things had started out so well today, she mourned.

"Matthew?" she asked softly as he stroked her hair soothingly. Her voice came out in a croak. She tried to clear it, but it felt dry and raw; she needed something to drink. "Why can't I see anything?" she gasped. She felt something wet press against her mouth. She parted her lips and took a couple of sips, letting it trickle down her parched throat. The coldness of it stung and she nearly choked in response. Coughing, she felt his hand leave her shoulder and she worried that he'd clamp it over her mouth again. She jerked her head uncontrollably to the side; a reflex to the previous smothering she had just experienced.

He shushed her instead and his hand started rubbing her arm. "I don't know how hard you hit your head or how much you remember," he said softly, trying his best to calm her down. "When we came in here, the streets were overrun, and I don't know how many more of those things are still out there. Any noise might draw their attention. We have to stay quiet. Our lives depend on it."

The water was tipped towards her mouth and she did her best to not get choked up this time. Her throat was still raw. It felt like she had inhaled an entire pack of cigarettes with one breath. Her clinical mind was trying to function, but her head was still heavy; her ability to reason impaired.

Concussion, her mind whispered.

She tried to think on all that had transpired since leaving the house, and a flood of memories gripped her, making her clench together in a ball between his arms. Her head flew back, and she nearly screamed. She flung her right arm into her own mouth, biting down on the rubbery surface of her suit.

The pressure.

Oh my God, her mind cried, and her hands frantically started to run up and down her body, searching for tears in the suit. She whimpered with fear, fingers running through every crevice, covering every inch. The panic had completely eclipsed her mind and controlled her every movement.

To his credit, her husband did not interfere.

She began to relax as her fingers found nothing bitten or torn.

"You are fine. I checked myself," he soothed.

She was taking another gulp of water, this time with the bottle in her own hand to control the short flow of it. "Then why let me go through that?" she asked softly, her mind still trying to make sense of things.

"You wouldn't have believed me until you checked yourself," he stated matter-of-factly. Something banged in the distance and Matt cut off whatever he was going to say next; his body growing tense. When nothing further happened, his body relaxed and his hand continued to stroke her, having fallen to her back now.

"There was an explosion. The blast threw you away from me. By the time I got back on my feet and found you, one of those things was clawing its way up your waist, trying to get through your suit."

She shivered with the memory and once again saw that old lady lunging.

"I got it off you, but you were unconscious. We couldn't stay on the street; those things were everywhere. So, I found a place to hole up until you were well enough to travel."

"How long?" she asked, some of the strength returning to her voice.

She could feel him shrug. "Hard to tell time in the dark like this," he explained. "It's been a couple of hours at least. Our phones have been updating. Most of the others are on their way, and someone is trying to hack our computer systems. Haven't heard much since."

"It's not night yet, is it?" she asked. "I know I'm not blind. I can see vague shapes, but it's pitch black in here."

"We're in a storeroom," he answered. "It has a small window on the door, but I covered it and turned off the light, so we didn't draw attention to ourselves."

There was a click and the beam of a flashlight suddenly lit up the room, making her eyes sting at the sudden assault. She covered them with her arm, squinting and letting them slowly adjust. The pain slowly began to recede, but her head pounded all the more.

They were lying on large brown sacks she hadn't noticed before, due to the suit and the presence of his body around her. At their feet was a large box of cups with green mermaids on the label. "Starbucks? Really? Zombies roaming the streets and the only place you can think of to take me is where you get your morning coffee?"

His chest rumbled with quiet laughter. "Not many choices, babe."

"Sure. So if I ask you to pass me your bag, I won't find coffee bags hidden away?" she asked, trying to lean forward and gain some of her balance back. She was picking on him out of habit. She really didn't care what he had stashed away just as long as it didn't end up in her bag. Those damn things were heavy enough as it was.

He chuckled but didn't respond.

That's what I thought.

A memory came to her then, and a need to be silent or not, it ached to be heard. "Remember that time after your second tour when you got this insatiable craving for Starbucks? Said you hadn't had it for so long you just had to have it? What was that flavor you made us drive all across town for?"

She felt the rumble of his chest while he tried to suppress his laugh. "Pumpkin Spice."

"That's it!" she exclaimed softly, grinning. "I don't know what you're going to do with those beans, not like we have a machine back at the compound to do anything with them."

"I like the smell," he answered simply, as if that's all he wanted them for.

Pausing briefly to collect herself, she looked from him to the door. "We're going to have to move," she whispered, her hand rushing to her temple and stroking it as her blood flow normalized.

"Can you do that?" he asked the nurse in her, knowing that every second she sat there she was analyzing her body, mentally running through a checklist of what was right and wrong.

Her thighs were sore. That was from the impact on the street and the fact some fucking monster had tried to eat her, but they were structurally intact and mobile.

Her arms were stiff, and she'd need to flex them a bit more to loosen them up. The suit had helped prevent most of the damage she would have otherwise taken.

Her head felt tender and when she ran her fingers through her scalp, she felt something damp. A small wound had bled a little, but she was otherwise fine, it'd heal. Her vision swayed a bit when she applied pressure to it, but she didn't think there was any internal damage. Not like she had an MRI just to make sure. There was no fracture at least.

Her earlier assessment was probably spot on; she had a concussion.

Well, she wasn't about to argue with the diagnosis of her unconscious mind. Usually she'd recommend bed rest, but that ship had sailed. If they didn't get moving, they might not ever make it out of town.

With his help, she struggled to her feet and put a hand out; grasping a wire shelving unit for balance. Her head was still a bit heavy, but the more she stretched and moved around the lighter it got. She began to shift her weight from side to side, testing her balance and her legs' abilities to keep her vertical. She seemed good. Her weapons were lying on top of her pack and she bent over to get them.

The world slid sideways, and she almost fell forward again.

"I think we should wait," he told her, concern heavy in his voice.

He came to stand by her side in case she needed assistance, but she had already regained her balance; the dizziness seemed to have eased. She was strapping on her weapons and trying to flex her neck to loosen the tensed muscles. She ran her fingers through the protective pads she wore, making sure everything was fastened. Then she grabbed her pack and wrestled it onto her back.

"I'm fine," she told him, reaching down and grabbing her Colt Rimfire. She held it firmly in the crook of her arm, but kept it lowered.

"We can wait. No one says we have to do this right now," her husband told her. He was eyeing her warily, as if expecting her to fall apart at any second.

It made her angry to be treated like a Jenga puzzle. "You know we can't do that. Let's go," she told him firmly.

He looked doubtful but didn't argue. He knew that she was the best judge of what she could take. Still, he took his sweet time getting ready.

"Really?" she asked, watching him, counting the passing minutes like they were the last of her life. "Women are the ones that are supposed to take forever to leave, you know," she said, ribbing him. She was doing her best not to snap, but it was a close thing.

He grunted in return and straightened up, taking his own rifle in hand. He was using an HK MP5 Rimfire and he held it firmly with the suppressor lowered.

She moved the cloth bag aside and felt the sting in her eyes as the light flooded through; the sun was still high in the sky. She didn't see anyone, or anything; not from this angle at least. She braced herself as she gripped the metal handle and opened the door a crack. With a nod from her husband, she raised her rifle and plunged back into the fray.

Chapter 11
Impact

Mark
West of Columbus, OH

Suddenly, living so far from Arizona seemed like a horrible idea. Ohio wasn't as far as the east coast but with the distance he had to cover, he might as well have lived on another continent. There was way too much America to cross in order to reach the compound, and he had no idea how he was going to do it. He had turned down Sean's offer to have a private plane on call; since he had no real intention of ever using it. Now he wondered at the stupidity of that choice.

He had gone along with things over the years, but never fully committed himself like the rest of them had. Always the quiet one of the group, he had kept his family distant from the rest; participating in body, not in spirit. It was a defense mechanism to keep himself separate and free to act as he wanted, to be able to break away if needed.

Now he regretted it and wondered if that choice would end up costing him his life and that of his family. He hadn't even caught up to his wife and daughter yet. He was texting her as he went but her answers were sporadic, and they were always just a little bit ahead of his position.

He had jokingly created several routes to get to the compound, but none of them were viable facing an infection of this magnitude. Yet, his wife was dutifully charging down one of the direct routes and he needed to pick up his pace if he was going to catch them. He had messaged her to keep on going; as getting out of the city had taken longer than he had been comfortable with. Since they were already on the road, he didn't want to endanger them by making them wait.

When he had gotten back to the firehouse, the dispatcher had told them that calls were coming in from all over the city and none of them were getting answered. His co-workers had tossed down their gear upon their return, each thinking of their families and rushing to get them to safety. He had told Debbie to get moving; to abandon the phones and get her family out of town. He wondered now if he should have offered to take them with him, but his wife was already on the highway; he couldn't afford to loiter around if he were to have any hope of catching up to them.

He was in his truck now with his gear on the seat next to him, barreling down the interstate as he made his way west. He held no hope in his heart for what was to come but giving up was not part of his character. Why hadn't he planned better? He had prayed that it would never come to this, but he had been naïve. How could he believe that those in charge would never push that button? That at some point, Mankind would grow so power hungry that they'd do anything to control the world?

As a fireman, he felt horrible that he was hightailing it out of there, abandoning his city at its time of need. He should be out there trying to save lives, attempt to fight off the hordes of undead that had begun rising around them. But he had seen several attacks since that fire and knew that it was useless. The most anyone could do was dig a hole, climb into it and wait it out.

His was twenty-two hours away from his destination and had to pass through cities larger than the one he was leaving. If getting out of Columbus was bad, Indianapolis would be worse. Then there was St. Louis, Springfield, Oklahoma City, and finally Albuquerque. He couldn't take a wrong turn, he had to stay focused and on track; that was his only hope.

His CB radio was on and the chatter was erratic but constant. Other than the occasional text from Ben and status check from his wife, he was alone with the voices. It was enough to drive a man crazy. The axe he had carried for years lay on the seat next to his high-powered rifle, the blood from that crazy ass woman still staining the blade. He had already decided the axe would be more useful in the future as really couldn't shoot for shit; best to stick with what worked.

Somewhere ahead, Joseph was on the move. He had been the one good friend he had made in their group; their similar professions drawing them together. They had both dedicated their lives to protecting strangers that would never even know their names. That made the bond between them stronger than the ones he hadn't quite formed with the others. Joe was a member of the Little Rock Police Department; a boy in blue, but who the fuck cared? He had more in common with him then some of those other nerds he had gamed with.

Roxanne had gotten along with the women of the group though, and she was the only reason they had continued on with this Doomsday shit. Regardless of his friendship with Joseph, he would have lost interest a long time ago if she hadn't kept pushing for them to stay involved.

He had taken up gaming on a whim; mostly as a way to blow off steam when a tour ended badly. He never expected to get so involved with it. Even then, he had kept to himself, only playing to relieve the built-up rage within. Killing made up orcs was better than being aggressive with an innocent bystander. Yeah, it could be fun at times, but mostly it served only as a way to occupy his mind on his days off.

His wife was an accountant and constantly had to run off to work for some crisis or another. He had restrained himself from reminding her that he actually dealt with real life and death situations, not her. But what was the point of opening that can of worms? His job had made his time at home seem more precious; not to be wasted on pointless bickering. Whenever he had a day off during the week and the house to himself; he had nothing else to do but amuse himself in front of a computer screen.

He glanced at the overpass ahead and saw a man standing on the edge; ready to jump.

He slammed on his brakes and swerved so he wouldn't be in the man's path; it was too late. A body pounded into his hood feet first, the impact causing his truck to buck wildly. He spun the wheel trying to maintain control but wasn't quick enough. The side of the overpass was approaching fast and he threw up his hands to brace himself.

His truck slammed into a concrete support column and his head struck the steering wheel so hard it knocked him unconscious.

Chapter 12
Vegas

Rosilynn
Las Vegas, NV

The streets appeared to be empty, but that could change drastically and without warning. The sun had risen towards its zenith; they must have been in that store longer than they'd thought. She held her rifle ready as she stepped over broken glass and onto the blood-stained sidewalk, her eyes sweeping her path for any sign of the undead.

The chaotic intersection they had been at was nowhere to be seen and she wondered how far Matt had brought her while she'd been unconscious. How had he managed to keep them safe while doing it? She didn't know how long she hovered there taking it all in, because her husband nudged her arm and was nodding his head down the street, insisting that they keep moving.

The road was littered with abandoned cars. Doors hung open; the resulting annoying tones reminding their long-gone owners to close them. She fought the ingrained behavior to step forward and do it for them; they didn't have time for such a useless act. If the sound was going to attract attention, it would have done so long before she had stepped onto this sidewalk.

Her eyes looked to a nearby road sign to try and get her bearings. The sun was hiding behind cloud cover and with all of the destruction the street had suffered, her mind was refusing to orient itself. The sign informed her that they were on Maryland Pkwy, and that meant that the accident had taken place south from their position.

Looking in the direction of Tropicana, she caught the occasional wisp of smoke and flash of movement. People were moving around down there, but she didn't know if they were friendly or the undead milling about waiting on some dumbass to just walk up on them. Either way, she wasn't going to take that chance.

She did feel a momentarily flash of anger that Matt hadn't taken them further south so they wouldn't have to cross between that massacre and the strip to the north, but it's not like she'd been conscious at the time in order to give him her input.

She sighed heavily and decided to move past it without saying a word. There was nothing to be done; the deed was done. Mentally, she ran their route through her head and realized that they would have to cut southeast through a cluster of buildings in order to make it to Spencer. It could not be a set path; it would have to adapt as they went as the world around them shifted with the chaos gripping it. She preferred to have every step worked out in advance, but that was impossible to do in a crisis like this; there were too many unknowns.

The route they were being funneled through would take them dangerously close to the airport, but it was the fastest way to the 215. She couldn't count on it being any safer than Tropicana was right now, but there had to be something for her to focus on; she could only deal with one dilemma at a time. The longer they remained immobile, the less the chance they'd survive.

She led the way as Matt covered her flank, his military training kicking in. Since stealth was paramount to their progress, and she didn't have a suppressor like he did, she shouldered her rifle and drew her sword instead. The blade was kept sharp, the polished surface reflecting the sun as she slid it free of its scabbard and held it ready.

Eyes alert for danger, she stepped carefully past an abandoned car that had its trunk up blocking their view. A twitching arm caught her attention and she paused. A man was bent over a body, hands tearing flesh and shoving it into his gore filled mouth. It must have just happened because the man he was ripping into appeared to be breathing. He was being eaten alive!

The zombie looked up and her blood turned cold. The undead man looked like a tourist. He had a name tag on his business shirt that indicated that he must have come from a nearby convention, but she couldn't make out the name due to the amount of blood on the creature's chest.

Why the fuck does that matter? Are you going to file a police report? Post it on social media? #asshattouristinVegas?

The zombie's eyes blazed with a mixture of fury and hunger, the mouth sliding open with bits of flesh falling free as drool dripped to the asphalt below. She could tell from his stance that he was preparing to spring at her, the man he'd been eating forgotten as new prey had arrived.

She tried to react, but her limbs were frozen in place; she was about to become his next meal.

Matt brushed past her and fired his rifle without hesitation. The head jerked backwards, and the zombie fell on top of the dying man, pinning him to the ground. Her husband lowered his rifle and fired again, ending the partially eaten man's misery; a head shot ensuring that he didn't come back from it.

"You okay?" he asked with concern. He had seen her freeze. It was not something they could afford; it would get her killed.

She nodded and tried to shrug it off; to harden herself against the world that was being born around her. It was hard after seeing such ugliness. She had seen her fair share at work and understood that the images would fade with time, easily recalled when needed but not as present with every thought she tried to conceive. She just had to ensure that she survived long enough to forget it. "Let's keep going."

They avoided broken glass, sliding carefully past open car doors, eyes watchful for more hidden undead. They masked their progress as much as they could with so much destruction and chaos unfolding around them, but there was only so much to do and keeping your head on a swivel still left you temporarily blind no matter how fast you moved.

A shrill scream came out of a building ahead, but it didn't even make them skip a beat as they continued forward. They were making their way past a neighborhood packed with closely built houses and the thought of what was hiding within made her too cautious to try to find the origin point of the terrified screamer.

It wasn't just the risen dead that was dangerous. People would defend themselves from anything at this point; even those that came to help. It was best to let them fend for themselves; for their progress to continue unabated. Her training as a nurse was pushing her to help, her Humanity driving her towards the pain in those screams, but her body kept moving away and to the south. There was a time to be a hero and a time to just get the fuck out.

She glanced behind her and saw that Matt was looking to their left, but she caught his eye and shook her head. His mouth became firmer, his eyes cold, but he nodded back; plowing his way past her and taking the lead. Having been in the military, it was not in him to avoid a fight but to face it head on. She let him stay there, knowing that it was distracting him from wanting to turn around. She needed them to keep moving, they'd lost more than enough time already.

They crossed the alley behind the houses and came to a halt at a long white wall on the opposite side. She looked around the corner at the parking lot beyond, taking notice of any indications of danger. After careful examination, she didn't see anything alarming, so she nodded to Matt and they began moving once more.

Tropicana was straight ahead. The accident site was to the west and she knew it had probably spread along the road in their direction. They listened to the chaos coming from that direction and tried to figure out its proximity to their location; looking at the casinos was misleading as they towered high overhead a mile away just as much as half. Most of the sounds floating upon the wind were echoing around them from multiple directions and it threw off her orientation, leaving her no clear idea of where the danger currently was or if there was any safe harbor to be had at all.

The screams that had been coming from their rear were suddenly cut short and Matt gave her an accusing look; like she was responsible for their sudden interruption and probably death. She returned the stare without flinching, trying to exude strength and confidence, but she hated herself for what they'd done and couldn't hold it for long.

"We need to keep moving," she whispered at him.

"That doesn't mean we stop being human," he responded coldly.

She glared at his stern face. "This isn't that and you know it. It's about our survival. You don't know what you'd be walking into going to help whoever that was, wherever they were. You could have ended up dead before you even got to them. You'd throw your life away for nothing. There are thousands of people dying out there right now, in this city alone, and you can't be Captain America and save them all."

"I'm not talking about all, just the one. And live or die, at least I'd die doing the right thing," he growled, but she knew that he understood on a deeper level what she was driving at. He just felt as helpless as she did and was taking it out on her.

He chanced another look at the parking lot beyond. Feeling confident that they were in the clear, he raised his rifle and stepped forward, not waiting for a go head or acknowledgment from her as he broke from cover. He was being driven by anger and she made sure to give him space as she covered his flank.

Moving as fast as they dared, they flung themselves against the backside of the building and took cover. They braced themselves, paused long enough to calm their nerves; fighting the impulse to just rush ahead and make a break for it. He checked the corner and she stepped out with him as he entered the side parking lot.

A man came flying down the sidewalk ahead and they froze; weapons raised. It didn't matter, he was oblivious to their presence. He was running full out and the look of terror was enough to get her heart pumping.

Half a second later another figure appeared, causing her adrenaline to flood her system; Matt's rifle tracking the corpse's progress. It was a scantily clad showgirl, judging by the costume she wore; or lack thereof. Her feet were bare and dark muck was flipping up from her heels; realization dawned that it had to be blood. The woman's hair had been pulled back when she was alive; strands popping out in all directions as they came loose from the woman's exertions. One of her breasts had pulled free of the costume and the lack of concern over the nudity drove it home that whoever that woman had been—she'd been replaced by a rabid monster.

Having seen the occasional zombie movie, she was stunned at how normal the girl looked. Her stomach began to churn as she realized that it was going to be hard to discern friend from foe in the heat of the moment. The creature showed no obvious signs of death, other than the blood that was pooling in her legs. When the woman died and her heart quit pumping, the blood had sunk to the lowest point and until the creature fell dead or was forced to crawl, there would be a simulated pair of purple boots below the woman's knees.

Her clinical mind wondered what was keeping that thing moving; what medical or scientific reasoning could be applied to this? She worked in the medical field and what she was seeing was just not possible. The showgirl was pale from the lack of circulation, but so were half the people who hid indoors with their air conditioning; avoiding the sun.

What else stood out that would help her make that split-second decision? It could mean the difference between murder and self-defense.

As the showgirl passed from sight, having not for one second looked their way with such an obvious prey in front of her, she let the breath out that she hadn't realized she had been holding. It came out in a rush and Matt looked at her with concern. It hadn't fazed him one bit.

For a brief instant, she hated him for that.

"Fuck," she whispered in frustration.

After so many years of movies, comics, and books, she had been anticipating a nasty ass monster that easily contrasted with the living. Where was the instant decay or the yellow eyes? These were supposed to be obvious signs, yet the medical part of her training insisted that none of that would ever happen. That it was more a tactic to make them seem scarier in the movies. People had no problem opening up on a hideous monster, but they might feel differently if the person looked completely normal. Now that she saw one that hadn't died in a horrible accident, she wondered how well she'd be able to handle shooting someone that looked ordinary.

"Damn it," she cursed her own naivetés. Matt glanced at her with curious eyes and she mouthed *"later"*, nodding for them to move on.

He nodded and she watched as he crossed the parking lot to a white sedan; the lone vehicle still parked at the Sherman Williams. He checked the lock and smiled; the door was open.

Well hell, someone out there was looking out for them.

He had begun to open the door when his head jerked, and he let out a surprised yelp of pain. Scrambling backwards from the car, he began cursing and stamping at his feet. Quickly moving around to his side, the first thing she saw was blood. It was leaking from where his suit met his shoes, right at the ankle. *Why the hell isn't he wearing his boots?*

Then it sank in; he had been bit.

Rage filled her soul as she fully came around the car, her rifle forgotten and her sword in hand. Crawling out from under the vehicle was a young teen, his skin red and scorched from lying on the hot pavement. Blood was dripping from his teeth; his hands clawing to pull himself in her husband's direction. Furiously, she swung her blade and cleaved the young man's head in half. The skull cap flew across the parking lot where it struck the side of a nearby pub's window; smearing the glass. As the corpse spasmed and the blood flowed, she sliced it several more times, her anger fueling her swings.

"I'm so fucked!" her husband yelled; not caring who heard. "I'm dead Ros, I'm dead." His eyes were looking at her with despair and in all the time she had known him, she'd never seen him so hopeless and defeated. The strength that he emanated was gone and the little boy who had escaped the ghetto at thirteen had returned.

She instantly loathed what she saw, and the words that escaped her were fueled by that hatred; he was supposed to be the strong one. "Shut the fuck up and pull yourself together or we both will be dead."

Forcing him to sit on the hood of the car, she inspected his wound, her gut twisting at the seriousness of the bite. "Why the fuck are you wearing sneakers, dumbass?" He huffed and she ignored it; probing the wound with her finger. Had any saliva gotten through? Was this thing transferred through body fluids? How could she know, when she wasn't sure of the cause or rate of infection? There were too many variables to consider and not enough information to make a diagnosis.

"The cat found my boots and decided to take a crap in them," he responded angrily. It sounded like a punch line to a bad joke. It was such a mundane act in the scheme of things, and it might have cost him his life. Gritting her teeth, she couldn't believe her husband, the love of her life, was going to be taken away from her by cat shit. "Take my foot off Ros," he pleaded, his usually confident voice trembling as he spoke.

"We don't know that it would make any difference," she told him, trying to keep her voice steady, letting her training guide her through the motions. Her eyes were focused on his ankle and it was quite a nasty bite. It had nearly torn his flesh completely off, parts of it hanging there loosely, only attached by a thin thread of skin. If he hadn't jerked his leg back as quickly as he had, it would have been a hell of a lot worse. "Your blood has pumped that shit through your heart by now. Its science fiction to think that you could cease the infection with a quick amputation," she replied, letting the clinical part of her speak over her heart, because at that moment it wanted to cut that damn thing right off.

They had all agreed on the steps that needed to be taken should one of them get bit and her heart sank at the realization that she was going to have to kill her husband. They had both made that pact three years ago. No matter who it was, if they were bit, they were dead already. Better to end it quickly and spare them the pain then wait for them to die horribly, reanimate, and kill one of them instead. But then, they were operating under the dogma that had been created around the zombie phenomenon.

After that half-naked showgirl, she was beginning to question what they knew versus what was actually true. She had seen a woman with a broken spine climb off a car and even though she was crushed by the wheels of their vehicle, had still come after them. However, her death was caused by the accident; not a bite. The showgirl had shown no obvious signs of infection. The old lady in the car hadn't been attacked. She had climbed out of that car with half a body, but none of the infected had gotten to her first. No, it had been that damn semi.

Who had she seen turn from being attacked by the infected? Nobody. So far it had been people that died from other causes. Could she safely judge that this wasn't some airborne virus that acted upon death, instead of a plague that turned anyone that got bit? It didn't mesh with what she had seen, and it wasn't enough for her to just end his life; not without proof.

She looked up at her husband and saw the defeat in his eyes. He was holding out his knife; the will to fight gone. He was ready to die. Her hand had already begun to reach for it, and she saw the tremble in her usually calm hands. Fast under pressure, sure of herself in the OR, not once had she experienced the shakes.

Taking a deep breath, she closed her eyes and tried to calm herself; to reconcile everything that had happened since her phone had gone off. Her mind was racing too fast to make any kind of coherent judgment. The showgirl kept coming back to her, constantly reminding her that she knew nothing about what the fuck was going on to be making a call like this. She poured Peroxide on the bite, watching as it foamed and went to work. Then she wrapped it tightly, trying to staunch the blood loss. She wasn't about to give up on him.

"We don't know if getting bit turns you. If you get sick and there's no other choice, then I'll reconsider. I'm not stupid, I don't want to die. But at this moment, I need you. I need your strength," she said, standing up and taking his face in her hands. She made his eyes meet hers. "I need you to stop acting like you're already dead. This is not some movie, not a TV show trying to get ratings. We don't know anything about this virus, if that's what it is, and what affect it has on the human body. Until we do, I'm not going to kill you. You are not going to die. You are going to snap out of this, get your shit together, and help get us out of this fucking city. If you don't, I might just kill you for slowing me down."

The forcefulness of her words drew anger and she smiled within, glad to see that there was still something there fighting to live. She hated that defeated look and if she ever saw it again, she'd forget he was hurt and kick his ass. It made her feel weak, and that vulnerability was not something she could afford.

"Do we have an understanding Matthew Patrick Miller?" Only his mother used his full name and his eyes flared at her words and the command embedded within. She was willing to bear it if it got him to man up.

"Yes, we do," he said forcefully. "But **when**, not **if**, that time comes, you are going to take that knife and end me, or I will eat a bullet. I will not become one of those things; I will **not** be the cause of your death."

"Agreed," she said, welcoming the anger; it had wiped the defeat away.

She heard movement from behind her and realized that in that intimate moment they had shared; they had forgotten that the world had gone to shit around them. A group of the undead was careening around the corner of the store in the direction the showgirl had taken.

She swiftly sheathed her sword and brought her Rimfire up. Flipping off the safety and applying just a modicum of pressure, she had fired a round before Matt had gotten back on his feet and brought up his own rifle in response. She didn't have a suppressor and she winced at the crackling sound of gunfire, but it couldn't be helped. She had no choice in the matter and found that she no longer cared. Right now, she needed to funnel her anger into something constructive and this herd had given her a target.

A large blade appeared in the head of the leader of the pack, Matt having thrown the knife he had only just recently offered her. Her bullet slammed into the one beside it. Both fell quickly and were trampled by the others. Matt now had his rifle up and was firing. It appeared his will to live had returned with a vengeance.

Her next bullet took out an overweight tourist with a flowered shirt, her second winging a naked man coated in blue paint. No blood exited the bodies on impact, the congealed legs obviously housing the majority of what they'd had when they died. She steadied herself as the distance closed between them and squeezed the trigger once more, taking the blue man's head off.

The last three fell quickly after that, Matt's aim truer than her own. His military bearing had returned. With the herd scattered across the small parking lot eating asphalt, he marched over and retrieved his knife, wiping the blood on the flowered shirt of the fallen tourist with a hint of disgust. "We can discuss this later," he said, as if she was the target of the argument instead of the other way around. "Let's get out of here and stop wasting time," he bit off, but wouldn't look her in the eyes.

She was happy enough to have her husband back that she didn't care to retort, only nodded in agreement. He was limping from the wound, but otherwise there was no obvious sign that anything was wrong. However, he was pausing as he walked, looking down at the corpses at their feet. She knew in her heart that he was imagining becoming one of them. It had crossed her mind as well, but she was not willing to give up; not now anyways.

"Matthew, let's go," she told him sternly.

His eyes snapped in her direction, and for a brief instant she saw the fear and hate dwelling within. Not for her, but for what might happen to him. Pissed, he balled his fist, sheathed his knife, and got into the car. The keys were still in the ignition; a miracle left unexplained and one that she didn't have the heart to question. Someone had ditched it. Probably the same son of a bitch that had bitten her husband. He had probably seen a zombie, hid under the car, and cooked himself to death. Her concerns that maybe it had been left because it didn't run was overridden by the sound of the engine roaring to life. She hoped it was an automatic because he didn't appear to be willing to sit in the passenger seat and let her drive. He had things to work out and needed a sense of purpose to push him forward. However, with the bite on his left ankle, a stick would prove problematic.

She wasn't even sure she remembered how to drive standard anyways.

Taking her weapons in hand, she got into the car, placing them between her legs where they were easily accessible. Their eyes met briefly, and she felt her heart begin to weep. Her defiance, his defeat, which one was more powerful? Which one would mean their death or their salvation?

Only time would tell.

She would have to keep an eye on him and monitor the bite, because he wasn't the kind of man that would complain over any discomfort. If things got worse, she knew she wouldn't hesitate to carry through with the pact they had made. She loved him, but she wasn't eager to die either.

As he flung them onto Tropicana, the thought of what she might have to do haunted her; an anguished tear leaking from her eye. She wiped it away quickly, lest he see it and the argument begin anew. Trying to keep her eyes on the street, her hands went through the motions of reloading their weapons; the whole time praying that one of the bullets she loaded wouldn't eventually find their way through her lover's head.

Not that prayers were worth a damn anymore.

Chapter 13
Rattlesnake Lake

Todd
US 191, AZ

They were finally approaching Rattlesnake Lake. Relief flooded him as he realized they had made it; they were safe. He had been driving close to four hours, the side streets that he had used to skirt the outside of the smaller towns had increased their travel time and added another hour to their journey, but it was better to be safe and make it, then reckless and dead.

The cities they had flown through showed no signs of panic; nothing to indicate that anyone was aware of what was going on in the world. They were blissfully hidden from the main thorough-fair and it was one of the reasons he had suggested this location for their compound in the first place. If you wanted to survive an apocalypse, you did not build your refuge outside a major city center. In fact, one of the places scientists suggested when asked was the Rocky Mountains outside Denver but fuck that shit; he hated snow.

His phone kept updating as they drove. Even though Tucson had begun to glow red, Safford and Morenci had remained in the clear. Maybe the decreased traffic and the locale had worked to their favor. It made him wish that he had moved to one of the smaller towns that his ancestors had once helped establish into a thriving community; it was still home to most of his family. He had been tempted to stop at their houses on the way, but he had been unable to take the chance with his kids in the van, or with Sam and hers close behind. Too many were depending on him and they had to be secured before he worried about anyone else.

He rubbed his chafed skin absent-mindedly, the skin on his wrist red from the friction. It was supposed to be more comfortable than a diving suit, but he felt claustrophobic with the tight rubber clutching at him. Sean had them custom made for each of them, but he swore that he must have put on some weight since the last time he had put it on because it was hard to breathe. His mid-section compressed against him, causing it to restrict his breathing.

Still, if it saved his life—right?

He had been worried ever since they turned onto US 191 and began their trek north. Superstition Highway went through Safford and the chance of them coming face to face with the infection scared the living shit out of him. It was almost a direct line to Phoenix, which had been hit far earlier than Tucson had. There had to be thousands driving in their direction, fleeing the capitol in search of a safe place to ride out the storm.

He had avoided the main part of the city by taking Herman road, which ran through the farmlands rather than the city center. Even then, he couldn't help but stress the entire ten minutes it had taken to get back on the highway and move further east.

His wife had been busy in the seat next to him, frantically sending texts to friends and family with rare looks at the land around them. He didn't know why she bothered. If the kid's cells weren't working, then it wasn't likely that anyone she was texting had phone service either. Whatever was going on wasn't limited to one provider. Still, she'd go stir crazy if she didn't try.

"I know my mother got one of my texts, it showed read on the bottom of it," she muttered.

"Just now?" he asked, his thoughts furiously wondering if the phones were back up and whether or not he could reach his parents. He had felt a flash guilt when he had passed his grandparent's turn off in Clifton but had kept on going. It had been the source of heated discussions over the years and one he ultimately lost. His wife's stance had been that no matter what; their kids came first. The rest were adults and could make it on their own. They had enough on their hands already without taking responsibility for every other person they knew.

That went for each other as well.

That had been the hardest promise he had ever made, to leave his wife if their kids' life hung in the balance. After seventeen years, they were inseparable; one not able to function without the other.

She was shaking her head at him. "No. It was one of the earlier ones. I wish I knew what was going on! Don't they realize that we can tell when they check their messages? That it's obvious they're ignoring us?"

He didn't have a response. He couldn't reassure her that everything was all right, because things didn't feel or look that way. How could he comfort her when he needed it himself? Her mother lived on the outskirts of Tucson and had more of a direct shot of getting east then they had. If she wanted to get out, she could have. There was nothing else he could say other than that.

She growled, then pocketed her phone and turned her eyes to the road.

"It's not just your mother, you know," he commented after a few seconds. "Sam's husband flat out ignored her advice to leave and actually **turned** his phone off. I'd say it might come back and bite him in the ass, but that might quite literally happen if what we're being told is true."

Monica glared at him. "I can give two shits about Ruben. I want our parents to get out of there, my sister to check her messages and get on the road, and for the few people we've told to take us seriously. It's not like we would just make this shit up. They have to have noticed something is wrong by now, right?"

"I know Babe," he answered simply, not wanting to push her any further.

The kids were usually a bunch of chatter boxes, always egging each other on, but as he looked in the rear-view mirror, he only saw passive faces watching the land pass alongside them. Their silence was a new and frightening thing; it helped bring the reality down upon him.

Without some outside impulse, they were at a loss of what to do or say; living zombies. Just—without the cannibalistic impulses. They were products of the information age and someone had pulled the plug. Their eyes were scanning the forest around them, but they were slightly vacant and disinterested in what they were seeing. He had worried that bringing them up in this kind of life might scar them forever; but what could be more damaging than what was going on right now? He might have actually saved their lives instead.

This was one time, however, that he hated to be right.

He was coming up on the turn off and he eased up on the gas. The road he'd be turning onto was well hidden; he would need to focus on where they were going if he wanted to find it the first time. No matter how many times he came this way, it was still hard for him to find. There were no markers to indicate where the dirt road was; their need for secrecy paramount to their survival. They didn't want the wrong people finding the place. Very few of their friends and family even knew about it.

Sam slowed to a crawl behind him, patiently waiting for him to indicate where they were turning, and even though he knew what to look for he had almost missed it. As he turned onto the road, he looked up at the surveillance camera in the large tree next to the road. He waved at it, sure that Ben was watching them from his computer chair in the compound ahead.

As if to emphasize that point, his phone became to vibrate.

Ben: Glad you made it. You're clear

Confident that the way ahead was free from danger, he drove down the narrow dirt road and started to relax. The tall trees to either side obscured the light and he almost had to turn on his headlights. The van barely fit on the road, the ruts causing the vehicle to buck as he drove onward. It was designed that way so that the canopy would obscure it from the view of any passing planes. Not that the compounds themselves wouldn't be seen or picked up by the satellites. They had a hard time over the years convincing themselves that it looked innocent when they looked it up on Google Maps.

"Mom, Sam is slowing down. I think her van is having a hard time with this road," Michelle spoke up from the back, her head looking out the rear window.

"She'll be fine. She can go slower if she needs to. There is nowhere to go but forward now; she won't get lost," Monica answered before he could.

He glanced over at her and smiled. She hadn't been overly eager to open up their marriage like he had been, and it had taken a few years for her to adjust to the added people in their lives, but eventually she came around and their marriage had prospered because of it. The rough parts had been smoothed out and now they were simply a larger family; acceptance achieved, and all earlier arguments forgotten.

The kids were calmer now as they realized that their second home was fast approaching. The safety it represented had a soothing effect upon them all. His wife's hands had stopped their nervous rubbing of her pant leg and she was now looking at him with a weak smile upon her face.

Even though they had practiced driving here using alternate routes over the years, it still felt like their first time and his heart beat rapidly in his chest as his destination drew nearer. The reality of what was going on in the world kept wanting to intrude, but enclosed in the embrace of this familiar forest, he couldn't help but forget it for a moment. The rush to get here had only been mitigated by the numerous times they had practiced this trip and the familiarity of the route they had taken. The routine of it had almost made the drive instinctual; like going to work the same way every day. It gave them more time to concentrate on what was around them rather than where they were going.

He remembered the first time he had come up here with Sean during their attempts to find a good site to build on. He had believed that this was just something to ponder, see if it were possible; not that they'd actually do it. He had been wrong about his friend's drive to make it happen and was surprised by the man's fervor to see it through, down to the smallest of details. It was almost like Sean knew that they'd one day need it, like insider information that only he had been privy to.

The night of the attack on Boston, he had been in the middle of a raid when one of his children had run in; flipping the television on. Barely distracted from what he was doing, he didn't even register what was going on until she turned up the volume. Unable to hear what was being said on vent, he had turned to ask her to lower it and the sight of what was on the screen had dried up his response instantly.

Queuing his mic, he had told them he'd be AFK for a second, not hearing the confused and angry replies. They were in the middle of a boss fight and none of them could believe he was walking away; they were winning. He turned his speakers down as he got to his feet and walked over to the couch, eyes glued to the television screen. There had been a terrorist attack at a Patriots game, and he couldn't put to words the horror of the videos being replayed; how devastated he felt inside. It was like someone had just sucker punched him while the most horrible nightmare unfolded before his eyes.

He had grasped his daughter's shoulders and she leaned her head against his hands and sobbed. The boys were away for the weekend with the Boy Scouts and his wife and younger daughter were out getting groceries. It was just the two of them in the house, yet it felt like they were the only two left in the world. That feeling of isolation and grief was overwhelming. It stayed with him longer than 9/11 had; the smoking ruins of that stadium forever imprinted on his mind.

The weeks following had thrown the country into chaos as even more of their freedoms were stripped away in the name of national security. Some things he could tolerate, but the more that the government clamped down; the less he felt like a free man and more like a rat in a cage. Using game console's virtual machinery to spy into homes? Webcams on computers keeping track of their private lives, watching them all hours of the day unhindered?

The fact that internet providers began to provide a constant connection so that people rarely turned off their devices wasn't lost on him. A computer always running, its webcam pointed at a couch, or someone's bed, watching. They welcomed that into their home for the entertainment it provided, yet no one thought of what nefarious purpose something like that could be put to. Making it so the only way to access a game was through an internet connection? It was another ploy to keep them online and trackable in the name of copyright protection.

His wife had thought he was paranoid, but somehow, he knew different. It wasn't even the increase of films like Enemy of the State or shows like Person of Interest that fed that paranoia; it was the feeling that someone was always monitoring him.

Once more they went to war against the invisible enemy who hated what his country represented. They made more enemies in the Middle East, if that was possible, and he spoke more often with his WoW buddies about their current national state. The impeding dread he felt was not his alone, and over the weeks following the disaster, the discussion turned extremely serious.

Sean had spoken up one night and asked what it would take to make a place safe enough in case things did go to hell. What had once been laughable had lost all its humor and a heated discussion began. He had made a flippant remark about winning the lottery and was surprised by Sean's silence; it turned out that money was not something their often silent guildmate was short of. Sean had always kept to himself during raids and although he was an officer in their guild, he never went into the details of his personal life. No one begrudged him that. Not everyone was comfortable sharing their lives with people they'd never met.

When his online friend had told them that he was actually a science-fiction/fantasy author, his jaw had literally dropped. He had written over fifty books under a pen name, and he actually owned most of them. This whole time he had been playing with one of his favorite authors and never even knew it. How had something like that escaped him? Sean claimed that it was the only way to keep his relationships on a realistic level; having seen what money had done to his previous attempts at friendships and needing some real companions that were interested in him as a person rather than his paycheck.

Still, he felt betrayed. Did he truly know any of them? He had heard of celebrities that played the game and wondered if any of them had ever revealed who they really were. He knew he'd recognize William Shatner's voice, or those of Trey Parker and Matt Stone, but would he know Macaulay Culkin's if he was on vent with him? He doubted it. And writers were even harder, because short of Stephen King's cameos, he had never heard a famous writer outside of their written word.

The joking had been light about the money since, the friendship they had formed preventing anyone from becoming greedy asses, but it had been a little different all the same. Casey would make a crack about needing help with his "gardening", but otherwise things just kept on as they always had been.

However, they felt liberated with their ideas. Even though they threw wild imaginings and crazy schemes at him, Sean just took it in stride and never let any of them know he was actually taking notes. The only time they got a negative response was when Casey suggested an underwater city off the Atlantic coast.

Sean had told him to be realistic.

He had wanted to ask, what was realistic about any of it?

It wasn't until he got a pair of cellphones in the mail with no return address that it dawned on him that Sean was serious about everything they had been discussing. The phones were top of the line and didn't work with any carrier that he had recognized. After plugging them in and letting them charge, he had dialed the number included in the box and Sean had picked up almost immediately. Having been asked to meet in person on his next day off, they had gotten together for only the second time in their lives.

That moment seemed unreal to him even today.

The first time had been at a comic-con. The mood had been light and their costumes silly in retrospect, but this was a serious encounter with the man and the first since finding out who he really was. That second time they were bereft of masks and he kept looking around, worried that someone else would figure out who Sean was, but no one paid them any mind. The crowds in the food court were exceedingly busy with their errands to take notice of them.

Sean had paperwork on places they had been discussing over vent and had detailed maps and research of those areas. Discounting the ones in New Mexico as too open, they had decided to look at a few places in northeastern Arizona. Even though Sean had insisted that they could take a trip out of state, he selfishly didn't want it that far from home.

He was surprised that Sean hadn't picked up on that and given him shit for it.

On the logical side, Arizona was between Utah, California, Nevada, and Texas, where most of them resided. Only a few of them lived further east and the more eastern the location, the further it became for those in the west. To him, Arizona was the logical choice despite his selfish reasons for wanting it to be so.

He used to make trips in the areas Sean wanted to scout when he was younger but hadn't been there in a very long time. He came from a long line of miners who had migrated from back east to Morenci and Clifton during the 1930's. He still had a lot of family there carrying on the family tradition and he'd been the first one born in a major city.

The road north of Morenci had originally been called Route 666 but had been changed by some Bible thumpers a couple of decades before. It wound its way from Morenci towards Alpine and Springerville in the northern part of the state. He remembered that fateful trip three years before as they inspected the land to build the compound; thinking then that it was just an exercise, something to pass the time. None of them believed it would ever amount to anything but talk, yet Sean had proved them wrong yet again.

It was fun at first; spending money on extravagant ideas and wild theories. The planning for what they would need was an ongoing process as each of them had their own ideas of what it would take to survive the end of the world. Things were constantly added and changed; evolving further as time passed. Upgrades were made as they became available, Sean not even hesitating to keep them ahead of the game. When war was declared in the Middle East, the fun had leeched out of their little project and they had all taken vacations from their jobs to help things move along more swiftly.

Sean had been in touch with an out-of-state contractor, not wanting anyone local involved, and the majority of the compounds were built through their direct supervision. That didn't mean they didn't do a lot themselves, but putting in sewage pipes or building concrete walls? That was beyond their means and they all knew it.

As the construction had gone forth, they had trained each other on skills they would need, most of which was first aid and self-defense. The kids were trained as well, causing them to mature faster than any of the parents had wanted; their innocence nearly lost with the firing of a Rimfire or applying a tourniquet to a bullet wound. His wife had argued against it, but once they were committed, her words started to fall short. It was one of the few arguments he had actually won in their marriage; though it wasn't one he would ever brag about.

In rotating shifts, all of them spent a couple of weeks there a year, refreshing themselves and helping to maintain what they had come together to create.

Sean had approached one of the families involved about living at the compounds full time. Rodger was on the verge of retirement as a truck driver and Sean offered to finance their move and stay at the compound, providing a nice salary to live on in exchange for maintaining the equipment and crops. Rodger's family would often take vacations when one of the other families showed up, getting them out and back into the world so they wouldn't go stir crazy.

Rodger's son Ben was their computer expert and he had been excited to have free reign over their computer systems. He spent most of his time upgrading their equipment and monitoring news from around the globe. He was a bit of a savant when it came to computer code. He could hack traffic cams and video monitoring systems, hence his being able to navigate them in case of an emergency. Todd had grown up with some of the earliest computers, having built a few himself, and still couldn't grasp half of what Ben did. Some people just saw connections in lines of code where he just saw numbers arranged in gibberish.

He slowed the van as they approached a large fence made of thick logs, rising twelve feet out of the forest before them. The barrier had wooden spikes angled outward at small intervals the entire length of the compound. A solid metal gate was before them and it had swung open at their approach, revealing the inner concrete wall directly behind it, a deep moat situated between, and a lowered drawbridge awaiting them.

Rodger was standing there waving them forward. He was around fifty-five with a crop of thick gray hair. He had a beard, blue overalls and a red flannel shirt. Tipping his ball cap at them as they passed, Rodger swung the gate closed as Sam's van eased slowly across the small gap and clear of the gate's arc.

The van bucked as it went over the lip of the metal bridge, relief flooding him as they passed over the drawbridge, through the twenty-foot concrete wall that surrounded the place, and into the compound beyond. This was only their first stop, but it was hard to not feel a sense of security fall into place with the closing of the outer gate and the concrete barrier now protecting them from the outside world.

He drove the van along the dirt road to the right and parked the van at the furthest parking space. As Rodger secured the gates, Todd's family got out and began to stretch, having not done so since the rest stop three hours before. He paused briefly to look around, taking it all in and angling his back at odd angles to loosen up. He soaked up the sounds of the forest outside the compound walls and took a deep breath of mountain air.

It was a large site, but only the first of three. The compounds were arranged in a triangular formation, the other two situated two miles further into the forest. It was hard to imagine that this wasn't the largest of them; despite the landing strip. You needed a lot of space to survive an apocalypse, the idea of living in a small bunker for years was ludicrous and nothing more than a plot device in a dystopian film.

They had livestock, crops, a small lake for fishing, and an above ground neighborhood to move into once the immediate danger passed. The underground complex was extensive, with living quarters, communal areas, and everything from armories to med labs. Anything they could think of that they'd ever need. There were large warehouses stocked with additional food to supplement the resplenishable resources they had created, as well as necessities like toilet paper and maxi-pads.

He glanced over at their hangar and felt reassured; Sean's plane was resting within. At least one of the others had gotten here safely. Leave it to Sean to be one of the first.

He really no leg to stand on as far as complaints, the guy **had** footed the bill after all, despite how crazy their ideas had been. Though, after today, he would have to make adjustments to what he considered crazy.

He looked left and saw the Huey and four tankers of fuel. One was jet fuel, the other three unleaded gasoline. It had been an offhand remark, but he was glad Sean had the foresight to follow through on it. The van was getting pretty low on gas and he would need to fill it up at some point.

However, he had no plans to go back out there any time soon.

He grabbed a nearby cart and loaded their supplies into it. Shouldering his pack, he turned to greet Rodger as he approached. "You'd pardon me if I don't say it's good to see you," he told his old friend, gripping the outstretched arm.

Rodger grimaced and put his hand on Todd's shoulder. "I know what you mean." Monica embraced the older man and Nick shook his hand. "Let's get you guys settled. Ben says it'll be awhile before I have to come back out here." As he spoke, his hand departed his right ear where an ear bud sat. His son had to be talking his ear off. "And it looks like you convinced your other lady to join us, that's good."

He nodded, sparing Sam a glance. She was busy trying to wrangle her kids, who were excitedly looking around at their new surroundings. "I see Sean made it," he observed, motioning to the Learjet, as they started walking towards the back of the compound. They crossed the airstrip and past the hangar beyond, his eyes sliding off the plane and towards his wife as she grabbed his hand; her sweaty palm letting him know she was still nerve racked despite their safer environment.

Hell, he could sympathize; he still felt it in his bones as well.

"Uh huh," Rodger acknowledged. "Got here about an hour ago. Ben says Casey is about five hours out and he's the closest."

Casey was a good friend of his, even outside of the game. They had kept in touch and had tried several other online games through the years, but they never really found anything worth playing. Maybe they had moved beyond it? He didn't know, but their past experiences and the time they had spent together had bonded a few of them for life. He hoped that Casey would make it, though, he'd have to knock that stoner shit off around the kids.

Sam strolled up on Monica's right, and she kept having to turn and encourage her kids to keep up. He had a feeling that it was going to be a long night for all of them.

They came to a building in the center of a small clearing. There were a couple of Humvees parked on either side that they had upgraded a year or so ago. He smiled at the memory; it had been a great weekend. Nothing but beer, barbeque, and the feeling of extended family coming together. What he wouldn't give to be back there with them in that moment, rather than meeting them all again with the death of the world hanging overhead.

They entered the small building. There was another set of doors with bullet proof black glass windows. He bent over and opened them, revealing the steps to the tunnel below. There was a ramp to the side for the cart to be lowered on. Michelle and Nick grabbed it and started down the ramp. He lifted Skye up and carried her down the stairs after them. His eyes adjusted to the electrical lighting as he carefully made his way forward, Monica close behind with their thirteen-year-old son in tow. He could hear Sam's voice echoing around him as she brought up the rear, a long chain of children between them.

As they neared the bottom, Rodger went over to the first jeep and the kids started loading up their supplies and other belongings. He hopped into another, Sam taking a seat beside him. Zeke, Bea, and Alan hopped in the back, Tammy opting to ride with Rodger and Nick instead. Monica hopped in the third and last jeep, the remainder of his children sliding in with her.

He turned the engine over, staring at the well-lit tunnel ahead. It wasn't overly large, but it was enough for two vehicles to pass on either side with just enough room overhead to keep them from feeling trapped.

When everyone was settled and ready, they drove a hundred feet down the tunnel and came upon a fork in their road. Taking a long deep breath, he turned his vehicle to the right, following Rodger's lead, and began the last leg of the trip to his new home.

Chapter 14
Trapped

Saint
Tucson, AZ

"I told your bitch ass we needed to get the fuck out," she scolded her boyfriend. Her brown eyes were filled with rage. As she strode after him, she whipped her shoulder length black hair back and balled her fists; nails digging into her palms. She didn't think being a Latina made her more pissed than anyone else; but she was sure it didn't help. "Straight up, this some bullshit."

She regretted stopping to pick him up; she should have gotten the fuck out while the getting was good. Now she was trapped at work, surrounded by fucking zombies, unable to get back on the road and out of town. It had been hours since Todd's last text and she was ticked that she was still in Tucson, and at her **work**—of all places. She didn't want to die here.

Jeremy was ignoring her as she ranted and that did nothing but fuel her anger.

"Seriously, what are we going to do now?" she asked, fury coursing through her. That's what she got for dating a white guy. It wasn't something that she did on a normal basis, but he had seemed so hot at first. He was six-four, slim, but well-toned. He had wide hips, a long face, and a great smile. His short brown hair was always covered with his green work hat, but she loved to take it off and run her fingers through his hair. Now, however, she wanted to knock him on his ass and throw him out those front doors. Maybe his wide hips would feed them long enough for her to escape.

She was sweating her make up off, the dark eyeliner streaking down the sides of her face. As she wiped it away, she realized she'd probably taken her painted eyebrows with it; not that she needed to look good when fed upon by the undead.

She silently cursed the day she was having.

Her eyes dropped to her clothes and her rage surged forward. Her black t-shirt and jeans were covered with blood and guts. This was beyond fucked up. Her glasses were smeared with gore and she took them off to clean them with her shirt, cursing when it was only making it worse. She was following close on her boyfriend's ass, just waiting for him to say the wrong thing and set her off. She had been pushing him since the last of those monsters had been killed and she knew he was close to snapping.

He didn't disappoint.

"I know, all right?" he yelled as he turned to glare at her, his voice a higher octave with the fear he was clearly experiencing. Bodies lay all around them and they were both working to at least clear the back aisle so they wouldn't trip if they had to run.

"Have you looked outside?" he asked, as he drug a body into the pet food aisle. "You want to go out there? Be my guest."

She was struggling to move an overweight Yaqui woman and grunted as her shoulder flared in response. "I'm not stupid, puto. Obviously, we can't go that way. But that's not the door out of here! Why not go up to the roof and take a look around, see which emergency door might be safe?" She was biting off every word; the acid sliding off each syllable she spoke. She couldn't help it; she liked to be in control of her life and this situation was really pushing her to the limit.

"You want to poke your head out the small ass trap door? Feel free. Personally, I'd rather know what's up there before I go sticking my head out," he growled, reaching to help her drag the corpse to the pile they were creating. "Not like we can't take some time to decide. We're not going to run out of food any time soon," he sneered, motioning towards the aisles of groceries around them.

"I've got this," she snarled, giving the arm one final tug and dragging the body into the aisle with the other corpses. She was hunched over, hands on her knees, her breath coming in short erratic gasps. She had stopped to pick him up, thinking it'd be a hop in the car and go. Instead, he kept putting her off and now they were trapped. "What sense does it make that any of them got on the roof? That's about the dumbest shit I've ever heard you say, and that's saying something."

Fucking dumbass.

She hadn't come inside at first. She had waited at the break table in the front, smoking cigarettes, and constantly looking at her watch. Then she had watched in horror as an old man suddenly clutched his heart while crossing the parking lot, falling face first to the asphalt with a loud thud.

People had panicked.

Management had come rushing out of the store to aid the dying man, calling for someone to dial 911 on the walkie hooked on their belt. Other coworkers had streamed out in response to the frantic radio chatter and she had almost gotten up to see if she could help as well; that irresistible urge to be involved. Then the guy was suddenly on his feet and attacking those that had come to his aid. Blood flew everywhere and she had nearly gagged with the viciousness of it. Knowing what Todd had told her through his texts, she made a mistake she might regret for the rest of her short life; she had gone inside to get Jeremy instead of jumping in her car and taking off. Those that died from the old man soon came back to life and began tearing into the people stupid enough to run their way; an endless cycle of death and rebirth that defied all laws of nature.

It had been a long-pitched battle to survive and now she was worn out and scared. Most of those that hadn't fled in those first few minutes, had died and turned, forcing them to have to deal with them as well. Now there were only a few people left. If the glass doors and windows gave way; they'd be toast. Her store manager had used the power lifting equipment to place pallets of dog food in front of the glass exterior, but it wouldn't take much to push those over. It was more to buy them time then actually stop those freakish monsters from getting in.

She went to stand next to the meat counter; letting the cool air wash over her. Caesar was approaching from the back room, trying furiously to get his cellphone to work, his face screwed up in a look of confusion and fright. She had already tried to get ahold of Todd and the rest of her family, so she knew that it was hopeless endeavor. Yet, he punched it repeatedly with both thumbs, like beating it into submission would make it work.

¡Imbécil!

"I can't get through to my wife," he said, almost like he couldn't understand why his phone wasn't working.

No shit, she thought as he pulled the battery out for a few seconds, then put it back in and turned the power back on. She shook her head in amazement. "No one's calls are going through. It's not your phone."

The look he gave her made her think that he was in shock rather than just being an idiot, and she suddenly regretted her harsh tone.

"I'm sure they're okay," she tried, not really believing it. If this shit was going on everywhere, none of them would ever be safe again.

She could hear David and Raleigh talking before they emerged from the end of the aisle on her right. They both looked at the cleared back aisle and she saw her boss grimace at the sight of blood on the floor. How could he be worried about that when the world was going to shit?

Fucking white people.

"Te necesita tener tu cabeza examinado, gringo," she muttered under her breath. Hell, this could all be a figment of her imagination. Maybe she needed to have her head examined as well. Jeremy was glaring at her, but she knew that he didn't understand a word she had said. "¿Tienes problema, Jefe?" she asked, rubbing in his ignorance.

"In America we speak English," he told her coldly and she wondered what she had ever seen in him. "**That's** my problem."

Well good for him, he half understood what she had said. "I was born here you fucking retard and now it looks like America is going to shit, doesn't it? Maybe we should make a run for the border; take our chances in Mexico," she responded, her temper flaring. She was sure that was one news story that would play over hilariously. Illegal immigrants fleeing to Mexico. What a hoot. If it weren't for the destruction being carried out outside, she might have laughed.

"Fuck that shit," Jeremy responded quickly.

She wanted to hit him so bad, that her fist were already balling themselves up in preparation. *Just keep it up,* she whispered within her mind; raring to kick his ass.

She looked to the two men approaching them and tried to cool off before she acted on her rage. David was just over six feet, bald, with wire framed glasses and a button-down white shirt covered in blood. His fists were hanging loosely at his sides, the knuckles covered in gore. A large wound on his right forearm was dripping blood off his fingertips. He didn't appear to have noticed it as he pushed by the larger Hispanic man beside him. Raleigh was 6'6 with big hands and a goofy grin. He weighed over 300lbs and had played as a starter on his High School football team. The green shirt he wore had earned the nickname of Hulk from his co-workers; something that he was proud to tell everyone he met.

The five of them were all that was left, and her heart ached at the friends that she had lost. Assistant Manager Tyler had been the first to die and he had taken out poor annoying Charlie immediately upon turning. Then Victoria had gone down. Within minutes all the cashiers were slaughtered and that new guy in dairy had simply disappeared. She still didn't know what happened to his ass; probably escaped through an emergency exit door; an idea she should have acted on right at the start.

There had been so much death that it still staggered her that it had happened so quickly. The customers fed the horde's numbers and overwhelmed the rest of the living. As one of the lone survivors, she couldn't help but wonder why she had lived while they had all died; the guilt was dealing a strong blow to her psyche and she felt her inner will tremble with doubt.

"We just checked the surveillance feeds. The back dock is clear," David told them, his will to move driving them towards the rear of the store. None of them had any intention of staying there. While there were supplies to last them for a while, there weren't weapons of any kind. The instant that horde got through those glass barriers, they'd be overrun. No, they had to leave while they still could.

"Let's make a break for it," Caesar said, his need to get home and be with his wife overwhelming the fear that had ruled the man since this whole thing started.

She could relate. If she had a family at home, she'd probably feel the same. But for now, all she felt was this urgent need to get the fuck out of Tucson, fast.

"And go where?" Jeremy asked and she wanted to sock him even more. "On foot? Shit, I'm parked in front of the store!"

Her stomach dropped as she realized she was as well.

Raleigh's eyes danced, his white teeth gleaming as the goofy grin swelled. "I'm not. The Beast is parked on the side." The dumbass loved the name he came up with for that junk heap he drove to work, and she wondered if he petted it every time it started. It was very likely.

She shook her head with bitter amusement. All she knew was that she didn't want to go anywhere in that piece of shit; she wanted her Lexus. She grunted and began to wonder if the side parking lot was empty or if there was something waiting in the cameras' blind spots. If there were, they'd have no clue until they came around that back corner. She had to get herself a weapon and soon. Why hadn't she applied at the Super Center instead?

"Can you take me to get my wife? They're probably still at our apartment. At least, they were an hour ago," Caesar asked desperately, his voice trembling.

No one answered, each considering what to do next.

She looked at them and cursed their indecisiveness. They needed to stop discussing this shit and just go. She caught her boss staring at her, and they shared a moment of understanding. While the others were still hoping to wake up and find themselves at home in their beds, both of them knew that this wasn't a nightmare; this was happening. And wasted time would only lead to a waste of life.

"I'm going," she told them, not caring if they followed. "If you're coming, you better hurry the fuck up. Porque si todos ustedes viven o muere, me voy a sacar el fuck de aquí," she told them, not caring if they understood.

Raleigh laughed. When the others gave him questioning looks, he just shrugged his shoulders. "She's going to take off without us if we don't keep up," he said, glossing over what she said.

"That's how it is?" Jeremy asked her crossly.

She was getting tired of his shit. "Damn straight," she returned, showing him her back. She'd gather some food and water, then she was gone. If he was with her, so be it. If not, then his ass could feed the zombies pounding on the doors when they broke through. At this point, she didn't give a shit. A part of her regretted that their relationship seemed to be falling apart; the other wanted to kill him herself.

Why the fuck had she stopped again?

Chapter 15
Fence walkers

Rosilynn
Las Vegas, NV

"Don't ask," he growled. "You keep on about it, I will pull this car over and do what you already should have, and you can go on alone."

He had been moody ever since they had left that parking lot of the Sherman Williams and it showed no sign of letting up. She had let him stay that way, the longer he was angry, the less time he spent feeling sorry for himself and dreading the worst, leading to a depression that might end with his suicide. She knew all of this mentally, but she couldn't help herself as she constantly asked him for updates, needing notice of the slightest change so she'd know if he was going to get better or worse.

The fact that he greeted her inquiries with disdain had slowly been eating her, though, and it appeared that the last bit was close enough to break that camel's back. "Don't you dare tell me what I can or can't ask about. My life is as much on the line as yours. If you're feeling hot, if you're losing feeling in your calf, if your heart is racing and won't slow down, these are things that I need to know that might indicate a direction this virus is taking, if any exists. You don't want to pull over so I can monitor it properly, fine, I'm down with that, but don't you dare act like I'm just a nagging wife who won't shut up about something inconsequential!"

"Whatever."

"Don't you whatever me," she growled back. She wasn't sure if the anger was actually due to his snarky comments, or if she was truly angry with herself. Even though her mind had tried to reason its way out of it, the simple fact was, they had made a pact and she'd broken it. If something happened now it'd all be on her. He had held out a knife and she was the one that gave it back.

She'd froze, and without a logical reason to act, she couldn't think or move past it. She needed irrefutable evidence that what they had always "known" would come to pass. Zombies were theoretically created from the transfer of bodily fluids, infecting the new host with a virus that corrupted the body's systems, transforming them into another one of the undead. That was the reproduction system that the monsters had always displayed.

Over the years since the Night of the Living Dead, fiction creators of the horror genre had branched out, needing new angles to keep the interest of their audience; to make them unique. There **had** been few exceptions from the accepted dogma. One had suggested that just inhaling fumes off of burned bodies could turn people. That those fumes could somehow make it rain and the water would then infect all the corpses it fell upon. No one accredited it with any realism, it had just been a plot device to make their zombies even more terrifying as they tried to step around Romero's films. In the end, it had just been another gory movie to take a boyfriend to on a Saturday night.

Now she began to question everything they had planned and theorized about; whether any of their promises should be kept. Until she knew how this thing worked, she wasn't just going to off someone because they got bit; especially her husband. Fuck that shit.

"Send more paramedics," she mumbled and got a severe look from her husband; he wasn't in the mood for humor. She sighed and checked his pulse, refusing to acknowledge his frustration. It was fast, but not erratic. He had no external temperature rise. She wouldn't be able to take an internal temp without stopping and getting a thermometer to ram up his ass. If he kept on acting like one though, she might consider that an option.

She had made him pull over a few minutes after they hit the road; his arguments to the contrary. She hadn't had time to attend to it before they got in the car, and she couldn't clean and dress the wound while they were driving. So far, she hadn't seen any obvious signs of infection. Was it possible that he wouldn't turn? Could she dare to hope?

They were approaching the airport and she felt dread start to settle in. If the strip had been bad, she didn't want to imagine what an airport full of undead was going to be like. It was a major population hub in the city, with tourists coming from all over the world to gamble at the casinos. With the apparent rate of infection, she knew it had to be one of the earliest places hit and they couldn't avoid it if they were going to get to the highway quickly. Any other route would mean sidetracking through more neighborhoods; something that she wasn't ready to do; not after that last one. She doubted she could keep her husband from rushing to the aid of another screamer; he was too suicidal to think straight. No, they had to take the chance and hope for the best.

Her heart sank as the fence surrounding the runways came into view. A large group of undead was spread across the fenced interior and were pounding on the wired barrier at the sight of fresh prey. It wobbled with the force of the blows and she cringed at the thought of what would come with their freedom. Luckily, this part of the street appeared to be barren with only a few abandoned cars lining the sides of the road, but she knew that could change quickly.

At any second those creatures could break through the flimsy wire barrier and the neighborhoods to the north would be swarmed within minutes.

"If Rick and his crew could hold out in a prison for half a year, I'm sure we'll be fine for the next twenty seconds," her husband told her dismissively.

She shot him a harsh glare. "Why the fuck did you just say that out loud?" In the time that it took for her to turn her head and look back at the fence, the very thing she feared, and he had denied took place; the fence gave way, spilling forth a mass of entangled bodies. "You just had to say something, didn't you?"

She felt the car surge and realized that her husband had slammed down on the accelerator, his hands gripping the steering wheel tightly as he ground his teeth in response to her heated questions. He hooked left with the road, coming awfully close to that large mound of undead and nearly tipping over with the force of the turn, then the car surged forward, and away from the freed horde.

The car was fishtailing from the violent turn and was beginning to straighten itself when something briefly impacted their trunk, causing them to veer to the left. She looked back at the zombies crawling over each other to get at them and saw a broken body on the ground. It rolled over, got back on its feet, and came after them with everything it had. Her heart was pounding in her ears as she brought her rifle up, ready to take a shot if the thing got close enough. More bodies had risen from the avalanche of claws and teeth and had joined the chase.

The fury on their faces speared her heart. They weren't passive zombies responding to sudden stimuli, these were fierce eating machines hell-bent on tearing their prey apart. She couldn't begin to guess what this virus did to their minds, but it appeared to focus all their rage and hunger with such force that it erased anything else that had made them human.

They look pissed off, she thought; not able to come up with a better description. She hoped that it was an automatic response to the virus at work and not a trapped mind fighting to wrestle control from the fury driving them forward; the thought too horrifying to consider.

The car rocked and her window shattered; jolting her from her watchful gaze behind and drawing her back into her surroundings. The glass didn't break, but it had shattered so completely that another push would bring it down upon her. A hand flashed by their back windshield and the horror of them getting blindsided like that; on her side of the car, enveloped her whole being. It made her aware that the danger was coming from all sides and as impossible as it seemed, she had to somehow keep a three-hundred sixty-degree awareness at all times.

A dead security guard had joined in the chase now and she prayed that the car didn't run out of gas. They'd never survive a fight with that many of the enemy raining down upon them. These things were everywhere! If they stopped, which way could they go? Where was there refuge that wasn't already infested?

The car had skidded a bit from the impact, but they were still racing down the back road, drawing slowly away from the crowd of hungry cannibals to their rear. Another turn approached and as he swung the car right, she lost sight of the horde as the shattered glass obstructed her view.

She could tell they were falling behind by how long it had taken them to come around the fence; even zombies were limited by how fast their legs could go. Her heart began to lighten with the thought they might just make it, daring to hope that they might yet escape. Her hands had been gripping the rifle so hard that her wrists were beginning to cramp, and she forced herself to relax; her fingers throbbing, sweaty, and swollen. She flexed them slowly, trying to breathe life back into them, but they resisted and stayed in a curled-up position. They groaned at the stress that she was putting them through, and though her gloves were practical in this situation, they weren't helping her flexibility.

Another vehicle was flying their way and hope swelled when she saw that it was a military Humvee with a soldier manning the gun on the back; locked, loaded, and ready to fire. There was half a dozen more following after, and as it rushed past, she flipped around in her seat to watch what happened next. A second man was hunched over the back and was using a pair of binoculars; speaking energetically into a walkie on his shoulder.

Swerving to the side of the road, cutting her view of the racing horde beyond, the vehicle leapt onto the sidewalk and came to an abrupt stop. She felt their own car buck as Matt had followed suit to get out of the way of the approaching formation of Humvees. They had spread themselves across the two-lane road and would have taken them out as they passed.

Her husband began to slow their vehicle now that the military was forming up behind them, his eyes glued to the rear-view mirror. They were staggered across the road and without ceremony, opened up on the large group of zombies that had been chasing them. She had no real account of how many had been behind that fence, but it had been enough to just push it over like it was a stack of hay.

She cringed at the destruction taking place, but a dark part of her enjoyed every second. She wanted to get out, rush back there, and help them mow those monsters down. Not just for what they wanted to do to her; but because they were an abomination and affront to everything natural in the world. She wanted to do her part; to erase them from this corner of her existence.

She glanced to her side and realized that the blind spot was more dangerous now that they had come to a stop. She used the butt of her .45 to knock the glass free and carefully plucked a few smaller pieces out. When she was satisfied that she'd gotten what she could she turned back to the battle just in time to see a hand reach up from in front of one of the Humvees. The man with the binoculars drew his side arm and a final shot rang out as the others had ceased firing. It had come that close to getting to them, even with all that firepower they had flung at those things. How would the two of them have survived if they'd been overrun? She shivered at the display of death and destruction; though from fear or pleasure, she wasn't sure.

"Oh, my God," she whispered and found that her husband was actually smiling.

"Hope they cut those bastards in half and they're still trying to crawl around, so I can have the pleasure of backing up over those fucks and killing them again," he snarled, speaking from the anger fueling his heart.

The guys let out a cheer in response to the fight and she caught herself cheering with them. One of them turned towards their direction and waved them on. Matt saluted in response, but she doubted they saw that through the smeared rear windshield.

"Let's get out of here," she said, patting his arm.

For just a moment she had forgotten the nasty bite on his ankle, and though she welcomed the respite, she abhorred the stress that the forgetting had caused. That she had lost that focus in the heat of things would only create problems if he did get sick during a fight and turned on her. She was beginning to sweat in her suit now that the window wasn't keeping the a/c contained and she wondered if the heat would increase the spread of infection.

She forced it out of her mind as they eased forward and continued on their journey. She'd worry about that when the time came. Until then, she was just tying herself up in knots. Her hand on her rifle, her eyes alert, they passed the airport and finally came to the interstate that would take them east to her friends; who were hopefully already awaiting their arrival. She prayed they were having an easier time of it than they were, or they might all be lost in the end.

She sighed, *so much for being prepared for this shit.*

Chapter 16
Hacker

Todd
Compound 2

He stepped into their communications room, having finally gotten the family settled and wanting to fulfill his need for information; he'd been in the dark long enough. He was on the first basement level of their new home; Monica and Sam had opted to stay behind and get the kids taken care of while he checked in with Ben.

Half the room was one long computer desk with eight computers; each with multiple monitors. The wall on the left had two couches and a recliner for comfort. One of the couches had blankets and a pillow thrown on it; Ben had been sleeping here rather than his own quarters. The boy was old enough to get one of his own and they didn't have enough people on the way in to force him in with his parents; privacy wasn't an issue. It had to be the amount of work he was putting in. From the looks of things, he had been sleeping in here for quite some time.

There were scattered Red Bulls loosely stacked on the floor and several empty bags of chips that never made it to the trashcan five feet from the boy's chair. The large refrigerator on the right wall looked well used and he knew from past experience that it was mostly filled with junk food.

Sitting in the center of the computer desk was Ben. His high back computer chair was turned slightly to the side as the young man hunched over his keyboard, eyes flashing between the eight monitors glowing before him. The boy had saved the life of his family and he wanted to give him a hug. But now that he was here, he figured Ben would be happy enough if he grabbed one of those energy drinks from the fridge and replaced the crushed can by his mouse pad.

Ben was dressed in a black T-shirt and jeans, and as Todd walked in, he flipped his long brown bangs back to see who had entered his sanctuary; a natural reflex and nothing more. His wireframe glasses barely turned as those bloodshot eyes quickly addressed him, then turned back to the screens dismissively. The monitors were set up vertically in four rows and he had no idea how the young boy kept up with what was on all those screens; he could barely handle two.

He walked over, opened the fridge, pulled out a couple of Red Bulls and grabbed himself a Coke. Gripping a computer chair by the headrest, he slid it over, placed the energy drinks on the computer desk, popped his Coke, and dropped into the seat next to Ben.

"Glad you made it," the young boy said, while absentmindedly opening one of the cans and downing it. Then he returned to his keyboard; typing furiously. He looked at the monitors, but Ben was alternating his windows too fast for him to keep up. He did catch glimpses of video on those closing windows and the brief camera footage was enough to make his stomach churn; things were going to shit out there. He was glad he had gotten his family to safety, but now he had to focus on helping the others get there as well.

He didn't want to linger; Ben had a lot of work to do and he didn't need to be responsible for causing an untimely distraction that would end up costing someone their life. "I dropped in to say thank you," he told him, taking another drag of his Coke. An ashtray was on the desk top and there were more than a few crushed butts there. When had Ben started smoking? "You been smoking backer?" he asked, attempting to say tobacco like they did back east. The glare that he got almost made him chuckle. Yeah, he shouldn't do that; it sounded wrong coming out of his mouth. He didn't think he had an accent, but then it didn't sound like one to you, just people from other regions or countries. He knew that he had butchered it and made a note not to go there again.

Best to stick with what he knew.

Ben's hand snaked out and grabbed a hot pocket on a paper plate to his left. His skinny frame must burn it up instantly and he wished that his would still do that as well. "With all this shit going on, I reckon you've been smoking non-stop." He was already fishing out a cigarette and the boy nodded. "That's what I thought. And you're welcome," Ben commented while munching his food. "Casey's closing in and Mark is off the grid."

The way he said that; the life and death statement just casually voiced like it was nothing, hit him in the gut hard. He knew that he shouldn't hold it against the younger boy. He was doing exactly what they asked him to do, but the indifference to whether or not their friends lived or died made him sick to his stomach. If something had happened to them on their journey to the compound, would they have been a casual side note in the boy's day? Ben had to be objective and disconnected to be effective, but Jesus.

"Is it possible Mark broke his phone, or maybe his battery died?" he asked and got a glare in response. There was no way to possibly know that for sure and he knew that before he had asked. Still, he felt like the man deserved more than a passing mention. "What about Roxanne?"

Ben nodded while typing. "Her signal is still coming in strong. She got out before Mark and is moving west right now. She lost touch with her husband as well and I haven't been able to provide her with any comfort on that regard. I don't think I should be the one to tell her," the boy said. He must have realized how cold he was coming across and Todd agreed with the assessment. But that was one task he wasn't going to commit to until they knew for sure one way or another.

No reason to upset her if they could avoid it.

"Best to tell her you're working on it then. If we find out anything concrete, I'll make the call," he told the youth.

Ben nodded and brought up a map with the GPS signals on it. He could see several at their present location and three heading in from the east. There were two sets of signals in California, Nevada, and Utah. From the maps he had seen on the way in, he was sure that the girls hadn't made it.

"Ros and Matt are slowly making their way east, but they still haven't gotten out of Vegas," Ben told him, bringing up a map of the infection's progress on the monitor in front of Todd.

Things had grown worse since the last time his app had refreshed and he wondered if Ben had quit updating his phone once his family had arrived. Flagstaff and Phoenix were heavily overrun, and Tucson's dot was beginning to grow larger with every new overlay. The west coast, from San Diego to Sacramento was completely red. Oregon and Washington were just showing signs of infection and he knew that the California portion of the plague would soon move north, as those to the south fled their way.

Southern Nevada was almost entirely red from Vegas to Bullhead City and he sent a silent prayer to the Gods that Ros and

Matt made it out of there all right. Texas was beginning to rival California and most of the mid-west was lost. Montana looked all right for the moment, but then their population was so small he doubted they'd have trouble until fleeing survivors converged on them from outlying states. There were only a few uninfected areas on the east coast; it was red from Vermont to Florida. Luckily none of their friends were coming from that area, with Mark and Roxanne being the furthest out, having refused to leave Ohio. Columbus had long turned red and he wondered if his silent friend had perished in his escape from the city.

"Are Ros and Matt going to make it out?" he asked, his eyes kept returning to that portion of the map. Rosilynn was the core of their medical staff, such as it was, and it would hurt them deeply to lose her. Matt had taught them a lot about self-defense, and they needed him here to help defend the compound from attack. His skills were too valuable to lose as well. Their group wasn't large to begin with and every person was vital in some way.

That was the cold way of looking at it and the heartache he felt at their plight was exhausting. Maybe the attachments they had made were a mistake; the pain he'd feel at their loss would be too much to bare. *You've got to get out of there,* he mentally told the screen, staring at the slow-moving GPS signals leaving Vegas.

"They've slowed, but they're steadily moving their way east. There is a military engagement at the site of their GPS signal, so they might get out. I don't know yet," Ben grunted, not liking the response he got from something he was trying to do. Traffic cams were floating by as Ben cycled through them, eyes quickly scanning and moving on faster than Todd could keep up. He finally stopped and maximized a video feed. It was a camera overlooking an intersection in front of an interstate off ramp. Cars were packed on both sides of the road, all of which were trying to merge onto the freeway on the other side of the overpass. Vehicles were moving slowly along the top and he saw a flash of light in the sky; six planes had just flown overhead. "That's where they are," Ben told him, leaving the screen up almost as a distraction to keep Todd from asking him too many questions.

"And the others?" he asked, his eyes not seeing the familiar vehicle that the Millers drove. He knew that they had probably ditched it and switched cars at some point. He prayed they weren't on foot. They'd never get out of there if they were.

"Paul and Christine are still in Utah. They are dragging their feet leaving and no amount of pushing is making them go any faster. Christine keeps asking if I'm sure," Ben sighed. "If one of those zombies took a bite out of her ass, she'd probably still ask me that. It's like trying to explain the simplest of apps to my parents, man. Its dragass slow and never really done."

He chuckled, that sounded just like her. "I could try calling them, speed them up a bit," he offered.

"Your dime. But I don't reckon they'll listen to you any more than they did me. Old folks move slow, that's all there is to it," Ben replied, then grumbled under his breath, "should probably tell her that there is a fifty-percent off sale at the local Wal-Mart. Bet that would get her ass moving."

His parents took their time when preparing to leave for any kind of road trip, so he understood what the boy was getting at, and the frustration that came with it.

Ben sipped his energy drink, then continued. "Joseph is making good time out of Arkansas. Linda and Jackie's phones never left Linda's work," Ben confirmed his earlier suspicion and his heart sank.

Although Linda had never really joined in on what they were trying to do here, Jackie had grown to be a large asset in their group. She had trained in first aid with Rosilynn and could fly their reconditioned Huey like she had been born with wings. She was a clerk at a law firm and spent her spare time flying a Cessna on her days off. If only they had gotten to her plane—he tried to shrug it off, but the loss was overwhelmingly painful and fresh.

It was easy to look at that map as a whole and not react violently to it, but when you considered the single lives being lost; it drove the horror home of what was going on out there.

He had pushed his family to get here without stopping, disregarding family members scattered across the length of Arizona. Now, as he stared at those growing red dots, he wondered if he shouldn't have at least tried to bring some of them with them. The infection hadn't even reached Safford yet. They could have made time to visit aunts and uncles, his grandparents, his cousins, but all he had thought about was the safety of his wife and kids.

Would it have made a difference? Would they have believed him without a firsthand experience to convince them? By the time that happened, it would have been too dangerous for them to be there. He was sitting in front of monitors, watching videos flash by of the violence and death erupting across the nation, and he still had a hard time believing it was real. How could he convince them, when he was still struggling with his own doubts?

Though, it wasn't all his fault; they had never considered the phone carriers going offline so quickly. "Why did the kid's phones go out?"

"Sean never set them up on our network. We share the satellite with a host of other companies and the amount of lines that we could use was limited. We could have gone with one of the mainstream carriers, but Sean was paranoid that they'd get shut down. He called that one right. Almost immediately after the shit hit the fan, the phone companies were offline. Most of the internet servers followed shortly thereafter. A few of those still online are porn sites. Their firewalls have protected them so far; but as to how long that will last? I couldn't guess. Someone tried to breach our network and I had to counter like mad to keep the fuckers off," the younger boy said, finishing off the Red Bull. He crushed it and hooked it towards the trash can to the left, missing it completely and slightly splashing the wall with the impact. "After that, the other networks began to crash. Cable and radio networks simply went to a standby screen and have yet to come back up."

"Why the hell would someone do that?" he asked, speaking to his feelings of isolation that had swarmed him back at Texas Canyon. "It only made the panic worse."

"If I had to guess? The government had all their top hackers kill the entire communication grid. For now, most of the cameras are still up," he said, indicating the slow movement of cars on that Las Vegas traffic cam. "But I suspect that's more for their surveillance benefit than anything else. They have to be keeping track of what's going on; much like we're doing here."

"I didn't know that was possible, shutting everything down remotely," he responded, trying to work it out in his mind. His hacker skills were non-existent, and he didn't get too far.

"If you had asked me that before, I would have told you there was no way they could either. This shit was massive and immediate. Either they knew it was going to happen or they have spent a long-time planning for it. If you put a lot of the top minds together long enough, you can really accomplish anything. They probably had a kill code written so that it really only took a press of a button, then instant black out. I don't know, I'm still trying to unravel and trace the intrusion attempt to its source. YouTube was one of the earliest hit though, looks like they're trying to minimize panic by controlling the information people are getting."

"Well, they're fucking up on that score," he said back. "That might have worked ten years ago, but now? When the whole world is interconnected the way it is? It's probably what is driving those people out into the streets!"

Ben was about to respond when his cell went off. "Talk to me," he said as he answered the phone, left hand tapping the Bluetooth in his ear.

He turned his eyes to the monitors, trying to absorb all that he was seeing. There were street cams from several cities hovering on one and his eyes refused to be moved away from them. The horror unfolding was too much for him to stomach. Suddenly, the Coke didn't seem like a good idea after all; it'd burn coming back up. People were getting torn apart on each of those feeds. The violence unfolding was beyond anything he had ever seen in a movie, and he had seen a lot of them. On a few, the cops and military were fighting shoulder to shoulder, but they were slowly getting overrun. New York City, Los Angeles, Tampa, it was everywhere, and the scenes so similar you'd think you were looking at one from different angles.

"Dude, I told you that you were clear through Socorro, which is as close to Albuquerque as you get. And this shit hasn't hit there yet. All for nothing bro," Ben paused, smiling. He began to wonder if the boy realized the enormity of what was happening. This wasn't a movie playing for his own amusement; this was life and death. Ben glanced at a screen, then up at him. His eyes were red and puffy and though his voice sounded calm, his soul shown clear from within.

Okay, he did understand.

"Yeah, dude, you're fine. Alpine is quiet as of right now, though I'd watch out for a bunch of rednecks driving around shooting mailboxes—and anything else that comes into range. They are not discriminating," he laughed, wiping a tear from his cheek. "I know you did, but Casey man, Roswell is gone."

The enormity of what Ben said hit him.

He looked to the screen above his head and saw a live feed; an intersection littered with corpses. Roswell, New Mexico, the labeled window said. He saw a little boy with a toy gun laying half out of a truck window and his heart broke. Before his eyes the hand moved, the head jerked, and the little boy raised his head at an awkward angle.

He couldn't take it anymore. He turned to leave and as he was getting ready to exit the room, he heard the boy ask Casey where his stash was hidden. As much as Todd hated that shit, he wondered what his friend from Texas said in response; he might need a hit himself before the day was over.

How was it spreading so fast?

Chapter 17
Run

Saint
Tucson, AZ

She took a long look through the bubbled window on the dock door. There didn't appear to be anyone out there, but she couldn't see directly below them. She nodded to David and he slid the door up. They could have gone out the receiving door rather than jumping down from the dock, but there was no way to tell if anyone was on the sides and the street was directly to their right. Anyone passing by would see them as they exited the store. At least this way, their field of vision was funneled by the large wall that ran the length of the docking bay. They felt reassured that the distance to the bottom would let them quickly step back in case something was down there that they couldn't see.

The store didn't sell backpacks, so they had packed as much food as they could carry in the reusable blue grocery bags they sold. They were made of low-cost material and couldn't hold much, but it was better than leaving empty handed. They would have to find more food later. Odd saying that, knowing what they were leaving behind, but even if they got the truck backed up to the dock, they couldn't assure they wouldn't draw attention just starting the engine. If those things funneled their way down here, they'd be fucked.

Now they were about to plunge back into the fray, after what only seemed like a short respite from fighting. David and Raleigh stood on the edge of the dock and held out their hands. She took David's and he held onto her as she slid down to the concrete below. Jeremy had Raleigh's help and Caesar was fast behind. Then the two men hopped down next to them. Her heart was racing, her adrenaline pumping harder, and she felt exposed now that they were out in the open.

David shook hands with each them and wished them luck. He had his wife and kids to look after and she knew he'd be taking no precautions to get back to them as fast as he could.

She was resolved to do the same.

Her own family was too spread out to be able to get to any of them and Raleigh's were already leaving the city. Jeremy's only family member was in prison and there was no hope of getting him out of there. Caesar was the only one that had immediate family nearby and they had all resolved to see him returned to them. If for no other reason than he had a shit load of guns at his place and she would finally have a way to defend herself. Caesar was cracking under the stress he was under and the quicker they got him to his wife and baby, the sooner he'd become his old self again.

With a final nod and look from everyone else, they all began to jog up the docking bay. They neared the top, the road opening up on their right, and she was immediately concerned about their flank. She did her best to push it out of her thoughts and poured on the speed; it was too late to do anything else. Her legs burned from the exertion, but she worked through it.

Jeremy was at her side and David was pushing ahead. He was going to make a break for his car on the side of the building, but it was towards the front. She had to give it to him, he had balls. He planned to drive around the front of the store and draw them away. While he did, they were going make a break for it around the back.

The others were falling behind, as Raleigh was big but not fast, and Caesar was not in shape enough to run for very long. She turned and the heaving Hispanic tossed the keys to her as he tried to catch his breath. She snatched them midair, her black hair whipping her face as she quickly turned and dashed towards his beat-up truck. She had a bag of groceries in one hand and the weight was slowing her down. She briefly considered dropping it. It wasn't worth her life, but she might regret it later; she couldn't be sure when they'd be able to stop again. Jeremy was carrying two sets of bags and was making it look easy.

As they cleared the rear wall and came around the corner, they were going at a full sprint on a downgrade. There was a long row of cars to her right and sitting on the ground by the first vehicle was a large Yaqui tribe member in dark blue soiled clothes. He raised his head and stared at them. His eyes were fierce, and his slackened jaw opened in a disgusting display of hunger. He lunged and her legs began to pump faster. She slipped right and darted towards the black pickup ahead. She was almost there.

Her head was yanked backward as something grabbed a hold of her hair and pulled. She couldn't help the scream that came ripping from her throat. Her glasses slipped and hung loosely upon her nose as she was almost flipped onto her back. The bastard had gotten her! Fear gripped her soul as she felt the constant tugging of the creature that had snagged her, and her momentum came to a halt.

Jeremy grabbed the sneering man, his teeth snapping at her neck, and she felt her neck hairs bristle from the touch of teeth. Her body shivered and she screamed again. A metal pole came crashing down on the head of the dead man and split it open with a sickening crunch.

Raleigh had caught up to them.

The creature fell to the ground, its hand still clutching her hair and pulling her down with him. She tried to pull away and felt Jeremy's hand on the back of her head trying to get the clenched hand to free her hair. She shook her head to quell her panic, but her nerves had been completely shot. She was ready to break down; she had been close to becoming one of those things. She wanted to vomit.

She turned to Raleigh and saw the large man gripping a bent pole in one hand. He was having a hard time catching his breath. She mouthed thank you and he nodded. Then movement caught her eye and a horrifying realization hit her; she had just alerted the entire horde at the front of the store that their food source was leaving. They came streaming around the front corner of the building and would be upon them in seconds.

David had just gotten to his car and she cried out a warning, but it was too late. They swarmed him, arms flaying, teeth tearing. A loud hoarse scream came out of the pile of zombies and her stomach decided it had enough. She vomited; the bile burning as she emptied the contents of her stomach on the asphalt below.

Jeremy grabbed the keys and bolted for the driver's side of the truck. She wiped her mouth as fear drove her towards the truck; her eyes needing a distraction, or she'd keep retching even as those things tore into her.

Jumping into the passenger seat, she felt the truck buck as Raleigh and Caesar climbed in the back. The truck vibrated noisily as

Jeremy turned it over, as if considering whether to start or not, then finally roared to life. Jeremy threw it in reverse and hit the gas. The truck staggered backward and rammed four of the closest walkers; the vehicle shuddering from the impact. The backend rose as they drove over the undead and came to a sudden halt.

"Shit, shit, shit!" Jeremy yelled, putting it into drive and swinging the wheel around. He floored it and they lurched over the bodies once more; she could feel the crunch of the bones through the floorboards.

Caesar suddenly screamed. She jerked her head around and looked out the back window. One of the walkers had jumped onto the back of the truck. The pole that had saved her life flashed through the air again, clipping Caesar, and slamming against the shoulder of the raving undead. The walker was flung free as Caesar dropped to the truck bed unconscious. The truck screamed forward, its engine pushing its limits and making sure they all knew it.

Two more leapt at them but came up short, falling face first on the asphalt behind them. Her heart pounded in her chest and her hands gripped the dashboard tightly. One hand absentmindedly adjusted her glasses, returning her sight, and relief began to flood through her.

The mob was falling behind.

Raleigh was checking on Caesar, his weapon ready to take another swing if needed. She heard Jeremy gasp and returned her attention to the road ahead. Two more zombies had come around the other side of the building and were heading straight for them. She flinched as they impacted the front of the truck, making it buck again. The undead corpses flew overhead, and the roof crumpled as they bounced off it. The windshield was cracked, but the engine was running, and they were still making their way forward. The momentum of the bodies must have lessened the damage to the truck.

"Get us out of here!" she screamed.

"What the fuck do you think I'm doing?" he snapped. "Look for cars, dammit!"

They cleared the Mexican restaurant and she finally had an unobstructed view of the path ahead. For the moment, they were clear; no cars, no zombies. Thank God for small favors. "We're good! Go!"

He grunted in response and jerked the wheel to the right. She stifled a scream as the two right tires lifted off the ground, and for a second she was sure that they were going to tip over. She turned and saw Raleigh gripping the side of the truck to keep from sliding, throwing his weight against the tilt in an attempt to force it back down—it helped. The truck slammed against the road and bounced, then finally stabilized.

She let out a sigh of relief.

Her blood pressure increased as she watched a herd of zombies streaming in their direction from the store's parking lot. Some of them had to have been following the sound of their truck, because they were closing in fast. Jeremy was trying to push the truck faster, but after taking that turn, it was taking a moment to regain traction.

The side-view mirror broke off as a zombie flung itself at them, its claws scraping at the window. The face staring at her, the flesh torn free, the eyes blazing, was that of her former boss. As the truck broke free and rushed down the street, she began to scream. Even when Jeremy assured her they were finally clear, that face continued to stare at her, her mind refusing to let go. She kept screaming, her hands on her head pulling at her hair. The vomit forced its way up and she dry heaved on the truck's floorboards.

She could hear Jeremy trying to comfort her, but she would have none of it. Those eyes continued to haunt her as they journeyed east and away from the horrors to their rear, a shiver running through her body as dread began to settle within; they were all going to die today.

Chapter 18
Settling in

Todd
Compound 2

"I'd ask if everything was all right, but I don't think I want to know the answer," Monica commented, as he walked back into their bedroom. Each of the families had similar size rooms and layouts, almost like an underground apartment complex.

Even Casey had four bedrooms, a kitchen, and a living room—they had to plan ahead. Casey might one day find a woman, and in fact had a girlfriend when they initially designed this place. Though, the thought of him procreating turned his stomach. One was enough, but three?

His wife saw the smile and he only shook his head.

Their rooms weren't large, but they were comfortable; the benefits of being on the design team. Their bags were thrown on the queen size bed, and he knew it'd take some adjusting after being on a California King for the last five years.

Their quarters were fully furnished and decorated, something that Sean insisted on doing for each of them to try to make them feel at home. A light always had to be on, but it was low wattage to keep the power drain to a minimum. The solar panels could only provide so much before the generators would kick in; and that would drain the exhaustible fuel supply they had.

He was glad that a gas line had been hooked up to that first compound because he'd hate to have to lug it back and forth every day. When the time came, they'd probably find plenty of gas out there unused, but that made his mind turn to those images on the monitors. He ground his teeth, shook his head, and tried to banish them from his mind. They went, but he knew it wouldn't be long before they returned.

He stood there admiring his beautiful wife. They had gotten out of the suits almost immediately upon arriving and had changed back into their normal clothing. She was wearing a canary yellow tank top and blue jeans, her hair pulled back in a medium length pony tail. She'd probably have to cut that soon, his aching heart thought. She was gorgeous and the long hair complimented her looks well. But it was also an easy thing to grab from behind and if a zombie got a hand on it—he shivered at the thought. In the zombie apocalypse, the less there was to grab, the safer you were.

"We lost Linda and Jackie," he told her. He watched as she paused to shift her gaze his way. Her eyes spoke volumes and he knew in his soul exactly what she was thinking; it could have been them. He went to her and they embraced.

"What happened?" she asked softly.

He held her tightly, not wanting to answer. "We don't know. Ben says they never left the school Linda worked at. Whatever it was, it had to have happened fast."

"Oh man," his wife responded, her hand stroking the back of his head. "And the others?"

"Mark is missing, but the others are on their way," he told her, still unable to let her go.

She pulled herself free but kept her arms on his shoulders. "Mark too? What the hell is going on? Are any of them going to make it?" She spoke straight from his heart, as she often did after nearly decades of being together. He didn't need to answer, the look on his face told her enough. She dropped her arms and went back to unpacking their clothes. He could tell without looking that she was crying and trying to hide it.

"What did any of this matter?" she asked, her arms thrown up in the air. "What good is it to plan if it's all for nothing, if they still die out there?"

"What would you have had us do? Nothing? Then **we'd** be dead as well," he spoke crossly, his feelings of loss making him angry. "They chose to remain in their home cities. How far they have to travel is on them, not us."

She shook her head, her ponytail swishing with the sudden movement. "Would **we** have moved? Could we just up and leave our families; our parents? Would you have left Sam behind in Tucson to move out here to the sticks?"

Even though he knew that he couldn't have done that, he still felt like it was the logical thing to do. California was one of the most populated regions of their country. What were Linda and Jackie thinking? Earthquakes alone kept him out of there. With all the shit going on in the world, it had never occurred to them they might be living in ground zero? They had all discussed this and they all knew the risk, but none of them had felt the need to move their homes. Each had felt secure enough in their belief that none of this shit was ever going to happen.

"You know the answer. Look, there's nothing we can do but wait and help when we can," he told her, summing up what he figured would be a very long week. She had begun to pile their clothes into the lone dresser, and he felt naked without the rest of the stuff they had collected through the years. He knew none of his movies got packed and he was suddenly glad he had backed up his computer files on the desktop in the living room. There were some video files on there at least. Even as his mind went there, he couldn't believe he was worried about that with so much death in the world.

He sighed and tried to clear his head. "Did the kids get anything to eat yet?" he asked, trying to change the subject. "How's Sam settling in? I'm sure her kids are freaking out."

His wife cracked a smile and wiped the tears from her face. "If there's one place they could find in the pitch dark with no directions, it's the kitchen. I haven't seen Sam since we got down here. I'm assuming she's finding everything all right, she hasn't coming knocking."

As if summoned, there was a knock on the door, and he turned expecting Sam to be standing there only to find Lucy instead. She was in her late fifties with short gray hair, her green eyes peering at them through her bifocals. Her face was round, and though she was a bit heavy, it looked good on a woman of her age. She had been the mother of the group since the beginning and everyone loved her. "Just wanted to check in and see how you guys were holding up."

"Just trying to unpack," his wife responded. "Won't take long, we didn't bring much."

Lucy nodded. "Yeah, there was hardly any warning at all. Everything just seemed to happen at once and before I knew it, Ben was sending out mass texts and typing furiously on that keyboard of his. Is it bad out there?"

"You mean you haven't gone to see for yourself?" he asked, surprised. He figured all of them would have been trying to keep up on what was going on. It was horrific to watch, but the future of

Mankind was being decided out there; they couldn't afford to be ignorant of it.

The older lady shook her head. "Not sure I'm ready for that yet. The very thought breaks my heart. So much death, it's too much for me to handle."

He wanted to sympathize with her. It was still hitting him in the gut every time he thought of it, but he couldn't not look; he couldn't not know. He had loved ones out there and he had to believe they were okay, that they'd make it, or he'd go crazy. Why hadn't his parents picked up their phones? Why had his sister ignored his text? The damn thing said she had "seen" them, so why the fuck hadn't she answered?

He wasn't a Christian, so he couldn't believe he'd see them again in an afterlife. He did believe in reincarnation; he just wasn't ready to give up on this life quite yet. He didn't think there was some all mighty being out there watching all of this; he couldn't believe that. There was no divine plan, because if there was, this was one fucked up part of the grand scheme and he wanted no part of it. If a deity had set this shit loose, he'd spend the rest of his life praying he'd get a chance to get revenge on the bastard for all those that were out there dying today. No benevolent God would be so cruel.

They were silent for a time, the unspoken thoughts weighing heavy upon them. Lucy finally sighed and said, "I will leave you to it then. I'm going to go next door and see how Sam is doing, the poor dear. You can hear her kids down the hall, she's going to have her hands full, especially without her husband to help her." Her voice was cracking, and he knew that she was excusing herself before she broke down in front of them; a sound of a sob echoing back at him as the door closed once more.

His heart wanted to go out to her, but her family was safe while all their friends and family were out there dying. He went to his wife, who he had seen begun to tear up, and knew that she had to be thinking of her own mother. He put his arms around her and held her close. He hated this. *Someone is going to pay,* he vowed silently.

"Mom? Can we go check on the dogs?" Caleb asked from the living room. They had bred and trained German Shepherds for the last two years. They were reliable, loyal, and most importantly, they'd only bark on command. That last had been a deal-breaker when deciding if they should try and breed them here. The walls of the main building were sound proof; the land around it was not. They didn't want unwanted attention drawn their way without cause, not if it could be prevented.

Monica broke away, wiping her face, then turned her head towards the living room and told them, "sure, go ahead. Go next door first though, see if any of the other kids want to go with." She had tried to clear her voice, but it was still evident to a trained ear that she was upset. She looked to him for confirmation that the kids would be all right out there and he simply nodded. For now, things were quiet in their part of the woods.

All things being equal, he hoped it stayed that way.

"It's okay, we're safe," he said, more for his benefit than hers.

"**We** may be, but what about everyone else?" she asked.

"Todd?" he heard Sam call from the living room and Monica smiled, shaking her head.

Go, she mouthed, pushing his shoulder and turning to the open bags littering the bed. "I've got this."

He gave her one last hug, then went to go find out what Sam needed. He should have found a way to just get them all to bunk together, maybe he'd have to take a wall out once they knew for sure there was no going home. That was a worry for another day though, there was way too much going on right now to be concerned with something like that.

"What's up Babes?" he asked, as he went towards his other partner, trying to look calm while his insides cringed at the horrid mental images that refused to depart his mind.

Chapter 19
Stall

Saint
Tucson, AZ

They'd only been driving for five minutes when the truck had begun to show signs of trouble. The engine ran like it was not getting enough gas and as they turned onto Mission, it began to lurch in sporadic movements, causing her already upset stomach to turn. There was nothing but desert to either side, the palo verdes obstructing their view of the terrain around them. Anything could be hiding in the darkness. She shivered at the thought of poor David and his transformation into that drooling cannibalistic monster. If she hadn't screamed, he'd still be alive.

"What's wrong with it?" she asked her boyfriend, not knowing much about cars, relying on the fact that he was a guy and should know all this shit automatically.

He'd been quiet since their confrontation at the store. His eyes were riveted on the road with his mouth firmly set and concentration undeterred by her efforts to get his attention. "How the fuck should I know? This is Raleigh's piece of shit, he'd know better than I do," he replied angrily. They had just barely escaped hell and now their vehicle was failing them. Would they ever catch a break? If this kept on, they'd have to find a replacement.

Part of her wanted them to go back and get her car. Surely, with the food source gone, those creatures had moved on. They could go up Drexel to Cardinal and circle around behind the store, come at it from the west. It felt wrong to leave a perfectly running vehicle back there while traveling in a junk heap like this one. Not to mention the little bit of personal items she had been able to pack. She didn't even have an extra-shirt to replace the gore-covered one she was wearing.

She sighed, it was a pipe dream; there was no way she was going to be able to convince them to go to the **one** place they were sure these monsters were; she'd have to go alone and on foot. Even though they hadn't traveled far, she winced at the thought of walking back there by herself; she'd just have to suck it up and move on.

Although they lived on the southern fringes of the city, it had not kept this shit from descending on them quickly. It had to be everywhere. How would they cross the southern-half of Tucson safely? It seemed impossible after everything that had happened so far. If it was that bad here, how bad would it be as they pushed through the more populated areas of the sprawling city? She couldn't let herself think on it or she'd end up throwing in the towel to face the inevitable. She wouldn't allow that to happen; she was not a quitter. If those things wanted her, they'd have a hell of a fight on their hands.

The truck surged violently, then sputtered and died. Jeremy was struggling to keep them on the road as they began to coast along the deserted roadway. He growled, slamming his fist against the wheel, a weak honk escaping from the hood of the truck. "Shit!" he exclaimed, running his hand through his hair, his cap lying forgotten on the floorboards below.

She glanced out the rear window and saw that Caesar was sitting up, a hand tentatively feeling the back of his head where he'd been hit. Raleigh had given her a thumbs up gesture after his initial inspection, and she knew that the wound was superficial; he'd be fine. Raleigh was climbing to his feet and the truck bucked as he hopped off the tailgate. Caesar was slowly making his way forward as her hand grasped the door handle and yanked it open.

She got out and left her boyfriend sitting in the driver seat, staring into the night through the cracked windshield. "It's dead and we can't stay here," she told him, grabbing one of the bags she had managed to bring along and slammed the door.

She met the other two at the back, watching as her defeated boyfriend finally climbed out of the vehicle and trudged his way to her side. She hated the weakness he was displaying, it did not help her confidence level at all. She wanted to slug him, to wake him the fuck up. They weren't dead yet and he was acting like they were pigs on a serving platter with apples thrust in their mouths.

"Your truck really is a piece of shit," she said, giving the larger Hispanic a dirty look.

The big guy grinned and shrugged. "The beast got us out of there, that's what matters."

"Well, your beast has been slain. Now what do we do?" she asked the group, hoping that somebody else had a brilliant idea on what came next.

"We find another car," Jeremy said in a deflated tone; his face downcast. The feeble light given off by the setting sun was still enough to show that he wouldn't meet anyone's eyes as he shouldered his way past to start the trek down the lonely deserted road.

Caesar was holding his head, eyes frightened, his mouth grimacing with pain every time he rubbed it in the wrong place. "You need to stop doing that," she told him. "Why make it feel worse?"

"It helps remind me that this is real and not some disturbing ass nightmare," he replied softly, his gaze falling upon her. "I need to get home." He said as if it was the only thing repeating through that injured brain of his; like a mantra that kept him moving. Would it be any different for her if she was in his place?

She envied him in that instant as she glanced at her departing, slump shouldered boyfriend. Sighing, she followed after, the two other men walking on either side. She hoped they'd find another car soon; there was no way they'd get out of town on foot. If they were faced with walking out of town, she would rather find a place to hunker down and wait it out. Suddenly being a criminal and knowing how to boost cars seemed like an admirable trait to being a law-biding citizen. How had they gained the edge in this world gone mad?

Each of them had bags to carry and she shifted hers from one hand to the other as her fingers began to hurt with the strain. The area they were passing through was owned by the Tohono O'odham tribe and there were no lights evident to the east or west of them; no obvious place to hide if the shit hit the fan.

They **could** brave the oncoming darkness in an attempt to blindly traverse the desert, but she was not a fan of that option. With their luck, the shadows would come to life and reveal the final moments of their short lives. The only choice that made any sense was to keep going forward, as going back was something none of them was willing to do.

"I have guns at my place," Caesar told them again, trying to bribe them to ensure he got home.

"We know. Would you relax? You'll be there soon enough," she told him, but didn't add that then she would push on without him. He was a nice enough guy, but during the fight at the store, he had shown that he was not made for this new world born of teeth and blood. He wouldn't last long, guns or not, and she couldn't afford to be responsible for him or his family if she was going to have any hope of surviving this unholy apocalypse.

Though, she might ask Raleigh to come along. He had shown the will to live and might be an asset when things got rough. Jeremy, however, she was seriously thinking of ditching the first chance she had. The attraction that she had felt had been purely physical and after all the shit that gone down throughout the day, it had slowly been replaced with disgust. The emotional connection hadn't grown between them and she had fooled herself into thinking there'd ever be one. He wanted what he wanted; regardless of the reservations of others. That kind of selfishness did not jive with the kind of person she was. She knew in her heart that when push came to shove, he would leave her in an instant if his life was threatened; chivalry never existed within the man. She would never be able to trust him, and the world was dangerous enough without willingly keeping that around.

She sent a prayer skyward to guide them in what came next and prayed that someone was listening. She had never been a religious person, had never gone to church or even read the bible, but with the dead rising it seemed like a good time to start. She hoped her prayers wouldn't go unheard. They would need as much help as they could muster if they were going to live through this.

The sun set on the horizon as they plunged forward into the oncoming darkness and the chaos of the new world beyond.

Chapter 20
Pissin' Bullets

Casey
Alpine, AZ

No matter how many times Ben told him that his road was clear, he couldn't help the jitter of his nerves as he passed that turn off heading north towards Albuquerque. His breathing had been ragged; his lungs needed something to soothe them. The cigarette he had lit burnt its way to the filter unsmoked, forgotten. His eyes remained fixed on the road, seeking any sign of trouble, ready to react the instant something out of the ordinary popped into view.

Ben couldn't be right all the time.

To his surprise, the intersection had been desolate and empty, and his heart began to beat again as he pushed forward on the final leg of his journey. He had kept his phone in his right hand, eyes dropping constantly to check for updates. Although Albuquerque remained clear, he had Roswell on the mind and how safe it seemed until that first shot rang out. He knew that he had gotten through minutes ahead of certain death and he was still shaken up over the experience. A small city was a few miles down the road and it would be the last, as he turned south on US 191. Then it was a short hop and a skip to the compounds and the safety they'd provide.

As he stood on the side of the road relieving himself, he couldn't help but take in the cooler mountain air and listen to the world around him. It was eerily quiet; an alien feeling for a city dweller. Even though it should've calmed him, it made him uneasy. Things could easily sneak up on you if you kept your head turned away long enough, and he was getting dizzy from constantly having to check his six.

Zipping up, he went to the passenger door, got out his bong and loaded it. He took a long drag, letting the fumes fill his lungs and blowing it out slowly; the calming effect spreading throughout his body, settling him. After a few minutes, he set it on the seat and went back around to the driver's side. He spared one last look at the silent world of northern Arizona, then hopped back into his car to continue on his journey to his new home.

He felt groovy now; he was close to being done and out of this shit.

His eyes were on the road and he was just getting back up to speed when his rear window shattered. He felt the rush of air on his face and his rear-view mirror exploded, sending glass shards in multiple directions. Blood began to trickle down his cheek.

"What the fuck?" he exclaimed, twisting the wheel. The car swerved, almost going off the side of the road and into the grass clearing beyond. Jerking it to the left, he barely kept control of the car as the rear tires bounced on the lip of asphalt.

He straightened out and punched it. He slipped the wheel left just as another gunshot tore into the seat next to him. If he hadn't swerved, it would have taken him in the back. "What the fuck is this shit?" he screamed, unable to comprehend what was going on. He was not a fucking zombie! Who the hell was trying to kill him? He chanced a glance to the rear and didn't see shit. Someone was trying to snipe his ass. "Goddammit, move!" he yelled at his car.

No matter what the speedometer said, he knew that it still wasn't fast enough.

His right hand was cut, and blood was gushing forth. There was a jagged green shard erupting from the palm of his hand and his anger began to rise; it was the color of his bong. "Oh, you motherfucker!" he cried, trying to keep his hand to his chest as he jerked the wheel left again. He was tempted to pull over and find this asshole, but his foot would not come off the gas pedal. Apparently, his body was smarter than his mind.

Cursing, he brought his hand to his mouth and gently pulled at the shard in his hand. Driving one handed, he winced at the pain as it slowly slid free, blood spraying his face. "Fuck that hurts," he grunted, quickly pressing his palm against his leg, trying to staunch the flow of the lifeblood fleeing his body. Doing what he could to put some distance on the shooter, he sped along the highway, not daring to drive in a straight line. For all he knew, there was a car back there racing to catch up with him.

Well, if he found a spot where he could ambush that motherfucker, he'd take it. No one broke his shit without getting an ass beating in return. There was a slight rustle of metal and he realized that the nut job had just missed. Triumph surged through him and he broke out in laughter. It was a horrible time for it, but he couldn't help it. He realized that he must have just gotten out of the sniper's range **and** the asshole wasn't mobile yet.

"Thank Christ," he muttered, still clutching his hand tightly on his pant leg. He had no clue what he had done to earn this shit and continued to pray that he wouldn't find out.

The car suddenly lurched. "What the hell?" he groaned. He glanced at his gas gauge and saw that it was quickly sliding towards empty. He had half a tank the last time he checked and spared a quick look in his side mirror. He was horrified to see that the last shot hadn't been a miss after all. The gas tank had been ruptured and was spraying fuel everywhere. Shit, he was going to run out of gas and be stranded with some maniac hunting him from behind. He was not a fucking deer, goddammit!

The engine sputtered and the car began to coast as he ran out of gas.

He was screwed.

Hastily he picked up his phone and grabbed his gear. He turned it on and hit send, hoping like mad that Ben would pick up and somehow get him out of this shit. Fear driving him, he slung his pack over his shoulder, spared one last look at his shattered bong, grabbed his stash, and slammed the car door.

He thought he could hear an engine in the distance, but he was still unable to see anything to indicate where it was coming from. Gripping his rifle, he made a quick decision, hunt or flee? His mouth firmly set, he set off for the trees with the phone glued to his ear. He feared that after all the crap he had been through so far, he was going to die in some hick town in Arizona.

What the hell was going on?

He reached the trees just as the phone picked up. "Ben, you've got to come get me right fucking now!" he nearly screamed, disappearing into the forest. He ran blindly south, with only a slim hope of rescue and the growing certainty that the reaper was closing in to try to drag his ass to hell.

Well, not today, he swore and kept moving as quickly as his legs were able.

Chapter 21
Friend in need

Todd
Compound 2

The intercom on the kitchen wall beeped at him. It felt a bit Trekish, and he had an urge to hit some imaginary badge on his chest. He'd never get used to that thing. He took another glance at his empty fridge and wondered if he shouldn't have the kids get to filling it. He closed the door softly then walked over to the wall and pushed the red transmit button. Monica was on the couch, alternating between checking her text messages and trying to read. She looked up at him, but he shrugged; he knew as much as she did. "Yeah?"

Rodger's voice crackled over the speaker system. "Casey's in trouble, he needs a pick up."

He rolled his eyes briefly, not used to this life and death crap yet. Then he realized he had to put that suit back on and he grunted. "Of course, he does. Be on my way in a minute," he responded. Monica was suddenly on her feet, following him as he quickly strode towards their bedroom. He was stripping as he went and threw the clothes towards her. They struck her chest and fell to the floor; she was in the middle of taking hers off as well. "What the hell do you think you're doing?" he asked, his hands fluidly putting his suit back on.

"What does it look like?" she asked as she slid her bra and panties free, grabbing her own suit in turn. "You're not going alone. It just ain't happening."

He grunted as the suit snagged him in the crotch; the wince unnoticed as his wife shimmied into hers. "You are not going anywhere."

"The hell I'm not," she told him, daring him to contradict her again. She was busy strapping her pads on and the veracity of her attitude told him it would be an uphill battle that he'd lose in the end. Still, they had just gotten here, and he wanted to know his family was safe before going back out.

"You are going to just leave Sam and the kids?" he asked, as she strapped on her weapons. He didn't want to orphan them should something go wrong.

She glared at him, her mouth set in a thin line, her blue eyes penetrating his resolve. "I'm not going to say this again. You are not going out there without me. You go, I go, period. You can't handle that? Tough shit. You can stay and I'll go." She stormed from the room, not waiting for him to grab his rifle and join her. "Sam is more than capable of taking care of the kids, and what safer place is there for all of them to be right now?" he heard as she opened the door and disappeared from hearing range.

He finally caught up to her in the communications room. She was at Rodger's side, the old man's suspenders given up for his own suit. Rodger looked more uncomfortable in his than Todd felt.

Somehow, that made him feel better.

His friend's younger daughter was in a chair next to her brother, her eyes glued to the screens. He wanted to yank her away from there; she didn't need to be seeing that. Rodger didn't seem to mind, and he wondered what Lucy would say if she were here. Ben was talking furiously through his Bluetooth and he heard the faint sound of someone yelling through the young boy's ear; the sound muffled and incomprehensible.

The fans on the servers below the long computer desk kicked on and he realized that it had grown hot in here since he'd left. It had to be the suit making his internal temperature rise. An overhead vent began to blow cool air and the sweat on his neck suddenly got chilled; giving him goose bumps.

The monitor on the right showed a live feed from Alpine and his wife was bending over, trying to make out what was on the screen. "It's an ATM cam," she muttered, cursing at the poor quality and lack of streaming video.

There was a gasp from the little girl, and he looked over just in time to see that a dead woman had come into view on that feed. The little girl whimpered as the corpse of a young teenager in a fetching blouse and skirt craned her neck at an impossible angle; staring at the camera. He doubted that whatever was running through that diseased mind understood what she was looking at. However, that didn't keep her from walking straight up to it, her nasty gore filled mouth filling the screen.

Wendy got off the chair, ran behind Rodger, clutched his pant leg, and hid her face. He had finally noticed the ghoulish face on that screen and muttered something to his son as he turned to his younger daughter, trying to soothe her. Ben moved his mouse and the screen closed, the flash of teeth vanishing from view.

He shuddered from the memory as it replayed through his mind and he felt for the little girl crying in her dad's arms. Rodger set her down in another chair but turned this one away from the screens. His hand was on her shoulder as he turned to Ben and the situation unfolding in the room around him.

"He's obviously still alive," Rodger commented, the shrill scream over the ear bud making it quite obvious Casey was still kicking.

Ben nodded, his head pointing towards his ear, not realizing they could partially hear the conversation unfolding. "I know man. Are you sure you can't just get another car? Or hell, push it to a gas pump? There's one right up the road. Oh, well you didn't tell me the gas tank got shot, asshole. Well, what are you doing in the fucking woods, you noob? Cover from what?" The boy paused, listening, then gave his father a worried glance. "He says a sniper was taking shots at him. You guys had better get moving, he needs a pick up."

"If he's in the woods, how the hell are we supposed to get to him? Can't he get to a road?" his wife asked, her hand on the back of Ben's chair. Her head was craned to the right, trying to hear what Casey was saying.

Ben shook his head. "There's no way. He said the guy must be hard on his ass. He won't turn back now. He's worried he's not far enough ahead and won't detour. No Casey, they can't hear you. I'm not going to say that. No," he stated firmly.

They needed to get going, but to where?

"Goddammit!" the young man cursed, giving them an apologetic stare. "He says, Todd get your ass in that fucking chopper and get out here now! His words."

He nodded in understanding. His friend was in trouble and he wasn't waiting any longer. "Send us the details," he said, holding up his phone.

Without waiting to see if anyone was following him, he strode back out of the room and towards the stairs that led to the upper level. Monica rushed to his side and his will to fight was gone. If she wanted to come along, he couldn't stop her. He heard the harsh breathing from behind and knew that Rodger was trying to keep up as well.

"If we're going to do this, we're going to do it right. There's no room for mistakes. If someone is after him, then I doubt they'll discriminate at taking a shot at us as well. Maybe you should stay here, take care of the kids." He said the last half-hoping she'd listen, but the grasp of her hand in his was enough; she wasn't going to stay.

Dammit, he thought.

"If you die out there, I'll kill you again," she muttered, her voice stern and making him flinch. He knew she'd do just that.

"Yes ma'am," he said as he emerged from the lower levels and back onto the ground floor. They had a lot more ground to cover and he felt time slipping away.

"How about we all try to come back alive and leave it at that?" Rodger remarked from behind them; startling him. He didn't realize the old man had kept up, he was practically pushing them along.

"Sounds like a plan." He tried to grin, but it faltered. This was going to be hell. How did this crap always happen to Casey? Maybe he didn't want the magnet for disaster back here with his family so close by. Sighing, he knew he'd never leave him to die out there.

They rushed down the steps to the tunnel that would take them to Compound One and his phone beeped, the map app opening on its own. Ben had found a clearing for a pick up. Now the question was, would they make it there in time?

Chapter 22
Survival 101

Rosilynn
Nevada/Arizona Border

Getting out of Vegas had been a close thing. Her nerves were shot, and her hands still trembled when she wasn't focusing on keeping them still. Several times she'd seen the reaper closing in and knew that they had barely escaped the outbreak trailing behind.

It had been infuriating at first, being stuck in that much traffic; it was beyond anything she'd ever experienced. She wasn't sure where they were all heading; they couldn't possibly believe it was limited to Vegas. With no communication to the outside world, they were blindly running, with no idea of where to go or what they'd do when they got there.

Several times their car had been nudged by vehicles trying to force their way past, but the congestion kept them from getting too far. They had inched along; the consistent crawl having destroyed any attempt at being patient. She had beaten the car door enough that the plastic cover had a permanent dent. Well it wasn't hers, so why should she give a shit?

It had been hot in the car, the broken window letting any semblance of cool air escape before it ever reached her. The air conditioner was a piece of crap and kept overheating the idling engine, so they ended up turning it off. She wished it was cooler out; fall was approaching but it wasn't quite there yet. The skin on her arms had to be red beneath the suit, the constant rubbing and scratching she'd been doing had made it sore as hell; the rest of her body feeling confined and sticky.

They didn't have much in the way of water, so they drank sparingly. She hated to do it, but she had used most of it keeping Matt's wound clean. Since they weren't going anywhere, she had gotten him to maneuver enough to let her clean and dress it again. There was a nasty aroma emanating from the gash and she didn't like how red the skin was getting around the fringes of the wound. He would need antibiotics soon to keep the infection from getting worse.

So far, it's acting like a normal infection, her mind spoke hopefully.

The human mouth was teeming with germs and she didn't want to think of what might happen if they didn't treat it in time. They would have to make the time to pull over. Not only to refill their water, but to find a pharmacy and make a non-prescription withdrawal. They hadn't dared pull off while they were still in Vegas, they might never have made it back on the interstate afterwards. Even the frontage road had been swamped and the vehicles swarming it weren't making much in the way of progress either.

The other side of the highway had been empty. It wasn't from the lack of people trying to come from that direction, but from the increased military presence dominating the freeway. No one had been brave enough to attempt it out of fear of an Abram Tank crushing them like Bigfoot at a Monster Truck Rally. Humvees were parked at intervals along the highway with their guns trained on the vehicles inching their way forward; hungry for action. She prayed it wouldn't come until long after they were gone.

The remaining windows shuddered from the constant barrage from the airplanes that roared overhead; a permanent fixture in the sky. They circled, let loose their ordinance and then disappeared only to be replaced by more. She recognized the Hornets and was surprised by the number of Warthogs flying overhead. Most of those were stationed in Arizona and had to have been in Nevada doing training exercises when the crisis hit. Explosions erupted in the distance and the dark cloud of smoke from the destruction of the city slowly drifted their way. Missiles streaked across the sky and the boom of tanks to the rear had shaken her so badly that she was about ready to just hop out of the car and make a run for it. It'd be a hell of a lot faster than their current pace.

"There's nothing I can do," Matt had told her, as frustrated as she was at the situation.

If only they had gotten out sooner. The explosion that had knocked her out back on Tropicana might end up costing them their lives.

"I know," she had replied, trying to reassure him. Regardless of the years of preparation, Death loomed over them, wanting to take them in his cold embrace. She could feel it edging ever closer and her mind was going stir crazy with the wait.

She had put her hands on the dash and peered over the tops of the cars ahead, but she saw nothing that would calm her nerves. All they could do was wait. A flash had lit up their rear window and the rapid explosion that rocked their car made it clear that the infected were closing fast on their tail. Her hand had reached for the door handle, ready to jump out and start running when her phone had gone off, making her squeal with the sudden movement on her leg.

Ben: lightening up, five mins

A rush of relief flooded her. Even though her eye hadn't caught it, they had begun to move at a faster rate; yards rather than feet. Matt had glanced her way and they shared a moment, they might just make it. Then she saw his eyes darken, his leg twitch, and the corner of his mouth firm up. She had constantly told him that he was going to be fine, but the look he was giving her said everything she needed to know; he didn't believe her.

Frustrated, she had clenched her hands and looked away.

Ben had been right; the traffic had lightened up shortly thereafter and they had finally been able to get their acquired vehicle up to a normal pace. The number of onramps had decreased, and the flow of traffic surged forward in an attempt to get clear of the city. The fact that Ben was still watching over them made her feel calmer. She felt reassured that if danger had come too close, that he would have warned them in an enough time to get away.

As if on cue, her phone buzzed again:

Ben: Take steps to avoid Flagstaff

"We kind of need to get out of Nevada first, Ben," she had muttered, shaking her head.

"What?" Matt asked her, his eyes on the road and oblivious to the text she just got. He suddenly braked as an SUV cut in front of him. She was glad that he hadn't checked his own phone, or they would've ended up pancaked or pinballed across the interstate with the cars behind serving as flippers.

She sighed, "he says to stay away from Flagstaff."

"How the hell are we going to do that?" he asked as expected and she didn't have an answer yet.

"Let me work on that. For now, just keep your eyes on the road," she ordered him. She reached for her map and unfolded it on her lap, eyes tracing the roads ahead in an attempt to find a way east without using the I-40.

"No shit," he sneered. "Like I don't know how to fucking drive."

Her hand slammed down on the map, impacting her sore legs. "Don't you snap at me! I know you're scared, but I'm not a fucking punching bag. Got it? We are doing everything we can. You can't fall apart on me now."

He shook his head, his nose lifting as his brows drew together. "Always about you, isn't it? You need to keep going. I need you to keep me alive," he mocked in a bad imitation of her voice. It was the hurt talking, but it still stung. The instant he said it, he glanced her way and saw the pain that he had caused, the firm set of her mouth, and the way she was kneading her hands. "Look, I'm sorry, okay? I know we need to keep moving. I just feel fucking stupid. Why didn't I clear that car before trying to get in? I fucked up. Even a rookie knows better than to pull that shit. It's the first rule in the Survival 101 manual."

"I thought that was don't die," she muttered, her eyes threatening to tear under the onslaught, her mind needing to focus.

He gave her an icy stair. "I'm not debating—"

"It isn't just on you. I didn't check it either," she said, cutting him off. "We are not perfect, we can't be. There's just no way to see every angle. That's impossible."

"Bullshit," he replied, but the anger had leaked a bit from his voice and her heart began to pump at a regular pace again. For a moment there, he looked ready to pull his pistol and end it. Her hands shook as they held the map tightly within their grasp.

"We might have to go through Havasu. We'll lose half a day, but there is just no other way without going through Flagstaff. Unless you want to hoof it." She instantly regretted it the second the words left her mouth. That was really out of the question and she wouldn't consider it unless they were left with no other choice; he wouldn't get very far. If the infection was spreading, the exertion would only make it worse. They'd have to stick to vehicles as long as they could.

"Maybe they'll pick us up," her husband offered, letting hope show on his face for the first time in hours. It lightened the load on her mind, and she welcomed it.

She looked up to the sky once more, watching the planes scream by overhead. "I'm pretty sure the airspace is closed down in this part of the world. If they're going to have any chance to come get us, we're going to have to get a hell of a lot closer."

He listened but she doubted he absorbed it.

Over the next two hours he had stayed hopeful and she let him; it was better than the dark brooding suicidal attitude he had been displaying all afternoon. If you believed you were going to die, you could sometimes manufacture the outcome you feared.

The sky was darkening as night approached and the lights along the freeway told them ahead of time that it was going to be a long evening. Signs began to appear for the Hoover Dam, and she knew that they were fast approaching the border. Traffic had begun to slow, and she was glad that the new interstate bypass was built a few years before; it would help them get into Arizona faster than that slow winding road through the dam. She had been there once or twice and after the initial awe, it had settled upon her that it was just a dam.

Hours later, she would recall that stray thought and wonder at how naïve she had been.

Chapter 23
Hot LZ

Todd
Gila National Forest, AZ

It took them twenty-five minutes to get airborne. It wasn't just the trip back through the tunnel, the Huey hadn't been flown in over a year. The area around it had to be cleared and the startup done from scratch; they couldn't just hop in and go. There was no point in going out there if they were just going to end up dead themselves.

Each of them had been taking lessons on flying; but some had shown more aptitude for it and had been certified by an instructor in Tucson. While he hadn't gotten his yet, his daughter had. Surprisingly, she had taken to the stick like she had been born in a helicopter instead of a maternity ward. Neither parent had wanted to encourage her. Even though she got certified, they had no intention of ever letting her fly on her own.

Using their GPS app as a guide, Rodger got the Huey off the ground and swung northeast. Judging by how close their two dots were, it wouldn't take long to get there. The question that weighed heavily upon their minds was whether nor not they'd be under fire when they arrived.

Monica was standing in the back, the door thrown wide on the Huey, her blond hair flapping with the wind. Her gear was fastened, her rifle held tightly with one hand, the other over her head gripping a bar to keep her balance. He was in the co-pilot seat next to Rodger during takeoff, but now he began to work his way to the back and went to his wife's side.

"I really wish you'd stayed behind," he yelled over the roaring wind. He hated that she was putting her life at risk, this was his job; not hers. That age-old thinking was hard to shake at times like this and he felt less of a man that she didn't trust him to do it on his own.

She shook her head slightly. "Wasn't gonna happen."

It was over and done with, it was too late to change it, so he decided to push it aside and focused on what was coming. He hadn't been able to convince her to stay but that didn't mean he was going to let her throw herself in front of a bullet either. He stepped closer to the doorway, the wind buffeting his face as he looked upon the forest below.

Apart from a clearing now and then, the unending pine trees gave them little intel on what lay below. Anything could be moving beneath that unending green canopy. His phone was vibrating and how long it had been doing so he had no clue. He'd never hear a ringer over the roar of the rotors and the vibration of the Huey offset what he'd feel in his pockets.

Ben: Casey says he's almost there, says all clear atm

Well, that was somewhat comforting.

The moonlight was bright tonight. Thank God for small favors, he hated going into this blind. Was there someone still chasing Casey? Were they waiting for the right moment to take their next shot? Would they land, see Casey for a brief second, then watch him die right before their eyes? Were they aware of the pick up and just waiting to see who'd show so they could take a shot at them as well? Too many questions and no way to answer any of them.

His arms were weary, and his body felt drained after the day they'd been through. He hadn't been in conflict yet, but the constant stress and emotions that had raged through him had caused an exhaustion to settle over his worn-out frame. He had to fight to stay on his feet against the forces buffeting him from without; both physical and spiritual.

He was badly in need of a nap. If all went well, he'd take one when they returned to the compound. He would need to be fresh tomorrow, more of their comrades might show up in need of their help. He couldn't afford to feel this tired then either. He should consider sleeping with Sam tonight, she was probably shaken up by her new surroundings and would be badly in need of comfort. He glanced at his wife and saw the strain on her face, the worry lines furrowing her brow. She was just as tired as he was; maybe they could all nap together. After the day they had, cuddling in bed seemed a nice way to fall asleep.

Though, he'd probably leave more than a few lights on. The images on those screens in the communication room had disturbed him on a deeper level. He wasn't sure that even if he tried, that sleep would come. Those images would haunt him for weeks and he wondered at how many more would be added to that horrific display by then.

His phone updated and a marker appeared on the map. Ben had found the fastest point for the two groups to meet. He noticed Rodger looking at the phone on the dash as well. The older man looked at him and nodded to the headset hanging on a hook by his head. He slid it over his ears, rocking slightly as turbulence shifted the Huey.

"Get the ropes ready just in case," Rodger suggested.

He nodded and immediately motioned for Monica to help him, grabbing the hooks and clipping them in place. "Casey's not a Seal, I'm not sure he can hold onto one of these. Ben said that he's got an injured hand."

Rodger shook his head. "There may not be a choice. We have to be ready for anything."

His older friend was just as worried about their mission as he was. The lack of confidence was detrimental to what they were doing, and he tried to flex his muscles, then relax them in an effort to ease the tension in his body. The map zoomed in as the two dots approached one another and he felt his anxiety increase at the size of the clearing they had to land in. Would they even fit or was the endless tree cover affecting his brain's interpretation of the clearing's size?

It ended up being a moot point as he saw their destination come into view through the cockpit windows. In the dim light, it appeared to be twenty yards across and there was a flash of white bouncing across the grass; probably a deer. Monica was checking their clearance on the left as he checked the right. They both nodded to Rodger, who began their descent to the grass below.

He was nervous about actually setting down; they didn't know how flat the terrain was beneath that flowing grass. He didn't envy the man's nerves at the moment and sighed with relief as they smoothly set down without incident.

His heart rose to his throat as he released his hand from the bar, grabbed the stock of his rifle, and jumped from the Huey to the ground below. His eyes scanned the tree cover, but the feeble light barely penetrated the dense forest surrounding them. He watched for any sign of movement and clicked on a flashlight, shining it in the direction Casey was supposed to be coming from. He hadn't noticed that his wife had jumped down at his side and he shot her a worried glance.

The Huey vibrated behind them, the speed of the rotors pushing them down, their bodies aching as they resisted. He checked his phone one last time and saw a red dot approaching their position. His grip tightened on his rife and he brought it up; prepared to fire.

Their arrival hadn't been covert; the beating of the rotors let anything within a two-mile radius know exactly where they were. If there was someone out there hunting their comrade, they had a definite idea of where to find them now. He hoped Casey got there quickly so they could get back in the air and headed south before the man hunting him closed the distance.

He wished that they had gotten a stealthier helicopter; but it wasn't as if there was access for civilians to buy modern technological crafts. He wasn't sure how Sean had arranged getting what they did have. The man claimed he had ordered the parts online and that it was assembled at the compound, but none of the others had fessed up to helping him do it. It was a mystery that never seemed important, until now; the more knew about where they were, the more chances of having unwelcomed visitors.

The amount of noise the Huey made when flying couldn't be adjusted or helped. When dealing with an outbreak of this sort, silence was key, and they were a beacon to any zombie lurking in the area. At least, that's what they were led to believe by decades of saturation from the movie industry. However, it had occurred to him that relying on that information could lead to disaster. They didn't know what was real and what was fantasy. How could you react right when you didn't know the difference?

His phone vibrated again, alerting him that Casey was finally reaching their location. He was coming on the run. He couldn't hear anything over the beating of the rotors, but he saw movement in the trees and his younger friend suddenly popped into view. He was winded and struggling to stay on his feet. The years of smoking was taking its toll as he stumbled and nearly fell over. Raising an arm against the beating wind, Casey gave him a pained look and Todd dashed forward to give him a hand.

Shouldering his rifle, he reached out and grabbed his friend by the arm. Monica was at their side, rifle in hand, and covered their flank as they made their way to the awaiting Huey. Casey threw his bag in, the handle covered in blood from his wound. He was having a hard time climbing after it. As he bent over to give his friend an assist, a shot rang out and Casey screamed in pain. Blood blossomed on his rear as he fell forward onto the chopper's deck. Monica began firing her weapon, sweeping the treeline.

His rifle was set to semi-automatic and he fired blindly into the trees, trying to provide cover as his wife stopped long enough to jump into the Huey. She got on her knees and began firing once more as he stepped back, put his hand on a handle bar, and placed his feet on the landing struts. The speed of the rotors increased, and the Huey began to lift. He tried to continue firing one handed, but the strain on his wrist was too much and the rifle fell to his side. Monica kept on though, her aim shifting as she blanketed the trees.

There were a few pops; barely audible, and the side of the Huey near his head erupted in small particles of torn metal. His face stung as a small piece sliced his cheek. Seeing two white holes on the dark green exterior, he realized that he had come within inches of getting his head blown off. He turned and dove into the rising Huey, his hand reaching. Monica grasped his hand and pulled, his dangling legs barely swept from view as bullets peppered the chopper's other door. It shattered the bubbled window and sprayed glass everywhere. He lay there on top of Casey, his lungs heaving, cheek stinging, wondering where the next shot would strike.

"Motherfucker get off me! This fucking hurts!" his buddy screamed, shaking Todd into the realization that he was putting pressure Casey's bullet wound. "That son of a bitch shot me in the ass!"

His cheek hurt like hell, his limbs felt like jelly after the brief conflict, but his funny bone was struck by his friend's exclamations. He couldn't help but laugh as he rolled over and fell on the Huey's deck. Monica had shut the door and was working on trying to inspect the wound on their fallen comrade. "You don't need to be touching his ass!" he yelled, laughing harder. They had survived and his joy only fueled his good humor.

His wife ignored him, and Casey screamed again as her fingers clamped a compress over the wound, the choppers first-aid kit lying open at her side. The Huey began to tilt, and his laughter suddenly died in his throat. As he began to slide towards the now-closed doorway, he turned his head towards the cockpit and saw Rodger's head sitting at an awkward angle. Had he passed out?

He got to his feet, adrenaline pushing him forward and helping to restore his strength. He grasped the seats and hopped into the copilot seat. They were beginning to lose altitude and he quickly made adjustments to right the craft and stabilize the falling chopper. His feet made small adjustments, the training he had limited but working in small steps to keep them airborne. "Monica, I need you!" he yelled, hoping that she could hear him.

She came to Rodger's side and he stole a quick glance, his stomach churning. There was blood sliding down the older man's head from under the helmet he wore. There was a dent in it, an impact mark that hadn't penetrated but still done enough to knock the old man out. There was a hole in the cockpit interior to the left of the Rodger's head and he knew that the helmet saved the man's life. His wife's fingers were placed over his jugular and when she nodded, Todd knew that his friend was stable enough to survive the trip home.

He grabbed a nearby headset and slammed it over his head as the compound appeared on the horizon. "Ben, get the med lab ready," he spoke into the mic and heard the frantic young man respond quickly to his commands. He knew that Lucy had to be rushing to the tunnels, the news of her husband's injury putting her into panic mode. She would meet them when they touched down and escort them back to the medical bay on the first basement level of the compound. He only hoped that his limited amount of time in the helicopter would be enough to set them down safely or they'd end up scattered across the forest below.

Despite his doubts, he felt a surge of relief when the helicopter jerked to a halt on the runway. It wasn't smooth, but they were down. He hadn't tried to land on the dirt pad reserved for the Huey; he could worry about moving it later. He flipped switches and began shutting it down. He was overjoyed that they'd made it in one piece, despite the gunshot wounds; neither of which appeared to be life threatening.

Though, he wouldn't know for sure about Rodger until they inspected the wound.

Casey groaned from the back and Monica was busy trying to remove Rodger's helmet. He put out a hand and grasped hers, shaking his head. "Leave it for now, the bleeding might increase if you remove it. We don't want him to bleed out."

They wouldn't be able to move both men at once.

He climbed out of his seat, hopped out of the chopper, and went to the pilot's side to give his wife a hand. Rodger's dead weight nearly drove him to the ground as he undid the man's seatbelt and lowered him out. Monica rushed to his side and together they carried him in the direction of the tunnels. After a hard few minutes of strenuous exertion, they had him in the back seat of one of the jeeps. He reached out and grabbed his wife by the shoulder. He wanted to hug her, but the time didn't seem right. They had survived, neither of them had been hurt; but to celebrate that while two of their friends were injured seemed wrong. "Take him to Lucy, I'll go back for Casey."

She didn't argue, just gave him a weak smile as she jumped into the driver side and started forward. He hovered there briefly, watching them go. He hoped his older friend had just been knocked unconscious from the blow to the head and that the dent in the helmet hadn't broken through his skull. It hadn't been that large, but it had been enough to break skin and cause the man to bleed. Though, he knew from experience that head wounds tended to bleed excessively despite the amount of damage it suffered. He hoped it was superficial, because if he had an inner brain bleed there would be nothing that they could do but sit back and watch their friend slip away.

Sighing, he tiredly climbed the steps out to the tarmac and approached the quieting Huey. Casey hadn't moved from the spot he had fallen on; too busy writhing in pain and shouting about his ass. The blood loss had slowed, and the compress was no longer getting soaked. It was a shallow wound, the extra flesh had probably prevented the bullet from going too far, or else Casey would have been in a lot more pain. He believed it was more psychological rather than physical that was making his stoner friend act like his life was coming to an end.

"Oh, shut up already, it's not that bad you fucking baby," he said, trying not to laugh at his friend's discomfort. Casey was lying across the deck spread-eagled, his face turned and his eyes glaring at him. "Seriously? Dude, it can't be that bad. Your ass has stopped leaking. Well, blood anyway," he commented, trying to lift the dread from his day in a vain attempt at humor. He waved his hand in front of his nose for effect and his young friend stared daggers at him.

"You are going to carry my ass to the jeep for that shitty remark," Casey said, trying to look serious and failing.

He broke into laughter; he couldn't help it. "Shitty? See? Your humor **is** intact, it can't be too bad," he remarked, slapping his friend's leg and making Casey yelp in feigned pain.

"Oh, you're definitely carrying me now, asshole," the younger man snarled.

"The hell I am. If you get your lazy ass up, I might just lend you a shoulder, but as to carrying you? We aren't married and this isn't our wedding night. You can carry yourself over the threshold, thank you very much," he returned. He had collected his rifle and was busy shouldering Casey's bag. He already felt laden down and wondered briefly if he should make two trips instead of pushing it with one.

Sighing, Casey slid his front side backward, his legs dangling from the Huey. He cried out in pain as his ass stretched, making the wound bleed anew. "Surprised you can keep track of who you're married to," he managed to grunt between clenched teeth.

He fought the urge to slap the man's other ass cheek to even out the pain. Bullet wounds were not really funny, but at times like this he could either laugh or cry. He had chosen humor instead of sorrow. He helped Casey to his feet, the man leaning heavily on one foot, arm draped around his shoulders for support. As they began to limp forward, the bag slipped and tumbled to the ground with a large clank.

Casey bent to pick it up. "Leave it. I'll come back for it later," he told his friend, feeling his strength starting to ebb. He wouldn't be able to support the weight for long; he needed to get them into that jeep and on the way back to the others.

"Todd, I love you man. And while I appreciate the save and assist, if you think I'm going to sit in that jeep, blood seeping from my ass, and not inhale something to distract my mind from this pain—then you are out of your fucking mind. Ain't happening bro," his young friend said weakly, taking the bag strap in hand and limping along.

"You know I can't be around that shit. You want to finish what that sniper started?" he asked, trying to smile. "You know I'm allergic."

"Better hold your breath brother," Casey returned, then grimaced as the wounds on his body began to take their toll. "Get me out of here man." They pushed forward and went down the steps at a slow pace. Casey was having to take it one at a time. "How's Rodger?"

"His vitals were stable when we put him in the jeep, but it's a head wound," he replied, not needing to explain any further. He leaned forward so that Casey could grab the door's edge and pull himself into the back seat where he could lay down.

Although he had joked about it, his friend did not bother going for the stash in his bag. Instead, he laid it on the floorboards of the jeep and tilted his head slightly, their eyes meeting. "Thank you for coming for me. If anything happens to Rodger—."

"If anything happens, we will do some hunting of our own," he replied, patting Casey's leg. The young man screamed, and he realized he had just made the pain flare up. "Oops, sorry," he laughed as he climbed into the driver's seat and turned the engine over. "I heard that's a million-dollar wound. Forrest says so."

"Yeah, fuck you too motherfucker. This shit hurts. Why not get us the fuck out of here and get me some morphine already?" his friend cursed from the backseat.

"Hooah that," he returned, shaking his head.

No matter what else happened today, at least one of his friends had made it. That provided hope that some of the others might as well. He stretched his back and neck in an attempt to loosen it up. He applied the gas and started the long trip to their new home, the moaning man in the backseat crying out every time his ass touched the seat cushions. His laughter echoed through the darkness behind them.

Chapter 24
Street Fight

Saint
Tucson, AZ

    A red light could be seen in the distance and her heartbeat quickened. She realized that they would soon be reentering civilization and the horrors that came with it. Drexel was ahead and though it was usually a quiet area, she wondered how much that had changed in the past twelve hours. The street light changed to green, but there were no headlights in view to signal that it mattered. She strengthened her grip on her bag and wished that she had a weapon; she hated feeling defenseless. All they had was Raleigh's bent pipe for protection, and that wouldn't last much longer before becoming useless as well.

    She had expected to see the bright red and white sign of a Circle K off to the left when the intersection came into view, but that side of the road was pitch black. Had it lost power? If so, how were the street lights still on? Not to mention the soft green glow of a Diamond Shamrock sliding into view on their right. The street lamps began to illuminate their way and her eyes searched the visible environment for any signs of life; or non-life as it were.

    As her eyes adjusted, she began to think the Circle K had completely disappeared from the corner it had occupied for most of her life. A glint of moonlight off a piece of glass caught her eye and she could see the dark outline of the building; barely visible to the naked eye. There had been an explosion at the gas station, the entire front of the store was destroyed and blackened from fire. There was a piece of twisted white metal near the center and the shell of what used to be a vehicle resting on top of it. From experience, she knew it was where they stored their propane tanks. What the hell had happened? It bothered her that there was a fire station right down the street and that no one had responded to the fire. There weren't any signs that anyone had even attempted to put it out.

The Diamond Shamrock however, was still intact. The lights were on and there were no cars evident in the parking lot. The hope of finding another vehicle quickly was looking slimmer by the second and she tried to fight off the feeling of despair descending upon her. They slowed at the intersection, trying to decide if they should stop off at the convenience store or not.

"We should get some water before we go on," Raleigh offered. It was the one useful thing he'd said since they abandoned his truck. From his size, she was sure that he was after more than that, but he did have a point. She nodded and the others didn't disagree. She began to move in that direction when a scraping noise reached her ears. She came to a sudden stop, ears attentive, and her eyes searching.

A large herd of undead shambled into view, not yet aware of their presence. They moved steadily forward on their cold dead legs and she knew it would only be seconds before they were spotted. She took a couple of hesitant steps back, trying to move without being seen; it didn't work. One of the dead men looked up, his blackened torso and work shirt making it obvious that he had been working at the convenience store at the time of his death. His eyes found hers and she nearly screamed at the look of joy that crossed his face. He made a slight noise and lunged at them. The others noticed the movement and all the heads came up, eyes fixing on them. The entire herd began to run their way; they were fucked.

They didn't have any real weapons, nothing but desert to either side, and a long empty road behind them. They dropped their bags and turned to flee. She hardened her heart against what would come next; her death at the hands and teeth of those monsters was almost a sure thing now.

A battle cry erupted from her right and out of the darkness charged a group of the living. They were streaming out of the parking lot of a tire repair shop behind the Circle K and were heading straight for the closing herd of zombies. Most of the creatures heard them and stopped in their places, turning to see the new source of food so willingly offering itself to them. The lone zombie that hadn't been distracted by the newcomers was the clerk and he was coming straight for her. She stopped trying to run and turned to meet the threat. She was not new to a fight and though she was terrified, the adrenaline pumping through her veins refused to let her back down.

Raleigh strode from her left, crossed in front of her, and grabbed the young man by the head. The hands clawed at the big man's arms as he lifted the zombie off his feet and jerked his hands to the left. There was a pop and the arms suddenly dropped. The teeth were still gnashing, eyes raging, but the body hung there limply. Raleigh tossed it aside like it held no further value or threat. "Thing barely had any muscles holding that head up, much easier to snap that way."

Maybe for you, I sure as hell couldn't do it.

Her blood was pumping wildly as she gave a small shriek of triumph and rushed forward to join the fray. The fighting was vicious, and she had nothing to lose by joining in. Anyone that died would only turn and reinforce the zombie herd, so it was better that they all worked together to ensure their survival. To her surprise, Caesar was at her side. She turned her head to see Raleigh and Jeremy working together to take down a half-naked female that had tried to tear into them.

She reeled around just in time to help a young man who was grappling with an older Hispanic lady in a nightgown. She was close to tearing out his throat and with a swift punch, she nailed the woman in the back of the neck. The sickening crunch sent a jolt up her arm, causing her wrist to go numb. It hadn't done any real damage, but it was enough of a distraction that the young man was able to bring a tire iron around, burying the tip in the head of the dead woman, killing her for a second time.

Another body flung itself at her and she found herself fighting a younger white male in street clothing. His hands clawed at her face and it was all she could do to keep those teeth from finding a piece of flesh to bite into. She screamed in fear, her heart hammering in her chest. That mouth was closing in and none of her efforts were making a difference.

A bat slammed into the head from behind. Disgustingly, the head caved in and teeth blew outward; showering her face with gore. She screamed again, the body pitching forward and falling dead at her feet.

Standing before her was a tall black man with glasses. He was bald and had a dark goatee covered in sweat and blood; mouth hung open in rage. For a brief second, she thought he was one of them, but then he raised the bat in triumph and howled at the sky. She had started to feel a tickle of recognition, but it struggled to come to her in the face of such naked fury.

"Robert?" she asked, unsure. What the hell was he doing there?

He didn't answer, barely even registered her presence as he turned and swung his weapon at another zombie. The head split apart and another body fell to the ground at his feet. He surged past her and continued fighting, rage spilling forth with every swing, every corpse a yell of triumph.

Heaving loudly, he brought his bat up again, but there were no longer any targets to swing at. The entire herd was lying dead at their feet. Some of the group were gasping for air as others kicked the corpses angrily; profanity following each swing of the leg. There were only ten of them now and a couple looked wounded.

Someone to her left let out a yelp of pain; one of the fallen corpses was attached to the man at the ankles, teeth tearing into flesh. Apparently, the celebration had been premature, they hadn't checked to make sure these things were down for the count. The younger man broke free, jerking his leg backward, and bringing a steel pipe down on the creature that bit him. He bashed at it repeatedly, rage pushing him far past the point of mattering. The thing would never bite anyone again. The man noticed that they were all looking at him with fear in their eyes. "What?" he asked, not understanding, his hand running through his hair, the steel pipe hanging limply at his side.

Robert stepped forward and without warning brought the bat down on the man's head. The look of surprise turned to sudden terror. Before an arm could be raised to block the blow, the bat caved in his head. The body fell to the ground and joined the pile of undead corpses.

Surprisingly, there were no cries of outrage from anyone. They just stood there, trying to catch their breath, stunned at what had just happened. None of them appeared as disturbed as she was by Robert's actions. Why had he done that?

Someone on her right suddenly started to back away from them. He was 5'9, thin, with dark skin, and frightened brown eyes. He wore a dark t-shirt, black pants, and he was holding his right arm behind him as he tried to move into the shadows. She saw wet liquid on the ground by his fleeing feet and a dark revelation settled upon her; he was bit. He had just watched another man get killed for that and must have realized he could be next. It dawned on her that she knew this guy as well. It was Erik, another coworker and Raleigh's roommate!

What the hell?

By this time, Robert had seen Erik's attempt to put some distance between them. He raised his bloodied bat and began to stalk his prey. The rest of the group seemed content to let it happen, watching with a combination of awe and shock. Were they going to let this go on? Robert brought the bat up and closed the distance. Erik began to scream.

"This is bullshit!" she yelled at him, choosing to break from the others and stand against the atrocity unfolding. "Robert!" she yelled, trying to distract the man before he could swing the bat, ending her coworker's life. These two were supposed to be friends, how could Robert do this to him without a hint of hesitation?

"Hey man, maybe you don't have to do this," a young man in a blue sweater and long black hair said. He had a guitar slung over his left shoulder and a large butcher knife held in his right hand. He was another one of her coworkers and she began to understand that they all must have been traveling together. None of them had been at the store when it came under attack, so they must have been hanging out when the shit hit the fan. It was too much of a coincidence to be just chance. Manny stepped in Erik's direction, but paused when he saw the dark look on Robert's face. He seemed uncertain and she felt the unease spread through her as well.

Those cold eyes looked at the others gathered around behind her. They were keeping their distance, but the horror of what they were about to do was finally settling in. It hadn't even been a day since this shit began and she wondered, were they that far gone already? The Humanity in their eyes told her that none of them had quite reached that point. The line had been drawn in the sand and they were hesitating before crossing it. How long before it was obliterated altogether, and murder was an acceptable part of this new life?

Well, if she had something to say about it, it wouldn't be tonight.

His eyes came to rest on her. He knew she was the real threat to what he was obviously convinced he had to do. "Stop trying to be a saint, Sabrina," he told her coldly; he had recognized her after all. They had spent numerous cold mornings at their break table, and she thought they were friends. She wondered if the events of the day had changed them so much that she'd might not even recognize herself in a mirror.

He raised his voice so the others could hear him loud and clear. "Just in case you're not aware of this, if you get bit, you die. You become one of them," he roared, pointing his bat at one of the corpses at his feet.

To make matters worse, Erik tripped and fell to the ground with a horrible squeal. He had tried to make a break for it while Robert was distracted and now, he was on his elbows, lips trembling, bloody arm exposed for all of them to see. It wasn't much of a wound, more of a patch of missing flesh. He wouldn't lose the use of it and if treated, the skin would heal over with only a slight scar. He could go on to live a long and fruitful life. At least, as long as anyone could hope for in a world gone mad.

She had taken a few steps towards her fallen friend and tried to maneuver between him and Robert.

"Jesus Christ! It's not even that bad! Not even a real bite. Come on man, you don't have to do this," Erik cried, trying to stay the swing of the bat hovering over his head.

"You're dead already," Robert responded without turning. He continued to look at his small group, then to the others that had journeyed with her from the store. Jeremy, Caesar, and Raleigh had worked with him and he glared at each, daring them to deny that he was doing the right thing. It came as no surprise that even her boyfriend wasn't coming to her side. Manny had begun to edge forward and was the only one of the group that seemed to want to stop it from happening.

"If you get bit, you die," Robert repeated. "It doesn't matter how bad it is. Do you want to wait for him to die; to turn and become one of them? We have to end this now, we can't take the chance!" he yelled.

To her horror, they were all nodding in agreement.

"You don't know that will happen! What makes you so sure, because you saw it on a TV show? This is real life Robert! At least wait to see if he gets sick before you kill your best friend!" she roared back, her temper getting the best of her. She had moved between them, her hands clenched, eyes flaring with her own inner rage.

"Get out of my way Sabrina," he told her firmly. Whatever friendship they had was now at an end, she could see that in his eyes. She thought she knew the man, that he was a sweet, quiet, strong man who could be depended on to always be there for you. What she saw now was a hateful angry beast who was about to kill her for standing up to him. The power and confidence emanating off him was stifling and she fought to stay in control; to stand her ground.

"No fucking way," she responded in defiance. She hadn't realized it, but Manny had come to stand beside her. She had never taken him for a physical sort of man, more of a stoner get-along type, but now he was supporting her when the rest of them wouldn't lift a finger. She would always remember that if they lived through this.

Raleigh had finally decided to make his presence known. He had given up his bent pipe and was walking forward with his large hands up in a display of peace. "Maybe she's right, maybe we should wait," the big man said.

Her heart thumped harder as she waited to see if it would make a difference.

Robert raised his bat and she prepared to duck should it come her way. How had he gone so far over the edge this fast? What was really fueling this manic rage? Or was she the one that was completely insane for trying to stop it. What if he was right? Was she saving Erik only to watch him die and turn? She didn't know; couldn't know. She was only sure that if she was going to die in this God forsaken world, it would be on her terms, not theirs.

Those eyes bore into her for a moment longer, then the bat lowered. He leaned towards her and kept his voice low so that the rest of the group wouldn't hear. "If he starts to turn, you get to end it. If he kills anyone else, I'll kill you."

She sighed and knew for sure that their relationship would never be the same; the hate flowing off of him in waves. She held her ground momentarily, then backed up and nodded, having to drop her eyes from that painful stare. Then she did what could be seen as either very brave or very stupid, she turned her back on him and went to Erik's side. She yanked a do-rag off a dead gangbanger's head, wrapped it around the flesh, and winced at Erik's cry of anguish.

As she cinched it, his fearful eyes met hers. "I am so fucked, but thank you," he said, voice shaking at his near-death experience.

She had no way of knowing if she was doing the right thing, but the grateful look in his eyes told her that for now it was. That might change should his health go south, but something in her gut told her to be patient and see. She didn't want to be the one to end it, but Robert was right. Erik had become her responsibility, and should things go badly, it would have to be her that righted what she'd done.

"You don't know that," she told him, her voice shaking from the forcefulness of the confrontation. She didn't know what she was doing, she didn't need another person slowing her down. Now she wouldn't be able to leave Erik's side for fear that once she did, Robert would finish what he'd started. But she had lost too many friends already and she wasn't about to hand another one over to the reaper.

"We need to keep moving!" Robert declared, ignoring the two of them now that the moment had passed. She knew that she'd have to watch her back; he would not forget what had just happened. At the very first opportunity, she'd do whatever it took to get away from him.

"There's a fire station down the road. We'll check the store for supplies then head that way. There's bound to be weapons there that we can use. Only dumbasses fight barehanded against a zombie!" The last remark seemed to be thrown in her direction, though he refused to look at her.

That was fine, she didn't want those eyes on her again anytime soon.

"You can't count on someone else to save your life. You fuck up, you die. Then I'll kill you again! Let's move!" he roared. He may not have been the group's leader before the conflict, but now no one was going to dare question him now. The others moved like cowed dogs after a severe beating; the fight gone from them as they began settling down.

She helped Erik to his feet and Jeremy finally came to their side, his face blank. The fucker had not even tried to help her, he was going to stand idly by while Robert killed her with that fucking bat. No matter what happened next, the two of them were done. She could see from Jeremy's face that it had already occurred to him as well, and he didn't look to shook up over it.

Well, fuck him.

Her hands shook, her breathing was rapid, and her eyes were trying to lose focus. She took a long deep breath in an attempt to steady herself, to prepare for the exertion she couldn't afford to be making after such a long frantic day. Manny put a hand on her shoulder, drawing her attention, and she looked into his eyes and saw the compassion within. He smiled weakly, then moved to help Erik walk towards the abandoned convenience store.

Caesar was hovering to her rear and she knew that he was thinking of taking off on foot, his eyes kept cutting north along that road. His apartment wasn't too far away, and he had to be thinking he could make it on his own. She could tell that he wasn't ready to do that. The idea of going it alone scared the shit out of him. There was fear in his eyes; he'd wait and see what happened next before chancing it.

"Shit, I thought he was going to kill you," Raleigh said, his teeth flashing in the moonlight.

"Thank you for the assist," she responded softly, brushing her legs off and walking slowly behind the injured man. Her eyes were on Robert as they walked, waiting to see if he'd turn and attack them anyways. There was no need, he was acting like they weren't even there, the stern face focused on what was ahead.

Raleigh chuckled. "I just didn't want you to die, that's all. But he's probably right, you know that."

"No, I don't," she countered. "The three of you live together, he's your roommate just as much as Robert's. You should have been the first to step forward."

The big man stumbled a step back. "Hey, he's the one bit, not me," he stammered as if it was a defense for leaving his friend to die. She was grateful for what he had done, but it had been too little too late. "Robert's a good guy. He wouldn't do it unless he was sure that it was the right thing to do."

Her heart had echoed that same sentiment only a few moments before, but after seeing the hate in the man's eyes, she wondered if any of them really knew him at all. He hadn't been like this before, it had to be more than what was going on that had changed him so drastically. He had a little girl, where was she? Had something happened to her? Was that what was fueling this rage? The more she tried to understand, the less she actually did. There were too many unknowns and she knew that getting answers from him now would be near impossible. That link had been severed.

Raleigh's eyes cut to Erik, who had stumbled a bit as they reached the sidewalk in front of the store. He had an uncertain look in his eyes, and she knew what was going on in there. He was questioning whether he should have stopped Robert after all.

"Just go on," she said, motioning for him to go with the others. The big guy hesitated, gave Erik another judging look, and then rushed inside with the rest of the foragers ransacking the store.

"He could use some water," Manny said. He placed his guitar against the glass window and watched Erik with concern as the injured man leaned against the side of the building, his face pale. He wasn't looking too good.

"I'll stay with him," she said to the young guitarist. He looked at her indecisively, but then nodded and strode away. "You two should get some food as well, we don't know when we'll stop again," she told Jeremy and Caesar, exhausted from the fight and in no mood to argue. Jeremy looked like he was going to say something, but then only shook his head and kept quiet. With a firm set of his lips; he set their bags on the ground and followed Manny inside.

Caesar didn't follow after them. He came to stand by Erik instead. "He was going to kill you," he said softly, the reflection of understanding leaking through his words. "I just can't believe it."

"The Robert you know is gone. That man is a stranger. You better start believing it, because he won't hesitate again. If you get bit, he'll kill you too," she told him, trying to break through that dense cloud of denial he was clinging to, like he was going to wake up in his bed at any second.

"Still, what if he's right?" Caesar asked. She didn't answer. She looked at Erik's pale and struggling form and was already asking herself the same question.

Chapter 25
Million Dollar Wound

Todd
Compound 2

The man that came to his side was of average height and build, his gray hair a signature of the life he'd lived. He was wearing a pressed silk red shirt and black slacks. In his right hand was a scotch, the other, a half-burned cigar. "How're they doing?" Sean asked, taking a sip of his alcohol. He had finally come out of hiding and was watching the girls as they went to work on their wounded. Nick hung in the background and tried to be useful. He handed them tools when they asked for them, eyes watchful of everything they were doing.

Their older daughter Michelle was alternating between Monica and Lucy, bouncing back and forth as the two women treated their two fallen comrades. Ben hadn't made an appearance, even with the news of his father's injury. He wondered how the young man was handling it. Ben was probably burying himself in his computer in an attempt to distract his mind from what might happen to his father.

There were three tables placed in the center of the room, they had never believed that they would need more than that. Their med lab looked no different than any other ER and the crash cart was close by Rodger's bed in case his vitals crashed. For now, they were steady, and he prayed those paddles remained in their places for a very long time. "Casey's on morphine, so he's not really feeling anything. The bullet didn't get past his fat ass."

"I heard that, asshole," Casey murmured from the table he was facedown upon. "This shit is better than what I got. Why not give me some more?"

"You've had enough already," Monica told him, as she worked to remove the bullet from his exposed rear. He didn't like it any more than she did, but it had to be done. It was not a fatal wound, but they couldn't just leave it in there; they'd never hear the end of it.

Casey however, never missed a chance to take cracks at them. "Always wondered what it'd take to get you to touch my ass." He suddenly yelped as his wife adjusted the angle that she was working at, obviously causing a bit more pain than what was needed.

He wanted to laugh. "I'd watch it bud, or I'll shoot you in the other cheek."

"I've got this," Monica growled, placing a fisted hand on the right ass cheek and pressing downward. The scream that erupted from the chair was drowned out by Sean's laughter. His buddy downed his drink with a smirk on his face.

"How's Rodger doing?" he asked Lucy. The helmet had been removed and though there was a slight amount of blood on the inside, it didn't look to be that serious of a wound.

The older woman only gave them a fleeting glance as she continued to work on her husband. "He'll be fine. He needs a couple of stitches."

"Why's he still out?" Sean asked, taking another drag on his cigar.

Lucy pinched her nose at the smoke flowing across the room but kept her face passive; it was hard to snap at the man footing the bill. "He has a concussion. He'll need some time to recover, but he should be okay." They didn't have an MRI so they couldn't be sure of that assessment. They'd have to trust in the training she'd received and hope for the best.

"I wish Ros was here," Michelle said quietly, watching over Lucy as she started to apply stitches to the wound. His older daughter had worked with Rosilynn more than the rest of them had; she had even considered going to medical school. He was proud of her and he felt a brief bout of sorrow fill him as he realized that would never happen now.

Sean was heading towards the door.

"Where you off to?" he asked his friend. Sean was looking haggard, like he had slept in those clothes the night before. His face was sunken, and his brow kept trying to draw together. It looked like he had a great weight was on his shoulders and was starting to buckle under the pressure. He wasn't the self-assured man that he had met so many years before and was proof that no matter how prepared you were, it was never enough.

His comrade glanced his way, but his eyes were unfocused, as if he was staring through rather than at him. "It's the end of the world as we know it," Sean sang, then walked away. It had a sorrowful tone behind the cadence, and he felt that his friend was trying to convey some inner turmoil that was waging within his soul.

He could sympathize.

So much death and destruction in the world; it was hard to keep hope alive in the face of such atrocity. He had sung those very words himself earlier that morning and it had been a much different world then.

Everything was under control here and with his head full of violence that he wished he could forget, he decided it was time to take a walk and clear his head. Sean had been a reflection of his own soul and unless he wanted to end up at the bottom of a bottle like his older friend, then it was time to take a break. Giving Monica one last glance, he turned and left. He knew that it would take more than fresh air to clear his soul of the evils that he had witnessed. That might just take a lifetime to sweep away.

Chapter 26
Suicide Cult

Rosilynn
Nevada/Arizona Border

Traffic slowed as they reached the Hoover Dam Bypass. Slowed? Hell, it had come to a complete stop; again. She squinted at the large flood lights and the flashing red and blue lights beneath them. It looked like a barricade had been set up on the state border. They were inspecting vehicles before allowing anyone to pass.

Shit.

"Get off!"

"What?" Matt asked. He was confused by her sudden need to go through the Hoover Dam rather than staying on the bypass. He knew how much time they'd lose detouring that way, but it couldn't be helped.

"Just do it Matt," she reinforced, not wanting to speak her fears aloud. In his current state, he might just drive up there and tell them he had been bitten. He'd let them do what he wanted her to hours before. She couldn't allow that.

Besides, there was a chance that the road through the dam would actually be faster. There weren't many cars breaking off to go that way and the traffic might be light. Of course, if they had road blocked this part of the highway, they surely had that part as well. She'd deal with that when the time came; no need to think about it until she had to.

When the highway had disappeared from view and those flood lights had winked out on the horizon, Matt turned and glared at her. "Now do you mind telling me what the hell is going on? Do you really think this'd be faster?"

She could only shake her head, eyes searching the road ahead for signs of another barricade. Maybe they should get out and try to cross the border on foot. She doubted they were watching the mountains as hard as they were watching the roads. They could find another car on the other side and continue on. She turned her gaze to the land around them, calculating what to do next.

"Ros!" her husband called, trying to get her attention.

She took a long breath and held it, closing her eyes and trying to clear away her thoughts. Finally, she turned to look at him. "Are you ready to die?"

He glared at her, a *what the fuck* look on his face. "Why are you asking me that now?"

"Do you want to die?" she asked, emphasizing each word, not letting him evade the question. Before she could plan on what to do next, she needed to hear what he was really thinking and wanting.

"No, I don't want to die," he said after a pause. "But it's not about what I want, it's about what is going to happen. I'm a threat to you. I don't want my selfish needs to be the reason you die I love you too much to let that happen."

Rosilynn shook her head in frustration. "You are not feverish. Your bite **is** infected, but that's normal! That happens to just about every bite wound and if you were in the hospital, we'd be pumping you full of antibiotics, not amputating your leg. If you were going to turn, don't you think there would be some sign of it happening? It's been hours Matt! Look at how fast this shit spreads! If it took hours to change someone into one of these things, it'd be easier to control! This shit takes seconds! You've seen that with your own two eyes!"

"I don't know what I saw. Maybe it takes longer to turn the living. Just because it's slower with me doesn't mean it's not going to happen. All I know is, everything we've ever read or seen says that bites turn people into zombies, period, end of argument," he stated firmly. His eyes showed that there was little doubt in his mind what his fate was, that it was just a matter of time.

"It sure as shit isn't the end of the argument. We do not know anything! This is not a TV show, it's not a movie. We don't know what bites do to you. Maybe it doesn't do anything! Don't you think that you would have already turned if it was going to happen? Las Vegas is gone, what makes you so fucking special?" she retorted, furious at how easily he was giving up.

"Maybe I'm resisting it longer," he offered, but there was a hint of doubt in his voice. He was trying to work it through, to challenge the beliefs that he had nourished, but he wasn't there quite yet.

"Matthew," she said, trying to get him to look her in the eyes. "We are not giving up until we know for sure that there is no other way."

He sighed, one hand on the wheel, the other fiddling with the top of the door frame, elbow waving in the breeze. It was a casual stance, but his face betrayed the turmoil boiling within. "What if—?"

She cut him off. "If that time comes, I'll take care of it. I promise you that," she told him, but she wondered even as she said it if it were true. Her brain said yes, but her heart refused to answer.

"You already broke one promise, don't make another you can't keep," he retorted in anger. Then he sighed and looked out the window for a long minute before turning back her way. "I still don't understand why you made me go this way. We could be getting closer to that roadblock, hell, we might be through it by now and on our way," he declared, but he didn't sound like he believed it.

"The only reason to put up a roadblock is to inspect people coming through," she responded. "Matt, how do you check for infected people?"

His mind needed a second to process what she was getting at. "Oh, fuck me," he said, hand running across his forehead, trying to wipe the thoughts away. "That's why you're asking if I want to die?"

"That and the way you've been acting since Vegas. Like I'm keeping you here against your will," she said, feeling her grief start to rise. She wasn't ready to give up on him yet.

"You'd be better off without me," he replied softly.

"Don't even think that. I love you," she responded and reached over and to put a hand on his arm. "I don't want to do this without you."

Red lights appeared in the distance and her stomach sank; traffic had begun to slow here as well. She chanced another glance at the terrain around them. Maybe they should ditch the car and start out on foot? Or was it better to wait and see the barricade first? "I need to know you're with me on this," she said, her eyes scanning for paths through the mountains.

He didn't answer right away. She turned to look at him, expectantly. "I'm with you until the end, I love you too." The cars had come to a complete stop and Matt swore as he hit the brakes, glaring at the immobile line of vehicles before them. "What now?"

People were getting out of their cars and walking in the direction of whatever blocked the road ahead. Should they get out here? Start up the mountain passes now? She looked at her husband. He finally relented and nodded his head. Her mind raced through what they'd have to do, but their options were limited. He wouldn't be able to do too much climbing; she'd have to find an easier slope that his ankle could handle. For now, they could skirt the road until signs of the roadblock appeared, then she could make a decision on what to do next. Why hadn't Ben warned them about the roadblocks? Did he even know about them?

They got out, grabbed their packs and prepared to set out on foot. The guy behind them honked his horn and gave them an ugly gesture that she threw right back. The man didn't like that and made a move to get out of his car. She shouldered her Rimfire and gave him a menacingly glare, a smile creeping upon her face as the man suddenly had another direction to cast his gaze and something on his seat to fiddle with.

That's right, she thought.

Her husband came around the front of the car and she moved to his side. She put a hand on his arm and watched as he put weight on his swollen ankle. He grimaced but he nodded that he could handle it. She knew that he'd do that no matter how painful it felt; he'd keep pushing it until he fell over or broke it. She'd have to make sure they took breaks frequently; he'd bitch but she didn't give a shit.

They were nearing a bend in the road; the start of the downward spiral that led to the bottom of the dam. They passed an empty parking lot on their right and she could see people congregating at the other one on their left. Just ahead was the edge of the cliff, a rail preventing cars from falling over the side. They'd be able to get a good view of what was ahead from that vantage point. Surely, whatever was drawing everyone's attention would be revealed. Yet, part of her didn't want to know, dreaded knowing, in fact.

A voice was on the wind and the echoing canyon side was distorting whatever it was trying to say. They approached the guard rail and glanced at the top of the Hoover Dam. A man was standing at the center of the large structure, yelling into a bullhorn. Lined up on either side were men and women dressed in black slacks and white shirts. There was a large cross being held on either end by large men; all heads turned towards the man at the center.

Below, the cars had come to a complete stop. People had come from both sides to see what had brought things to such a grinding halt and to listen to the ravings of the man above. She heard the sound of rotors and saw a military helicopter hovering over the canyon to her right, shadowing the crowd below.

Something about this was off and she felt panic begin to rise within. "Matt, we need to get out of here," she told him. His eyes were fixated on the man giving his sermon and he refused to acknowledge what she'd said.

"Matt, we need to go!" she tried again. He nodded but stayed rooted in place. Her rifle rose and for a brief second, she considered shooting the preacher; to end the spell he was weaving over the stunned onlookers. Then the people lining the top of the dam took one large step forward and began to fall to their watery deaths below.

Chapter 27
What was that?

Saint
Tucson, AZ

Everyone had a bag in hand as they left the convenience store. The junk food had been hastily eaten and what little canned food the store had was thrown into double layered bags to take with them. She had grabbed a case of Rockstars and had downed two in an attempt to rejuvenate her weary muscles. She felt pumped up as the caffeine coursed through her system and the view of the world seemed less bleak.

Erik was on one side, Manny the other. It was odd that the two of them had gravitated towards her, while those that came with her had begun to draw away. Jeremy wouldn't meet her gaze and though he strode a few feet to her left, he acted like he didn't know she was there. Maybe it was better off that way. Caesar was bringing up the rear and he kept looking north. She wondered how long it would be before she turned around and to find that he was no longer with them

Surprisingly, it was Raleigh that had done a one-eighty on her. The towering man had made his way over to Robert while they were in the store and they were now walking side by side as they headed east towards the firehouse. Their heads were inclined towards one another, as if having a deep conversation. She had no doubt at all about who they were talking about. The big man was holding a box of Twinkies and as he spoke, she could see white and yellow mush between his teeth.

Disgusted, she had turned away and tried to think of what to do next. Would Robert notice if she just faded away? If the four of them hung back and melted into the shadows, would he try to stop them? She could feel his eyes constantly drifting her way and she knew that he would. She wasn't ready to force another confrontation; she needed to wait for the right time to present itself.

As they entered a wash, everyone paused to listen to the neighborhood ahead. They didn't hear anything; the silence an alien thing in the world they lived in. Where was everybody? She imagined that most of the people had to be hunkered down in their homes tonight, waiting things out; praying for rescue. But there should be others like her roaming the streets, trying to make their way out of the city.

On the other hand, they also hadn't seen any sign of the undead since that confrontation in the intersection an hour before. She didn't welcome the sight of another abomination, but she did wonder where they were hiding as well. Why were things so quiet? It felt like the shadows were watching them, preparing to spill death from their bowels the instant their guard dropped.

"Maybe we should check some of these houses," Raleigh said loudly, pointing towards the neighborhood approaching on their left. He was eyeing them like they held precious treasure, but she was more worried about getting shot by someone defending their home.

Robert must have been thinking along the same lines and that scared her more than any zombie hiding in the wash behind them. "If there are people in there, they won't take kindly to us trying to break in. It's a good way to get shot. And if a gun goes off; it'll just attract the walkers. You might even walk into a house full of them. You want to do that? Go ahead. Go ring the dinner bell. I'm not that stupid."

It was the first level-headed thing she had heard escape his lips since that brawl in the street. Maybe now that the rage was gone, he was returning to his old self? He carried on like he was their leader and knew exactly what he was doing. She could see the allure to those that blindly followed him, but she refused to give into it. What exactly did he know? What made him the expert? Would that self-proclaimed knowledge end up being what gets these people killed?

She didn't know what they hoped to find at the fire station coming into view. They wouldn't have any guns; the best they could hope for was some axes and she doubted very much that Robert would allow her to get her hands on one of those. Her eyes began scanning the parking lot as they started to cross the intersection in that direction.

"We need to find a place to hunker down," Robert continued. "Maybe get to Davis Monthan and help them defend it. We can't stay out in the open like this." The others nodded their heads, liking the idea of letting the military do the fighting while they hid behind the large fences surrounding the air force base.

"Going to need something closer than that, maybe the Super Center," Manny muttered. It was just a mile to the south and she knew for certain that as long as it hadn't been looted, that there'd be plenty of weapons for them to arm themselves with.

Robert was shaking his head. "The store has long been stripped. I doubt there's much left and it would be a horrible place to try and defend. Besides, others are probably thinking the same thing and the more people that are together, the more chance that an outbreak will occur. It's a good way to get everyone killed. Smaller groups are better; more mobile."

They were all talking in whispers now and each paused after talking to listen for anything approaching their location. Crossing the road, she instinctively looked both ways, a habit that was too ingrained to break.

Erik was starting to lag behind, but so far showed no sign of infection. It was not an indication that she'd made the right choice, but it was making her feel more hopeful about his chances. But then, what the hell did she know? She never watched that zombie shit; it was exceedingly gross and unrealistic.

Caesar suddenly appeared at her side. He was no longer nursing his head and his beady eyes shifted nervously as he walked. He looked uncomfortable and she didn't have to ask what was wrong. "As soon as we check things over, we'll head out, I promise," she told him, trying to sound sincere. It was hard to sound confident when things were constantly erupting into chaos. The madness of the world seemed to be hounding their every move. The odds that his wife was all right were slim, but he wouldn't give up until he was absolutely sure.

"And if the Lord of the Flies over there decides not to let us go?" he asked, nodding at Robert.

She stared at the tall black man for a minute as Robert continued talking to the hovering Hispanic man at his side. Maybe he had been right, maybe Erik would turn, but that was on her now. If she was wrong, so be it, she'd handle it. At least she tried. She had to believe that in the end, that would count for something. However, she knew that it was the last time she'd survive a direct confrontation with the power-hungry man and his bat. "Then we'll ditch them and go on our own," she assured him.

He nodded gratefully and seemed soothed by her words.

"Once we get my car, we can get the hell out of here and make a break for Todd's doomsday bunker," Caesar said, letting the hope in for the first time that day.

Panicked, she made an effort to cut him off before he finished speaking, but it was too late. Slowly, she turned to look at Robert and hoped that he had missed it; he hadn't. He had stopped and Raleigh kept walking, oblivious to the fact that the man at his side had come to an abrupt halt. "Shit," she swore, watching as he turned his head and looked into her eyes.

Those brown orbs burrowed into her soul, crushing her hopes of ever making out of this alive. "What was that?" he asked.

Chapter 28
Leap of Faith

Rosilynn
Nevada/Arizona Border

  The preacher had started to ramp up his speech and she ignored his Book of Revelations rhetoric as they began to run downhill to the street below. She had a bad feeling about all this, and Matt was no longer resisting her insistence to get some distance from it.

  The fact that all those people had jumped without a pause in the preacher's sermon made her ill. *Something worse was coming,* her heart told her. They had to get out of there, but where could they go? They were trapped amongst a crowd that had funneled together from both ends. There was no way to get anywhere quickly.

  They ran across the road, through the parked cars, and slid down the dirt hill on the other side to the switchback below. She looked left as she realized the only way to get around the river was to go towards the dam; right where the cult members would be reanimating. She could already hear screams echoing from that direction and made a split-second decision. "The river," she told her husband, working her bag open and bringing out a zip lock bag. She held it up and motioned to Matt.

  He still didn't understand what she meant, but he gave over his phone and she sealed it within. Then she placed it back into her bag. They were running out of time, they needed to hurry. "We have to jump," she told him, trying to make sure he heard her over the chaos approaching.

  He had also been looking in the dam's direction and she saw that he had come to the same conclusion. "Let's do it."

  Backing to the edge of the road, they braced themselves for what was about to come. They'd probably die, but at this moment, there was nowhere else for them to go and no other way they'd make it out alive. Her phone was going off in her bag, but she ignored it. "I know Ben, get the hell out. I'm trying," she uttered, already knowing what he'd say; not needing to check. This was it. She kissed her husband, their lips connecting passionately, the feeling lingering as they parted. "I love you."

"This isn't goodbye," he returned with a smile. The defeat that he had been displaying all afternoon was gone. This was the husband that she knew and loved. Why he had decided to show up now of all times was beyond her, but her hope was fully restored, and she loved him all the more. "Let's go for a ride," he winked. He ran forward, jumped on the guard rail, and then leapt off the edge of the cliff to the river below.

She took a couple of quick breaths, trying to ready her lungs for the pounding they were about to take. She could hear the screams growing nearer and steadied herself against the panic within. She surged forward, jumped onto the rail, and then plunged outward, not bothering to look down for fear of losing her nerve. She floated forward momentarily, then she began to drop, her legs and arms flailing. Her grip on her rifle tightened as she brought it towards her chest so she wouldn't lose it. She tried to brace herself for impact but the sudden rush of water, the cold fluid smacking her body, drove the breath out of her and water flooded in to replace it. Her lungs burned, her limbs flared, and she fought her way back to the surface. Her vision was gone. She was disoriented and had no sense of direction. Her feet kicked and her hand broke the surface. With another burst of her legs, she surged upward and breached the water pressing down upon her. She only got a brief gasp of air as her feet were swept forward by the current. She was dragged back under and into the blackness beyond.

Chapter 29
Best laid plans

He had been planning this for more than a decade. It wasn't what he had originally imagined, but it would have to do. He had strategized and maneuvered, doing everything within his power to carry out God's commandment. He had heard His voice since he was a little boy and had been utterly devoted to it ever since. This mission had been given to him by the Lord; a reward for his unwavering faith. A new Babylon had sprung up in the Nevada desert and the City of Sin need to be cleansed from the Earth.

It was God's will.

He had formed his congregation gradually, never revealing the truth behind the purpose for which they would one day serve. Viewed as a cult by misinformed heathens, he had strived to keep his ultimate goals a secret from all but a select few. Secrecy was paramount in a world of cyber invasion and infiltration from outside forces. Satan had agents in every part of government and would do whatever it took to keep him from carrying out God's will.

He had received a sign from God recently and any doubt he or the congregation had that they were doing what He wanted was forever silenced. When the package had arrived on his doorstep, his soul had trembled, knowing that the time was at hand. Attached was a letter with printed text, telling him where to go and when. When he had seen what was inside, all his doubts had vanished. This was His plan and he was to be the instrument of God, raining brimstone upon the City of the Godless.

A sane man would have questioned how it had come to him, why that specific time or date, but not him. The Lord's voice had spoken, and he had never looked back.

It was his duty to serve, not to question the will of God.

Calling his followers to him, he finally revealed God's plan for them and together they had said a prayer praising His name. They were on their way to the Den of Whores when Armageddon had begun. They hadn't left in time; he had failed. Maybe if they'd left sooner, he could have saved the billions that were dying tonight. The apocalypse was upon them and all that was left was to join the rest of the faithful in heaven. He was not able to take Babylon with him, but he could cut off its water supply; kill it through attrition.

One of his followers approached him and nodded, handing him the device that would send them to their brothers and sisters awaiting in the afterlife. He lifted the bullhorn and began his sermon, the trigger in hand. His followers prepared for the last leap of faith that would spirit them out of the mortal life and into the rewards waiting for them in heaven.

"I looked when He opened the sixth seal, and behold, there was a great earthquake; and the sun became black as sackcloth of hair, and the moon became like blood. And the stars of heaven fell to the earth, as a fig tree drops its late figs when it is shaken by a mighty wind. Then the sky receded as a scroll when it is rolled up, and every mountain and island was moved out of its place."

"And the kings of the earth, the great men, the rich men, the commanders, the mighty men, every slave and every free man, hid themselves in the caves and in the rocks of the mountains, and said to the mountains and rocks, 'Fall on us and hide us from the face of Him who sits on the throne and from the wrath of the Lamb! For the great day of His wrath has come, and who is able to stand?'"

Chapter 30
Oh shit

Todd
Compound 2

"Holy shit! Get out of there!" he heard Ben yell, his voice echoing down the long hallway. The terror in those words chilled him to the bone.

He rushed into the communications room and came to halt in front of the bank of monitors. He wasn't sure which one to look at first. "What is it?"

Ben motioned to one on the left and his heart skipped a beat. It was a security cam overlooking the roads through the Hoover Dam.

He groaned and felt bile fighting its way up his throat. "Fuck me," he said, each word coming out soft but severe.

There was a single man left on top of the Hoover Dam. They had watched in awe as the rest of his group leapt to their deaths while their leader remained where he was. He had a bullhorn in hand and continued on for a couple of minutes, not missing a beat in his sermon. Then he lowered it and tossed it after his comrades dying below. Crossing himself, the man began to yell once more, raising both arms into the air. Whatever he had said was causing a panic below and the chaos unfolding told him all he needed to know; things were going to shit fast.

"Can you zoom in?" he asked. Doing so would obscure the mass confusion taking place on the right of the screen; it was too gruesome to watch. He looked at the map on the right and saw that Ros and Matt's GPS signals were emanating from right there at the dam. The signals were moving south, but it wasn't fast enough. "Text her and tell her to get the fuck out of there."

"I'm trying!" Ben responded, frantically punching keys, the mouse pointer flying across the screens.

The leader of the group was holding something in his right hand, and he was fiddling with it as he finished his sermon. He was glad that there was no audio, but he wished the pixels would tighten up on what the man was doing. His eyes were drawn to whatever the guy was holding, and he felt his gut wrench in horror. The man screamed a final time, then the screen went blank.

"What the fuck? Get the picture back!" he yelled, wanting to shove Ben out of the way and do it himself. That helpless feeling had returned, and he fought against it, but he was not winning the battle. The problem was, there really was nothing he could do. Ros and Matt were left to their fate and all he could do was stare at a blank video screen.

Ben sat back in his chair and shook his head, a tear sliding down his young face. "I can't, there's nothing to go back to."

"What do you mean?" he asked, still not getting it, or not wanting to.

The youth had tears streaming down his face as brought up camera footage playing on the lower left screen to the center monitor. It had been blocked by the boy's body and hadn't caught his eye until Ben shifted it over and enlarged it. You couldn't miss the mushroom cloud rising from the desert floor.

"Oh, my God," he whispered in terror. He couldn't tell how large it was, there was no context to allow that, but the sight still horrified him.

They sat there and suddenly embraced, the mushroom cloud slowly lifting into the air. The tears flowed, sobs ripping from their chest. So many lives had just winked out of existence, including two of their own and it was overwhelming their souls with grief. Even after the loss of life the day had wrought, the millions dying in the streets, it still wasn't enough; the hits just kept on coming.

What the hell was going on? How did it all go to shit so fast?

The radio on the right wall began to sputter and they paused, pulling back from each other and glancing its way. He wiped the tears from his cheek. "What the hell?"

A familiar tone began to repeat over the airwaves and in the moment of grief, he thought he was imagining it. There were three whirs and then a long tone. Ben's face confirmed for him the reality of what he was hearing. "This is the emergency alert system. This is not a test. The United States Government has declared martial law in the following states," the voice told them, the quality of the sound crackling in their ears. He listened in horror as the long list was rattled off in that droning voice. He had seen it on the updating maps Ben kept, but now they were getting outside confirmation; this was really happening.

"All residents are advised to stay indoors. Anyone caught on the street after nightfall will be dealt with in the harshest manner possible. There is nowhere to go that is safer than your own house. We repeat, stay indoors and await further instructions on evacuation procedures and triage sites. This has been a broadcast of the emergency alert system." Then there was another long beep, and it began to repeat. When it finished, there were three more alert tones and then the radio went back to static.

"A little late, don't you think?" he asked before considering what he had heard. His voice was cracking from the grief he felt.

Ben either didn't hear him or didn't have an answer. He looked stunned, completely broken, and the tears were still flowing down his face. Exhausted, stressed, and seeing the things he did throughout the day, it was a wonder this hadn't happened sooner. Ben needed a break.

He rose to his feet and helped the young boy to his feet. He led him towards the door. "But—," the young boy stammered, trying to resist.

"I'll take care of it. You've done enough for now," he soothed. He wanted some time to think things over and solitude was always the best way to do that. Besides, Ben needed rest if he was going to be any good to them tomorrow.

He had a feeling that it was going to be an even longer day than this one had been.

Ben simply nodded his thanks, the resistance already gone. He shrugged free and began to walk down the hall, the sobs echoing in his wake. He stood there and watched him go, then turned and walked back to the computer station.

Well, what was he going to do now?

The phone began to ring, and he fumbled at the Bluetooth, it didn't want to sit in his ear. He pushed the button before getting it all the way in and thought he heard someone whispering on the other end. "Hold on," he growled.

"Ben?" a voice inquired from the other end of the line.

"Do I sound like Ben?" he asked, getting it seated finally and trying to force his grief down. His eyes drifted to the monitor screens and he wondered which was linked to whoever was calling. There was no apparent order to anything. It was like sitting at a desk of clutter and only the one that created it would know where to find anything quickly.

Someone was grunting on the other end. "No, it sounds like Todd."

"You should have put in for detective years ago," he snarked, trying once more to lift his mood. Then his eyes fell on the screen where the bomb was still flowing towards the heavens and he quickly moved the cursor to the window and closed it, the sorrow threatening to overwhelm him. "What can I do for you officer?"

"I swear, between you and Casey, I am saddened by the amount of wise-ass that is surviving this shit intact. Look, I need Ben's help. So get him for me. We are pinned down and I need a route out of this joint," Joseph snapped.

He thought he heard someone screaming in the background and he quickly started scrolling through the windows. "I sent him to bed. He's been working non-stop since all this shit began. You're stuck with me."

"Fuck me, we're dead," Joseph groaned.

"Hey, where's the faith?" he retorted. Ben had a window with names and GPS locations. He scrolled down to Joseph's name and clicked. A new tab opened, and a map began to load. A view of the United States came into being with a glowing red dot pulsing in Arkansas. He clicked on it and the map zoomed in so fast he felt vertigo threaten nausea.

"It's the wrong day to be taking anything on faith, brother," Joseph returned. Gunfire followed after and the man's breathing was heavy upon his mic. "I need an exit. Are you able to find me one?"

Camera feeds began to load on one screen, another tab showing the satellite images of the area on another. Joseph was in Hope, Arkansas, just off the interstate, stuck in a warehouse by the looks of it. One of the feeds was from a traffic cam and there was a very large herd rushing the side of the building.

He quickly scanned the screen and double checked every angle. Whatever he told the man would lead either to his safety or his death, he did not want to get it wrong. "Looks like the southern-most wall has an emergency exit. Go through it, across the alley, and over the fence at the border of the property. The street on the other side appears to be empty and nothing from the front of the building has wandered around there yet."

"One of you get Bronstein, we're blowing this popsicle stand," Joseph said to someone off mic. "I'll cover you, make for the emergency exit behind us. Yes, I've got eyes on. Now move! Todd, if I make it through this, I take back every mean thing I've ever said about you."

"You've said mean things about me?" he asked, grinning.

A few more shots rang out, then he heard a bang and more heavy breathing. He waited patiently, knowing that Joseph would not dare say a word if they were out in the open, as it might alert the undead to their location. He switched through the feeds and brought up the one from a street camera in the direction they were heading. A silhouette was walking into frame from the east and his breath caught. "Got a bogey at your nine o'clock."

He watched as three men came into frame, one limping with an arm around his companion. Joseph, the untethered man with his weapon up, moved towards the shambling creature that had just noticed the new food source landing in his lap, and hit it with the butt of his gun. Then a knife flashed as it plunged into the creature's head. "Got it, thanks. I owe you one."

"Just get back here safe, that's all the reward I need," he answered back, watching as Joseph turned towards the street cam and waved.

"That's the plan. I'll hit you up if I need anything else. Stay safe," Joseph returned.

He was about to respond when the line went dead. Watching as the three men moved towards a nearby truck, he let himself feel a brief spark of hope; at least someone was still alive and heading their way. Despite his lack of knowledge of Ben's systems, he had still been able to lend a hand, to be useful and that made all the difference in the world.

Chapter 31
Resurrection

Mark
Bardstown, KY

He didn't know how long he had been out, but it was long enough for the sun to have set. His chest still hurt from the deployed airbag, his face swollen and tender to the touch. The fact that he had survived was only the first surprise waiting for him. He had been stunned by the fact that nothing had gotten to him while he was unconscious. Someone had been looking out for him after all. Though, after the events of the day, he hoped it was good rather than evil. The thought that he was being saved for some nefarious and ugly death was too horrible to consider.

While taking gear from his truck, he had noticed that his phone was smashed to hell; another casualty of the car accident. The first had been the fucking asshole that had chosen to end his life by falling onto his truck. He saw a couple of legs underneath the front end. The rest had leaked from the front corners of the wrecked vehicle; providing the glue that kept it lodged to the concrete overpass.

He had lost part of his lunch at that point.

After he had collected himself, he had stood there, stunned that he was walking away from such a horrid accident alive and intact. There had been a flash of light; a cargo van was slowing as it approached the accident site. An older couple were on their way to Lexington and offered to take him with them. Having no other alternative other than walking, he had accepted. They had made space for him to sit amongst the supplies they'd brought and though it was a bit cramped, it was still preferable to making his way on foot. On guard, he had kept his eyes glued to their surroundings every second of the trip, prepared to warn them off should he see anything that looked threatening.

There had been a roadblock at the state line, but they had passed easily enough; none of them had been bit or showed any signs of infection. There'd also been a couple of assholes riding around in trucks, shooting randomly into the forest at some imaginary foe; they hadn't stuck around in case they got bored and wanted a real target to practice on. Otherwise than that, it had been a quiet journey west.

He was surprised by the lack of traffic on the interstate, sure that the roads would be packed no matter how late it was. Without his phone, he wasn't receiving updates from Ben and the couple's phones weren't in service. His wife and daughter were out there somewhere, possibly in trouble, and he could do nothing to find them. It bothered him every passing minute of their journey, causing him to be restless and short tempered. The older couple had been understanding and kept the conversation steered towards mundane stuff, trying to stay distracted from what was going on in the world around them.

Then they had gotten to Lexington.

Coming down the 75 they noticed vehicles pulled off on the side of the road and sleeping forms hidden within. Curious, but overly cautious, they crept around them and kept moving. As they progressed further, he began to see a glow of light in the distance.

They passed through the abandoned city of Georgetown and the landscape opened up, revealing the source of light at last. A makeshift runway had been created and the constant moving lights overhead told him how busy the temporary base had become. Planes large enough to carry military vehicles had opened up their cargo bays and unleashed the military war machine into the plains around them. A pair of Humvees were parked on the side of the highway and they were flagged down by a uniformed man waving a large flashlight. They were advised of the curfew and were commanded to turn around; to find a place to hold up for the night. Lexington was under quarantine.

The couple had tried to negotiate a detour, but the weapons trained on them swiftly ended the discussion. They had retreated, their eyes glued to the tanks that were starting to roll down the interstate heading south. The sight of those Abrams brought hope where there hadn't been any before. The military was reacting to the outbreak with everything in their arsenal and were holding nothing back.

Backtracking towards Georgetown, they had stopped at an empty gas station to refuel and resupply. They had discussed their options and after a lengthy debate, it was decided that they would travel with him to Arizona. Up until that point, he had held onto the belief that he would find his family somewhere along one of these roads held up for the night, waiting for him to catch up. But the chances of that happening without his cell were exceedingly astronomical. There were just too many places they could be hiding.

After a series of highways and numerous exits, they were now on the 9002, heading west once more despite the curfew. Hours had passed and they all had needed to make a pitstop. Parked at the closest and quietest rest stop they could find; they took turns using the bathroom while the others stood watch. A payphone caught his eye and he took a chance and picked up the receiver.

There was a dial tone.

Holy shit, the phones were back on.

Relief flooded his soul as he frantically dialed an eight-hundred number they had set up in case the cells didn't work. Things were beginning to look up. The military was on the move, he hadn't seen a zombie since Columbus, and now the phone networks had been restored. Was there a chance he could find his wife and daughter after all? The phone began to ring, and his heart tripled in speed.

Chapter 32
Needs of the many

Saint
Tucson, AZ

"What are you talking about?" she asked Robert, ignoring the *oh crap* look Caesar was giving her. Yeah, he had just fucked up, **royally**. He just couldn't keep his damn mouth shut; she should have never told him. When they were stuck in that store waiting on David to review the camera footage, he had talked endlessly about going after his wife and what to do once he found her. He was friends with Todd, so she had thought he could be trusted, now she was regretting that decision and cursing herself for not keeping a tighter lip about where she was going.

Robert stepped towards her. The rest of the group was busy heading into the fire station, but a couple had hung back when noticing their leader's halt. Jeremy cowered off to the right, committed to neither side. Erik and Manny flanked her while Caesar tried to back away from both sides.

She glanced at the wounded man on her right and knew that if things went south, he wouldn't be able to put up much of a fight; he was too vulnerable at the moment. She had to try and calm this down before it spiraled out of control. Raleigh had turned and was hovering at Robert's side, his choice obvious by his stance. At least she had the foresight not to tell him anything, he had a bigger mouth than Caesar did.

"What bunker is he talking about?" Robert asked and she knew that denials were wasted; he had heard their entire conversation. When she didn't answer right away, she saw his eyes lose focus, no longer seeing her, withdrawing to some inner recollection. Then understanding dawned and his gaze narrowed. "Are you so stupid to think that Todd and his doomsday prepping bullshit was actually real? He's probably hiding in some house somewhere, not some ultra-secret bunker that a rich author swooped down and built for him. That's just insane! It has to be bullshit," he said, his voice losing steam at the end. He was starting to think it through, and blood rushed to his face. She kept silent, refusing to give him the confirmation he was searching for. "There's no fucking way it was true."

The two men at her sides stood their ground and she suddenly wished that one of them had a weapon, not a bum hand and a guitar case. "I don't know where he is, nor care," she bluffed.

"You're lying," Robert said, taking another step closer.

"Fuck you. I haven't been talking to Todd." *Not since this morning anyways,* her mind interjected. It was partially true, she hadn't **spoken** to him in quite some time. "The phones are out," she reminded him, waving hers in the air for effect. "I work nights, remember? We haven't talked in weeks."

The black man standing before her kept his face passive, thinking it through. "Why are you guys out here? Why didn't you hole up somewhere? Where were you going when we found you?" He directed his questions to Jeremy, knowing that as her boyfriend she would have confided in him anything. The neutrality of the expression on his face stung her. Things were definitely over between them.

"She wouldn't tell me anything," Jeremy finally confessed. Fortunately, she hadn't gotten the chance. Things had been so chaotic during the day that she hadn't had a moment alone with him since things went to shit, but she would have told him had he given her the chance. Thank God that never happened. "But she knew about this shit before it went down," he continued. "She came to the store to pick me up so we could get out of town, but we got stopped by an outbreak in front of the store. And I saw Todd earlier this morning. He got a text, totally freaked out, and took off like a bat out of hell."

Robert's face grew tighter, his blood rising, his anger starting to show. "Is that right? Did you know about this shit before it began? Did Todd?"

She couldn't guess at the source of this newfound rage and stepped back from the force of the onslaught. She was trying to remain quiet, but the gravity of the man's gaze was starting to shatter her resolve. Her heart sped up as the bat began to rise. "I don't know how he knew. Maybe something happened that tipped him off. I got a text telling me to get out of town and I knew that he wouldn't lie about something like this. I believed him," she offered, giving him a slice of truth in hopes it would be enough to end this conflict before it escalated.

"Did you see him at work today?" he asked Caesar, who yelped at being the new target of Robert's rage. "You work in his department, you'd know better than anyone what is going on."

"He was there," Raleigh replied, interjecting himself into the conversation. "He looked flustered, said he had a family emergency, but then took the time to fill an entire shopping cart full of junk food," the big man finished, as if he was finally putting two and two together. "That motherfucker."

"This **morning**? He knew this **morning** that this shit was going to happen?" Robert screamed. Those that had been heading to the fire station had stopped and were starting to turn back. "And he didn't warn anybody? People he worked with? His coworkers, his friends, only you? Why were you the chosen one? Are you fucking him?" Now the bat was rising, and he was beginning to close the distance between them.

She fought the urge to flee. She knew that when facing rage like this, running would only make things worse. He'd catch her and beat her to death with that fucking bat. "I'm not fucking him," she snapped, noticing a stunned look cross Jeremy's face. Great, now he thought their problems stemmed from cheating. *What a fucking moron*. "I told you everything that I know. The phones are out. He hasn't texted me since this morning. I don't know anything more than you do," she tried again, but the chances of things cooling off were rapidly disappearing.

"I don't believe you," Robert roared. "Do you know that my daughter died today, that our neighbor broke into our house and attacked her? That she was already long gone by the time I got out of my bedroom and got that fucking thing off her? If Todd knew about this shit, if he could've stopped my little girl from dying, I will fucking kill him and his whole fucking family. Every—single—person—that bastard saw fit to save, while my daughter turned and attacked her crying father—will die," he was coming closer now. She knew the time was approaching where she would have to choose to either run or die. "I had to kill that thing that used to be my daughter!" he raged.

The blocks were starting to fall into place. The rage, the need for power, everything that had changed him from who he had been into the man he was now became painfully clear. "I'm sorry," she said softly, sympathizing with the anguish that the man had to have been feeling, doing her best not to imagine how'd she react in his place.

The apology stopped him, his eyes penetrating her soul.

"Let's take a second, man. Calm down a bit," Manny spoke up, hands raised, taking advantage of the momentary lag in conversation.

"Fuck—you," Robert responded, biting off every word. "This is what we're going to do. We are going to go in there and check for weapons. Then we're going to see if there's any trucks left that still run," he said, speaking angrily to the group around him, wanting them all to understand who was in charge; including her. "Then we're going to get on the road and you," he paused to point the bat at her, "are going to take us to this fucking bunker he's hiding in. I don't care if you are going to willingly cooperate or not, you **are** going to take us there," he assured her. The look he gave shocked her to the core. She saw in those eyes how far he'd go to make her tell him anything he wanted. He had become a monster.

Manny was looking behind Robert now, leaning over to glance behind the angry man with a bat. No one paid him any attention.

"We are seriously outnumbered here, and we need weapons if we are going to make it out of the city alive. If we stick together, work together, we will survive. Apparently, there is a secret hideout where we could be safe, hidden deep in the woods and heavily defensible. We are going to find it and take it from the people hiding inside. Why shouldn't they suffer as we have suffered? Why should they get to survive while the rest of us are left out here to die?" he continued on, the others nodding as he spoke.

The fear that had started to grow now blossomed. The first chance she had to break away, she was taking it, regardless of anything or anyone she'd leave behind. What she had seen in those eyes was pure unadulterated rage with no inhibitions, no morality, and she knew that no one would stop him from killing her when the time came.

Manny was leaning sideways again, and Robert finally paused in his speech and raised his bat at him. "What the fuck is your problem?"

"This is the part of the movie where something pops out and eats the guy making the long-winded speech about how they're going to survive. Just want to make sure I get to see it when it happens,"

Manny replied with a laugh. Everyone paused, eyes on the guitarist, so caught up in what Robert was saying that the sudden laughter was leaving them too shocked to respond.

"What the fuck are you talking about?" Robert asked, obviously confused. He was trying to rally his troops and the sudden outburst was destroying his momentum.

The young man at her side coughed. "You're having your Samuel L. Jackson moment, and this is the part where he gets eaten by the shark." His laughter rang out again, but as Robert began to move his way, it petered off. "Hey man, my point is, you need to chill out," Manny told imposing figure, hands up, making sure that everyone knew that he was defenseless. "I'm sorry about your daughter and shit, but that doesn't justify murder in cold blood."

"What the fuck do you know about it?" Robert thundered.

There was movement in the distance and at first, she dismissed it. Then the shifting shadows began to near the overhead streetlights and her brain instantly told her limbs to run. She was in motion long before her brain caught up to what she was doing. She brushed past Robert, who had responded by raising his bat, probably thinking she was attacking him.

When she swept past him and kept going, he turned and saw what had created her sudden urge to run. He was instantly on the move as well. "Get inside now!" he yelled at his people. Most were already near the building, only hovering outside to watch the argument taking place, and quickly disappeared from sight.

She was outdistancing those behind her and for a brief second, she thought about Erik. It was fleeting, her survival instincts overtaking her need to protect anyone else. As she dove inside, she turned and watched as the others dodged her way. The undead horde had realized their food was escaping and sounds of their approach grew louder by the second. One leapt into view and Robert's bat finally finished its swing, connecting with the head of the zombie. The crumpled body fell behind him as he leapt forward and kept going. She was surprised as Erik reached the door first and pushed past her. Holding it open for the others, she watched in horror as the horde came into view. Realization struck her in the gut, they wouldn't make it in time.

She saw it dawn on Robert's face that he had come to the same conclusion and she instinctively knew what he was going to do before he turned, grabbed Jeremy by the shoulders, and flung him at the approaching horde. Jeremy tried to fight back, but his momentum worked against him as his direction shifted and he ran face first into the awaiting teeth and claws. Screams penetrated the air as the undead tore him apart, the snarling monsters congregating in a large pile of flesh, each trying to get a piece of him.

Only a few remained fixed on their course and they were closing the distance swiftly. If Manny hadn't been close on Robert's heels, she would've slammed the door and left the son of a bitch out there to die. Unable to watch any longer, she backed away and began to look around for a weapon. She saw a fireman's axe lying forgotten on the floor just waiting to be picked up. As her hands closed around the axe handle, the door opened, and the other three men pushed their way in. They slammed it quickly and turned the deadbolt as bodies pounded against it from the other side.

"You son of a bitch," she cursed at Robert. He had his back against the door, his chest heaving. The small window broke as the creatures outside tried to break through, but the wire mesh kept them from reaching in. It would not last long and she knew that she couldn't stay here; not in the same place with him. If she did, she'd kill him.

"It was him or all of us," Robert responded, his hand gripping his bat.

"Bullshit! He was your friend, you fucking asshole!" she felt the tears welling up inside. They might have begun to fall apart as a couple, but that didn't mean that she didn't still care for the man. The fat ass remark she had made earlier was coming back to haunt her and she was horrified at what it might represent. Was she capable of the same evil as Robert?

"So are they!" Robert said, waving his arms at the people around him. "He gave his life so the rest of us could live. His sacrifice has meaning!"

"You really are a self-absorbed puta. That doesn't give his death meaning, it only shows what a monster you truly are! There had to be another way," she spat, the rage boiling over. Robert's eyes finally caught sight of the axe she was holding and how tightly she was gripping it.

"You hate me, that's good. It might just save your life. You want to kill me? Do it, I'm right here," he challenged her, arms spread wide.

"You don't think I will?" she returned angrily. There was no one else in the world right now but her and Robert, no one dared to interfere. "I've had enough of your fucking bullshit. How many lives will I save by putting you down?" She had her axe raised and was battling against the urge to swing it.

He leaned the bat against the wall and swung out his arms. "I'm not armed. You want to kill me, kill me. Show us all how much of a hypocrite you really are. My daughter's dead. What do I have left to live for?"

Her inner turmoil increased, and a flurry of images raced through her mind. Tyler, Victoria, Charlie, David, Jeremy, so many deaths today, could she bear to add one more? "We do not kill each other, pendejo! There are enough of them out there willing to do that! Are you so fucking power hungry that you can't see that working together, rather than against one another, might have changed how all of this went down? You ain't right in the head. Maybe you never were," she said, dismissing him. "All of you had better ask yourselves, will you be his next **sacrifice** for the greater good? Seguro que no será!"

None of them were responsive, only Erik and Manny would even look her in the eye. Caesar was non-committal, choosing to stand to the right of the door with his head down.

"I'm done with this shit," she spat, turning from Robert and letting him get a good look at her back. He could take a swing at her; she was daring him to do it. It would give her a reason to end his sorry life once and for all. Yet, she knew that he wouldn't. The instant he swung that bat he'd lose whatever trust he had earned with them. That would be worse than letting her walk away.

"We're not done here Sabrina!" he yelled, as she walked down the hallway to the rooms beyond.

"And we never will be," she whispered in response, her voice finally cracking and the tears beginning to flow.

Chapter 33
EAS

Todd
Compound 2

The EAS had come on again to announce that the President would address the nation shortly and he had gone to the med lab to tell the others the news. Ben was too exhausted to get out of bed, Sean was nowhere to be found, and his two younger kids were passed out in their beds; he let them sleep. There was a television set up in the room. He turned it on and waited with the others for their President to appear.

Rodger had finally woken up and was propped up in his hospital bed. Casey was still flying on his pain meds and he seriously doubted his friend would remember anything the next morning. Nick and Michelle sat by their mother, and he made no move to remind them that it was past their bed time; such things didn't seem to matter anymore. Samantha came to sit by his side, her children down for the night.

The static fluttered and the seal of the President appeared on the television screen. All of them quieted at once, each with their own expectations of what she was about to say. When the Seal faded to the familiar scene of the President's desk, the exhausted face of their country's leader was there to greet them.

"Michelle looks like shit," Casey said, smiling. He must have had another dose because he seemed to be blissfully unaware of the gravity of their situation. Monica shushed him as the President began to speak.

"My fellow Americans, today I address you not only as the President of the United States, but as a citizen of the world. An unknown terrorist organization has launched a series of deliberate and deadly attacks upon our nation with only one viable purpose behind their actions; the total annihilation of the world as we know it. Every nation across the globe is currently working on their own way to fight back, to survive. None have been spared this evil loosed upon the world. Tonight, I ask that you pray with me, pray for us all."

"Here is what we know. Yesterday morning at 10:00 a.m. Eastern Standard Time, a biological attack was launched upon the United States in an airport in St. Louis, Missouri. By the time the response teams arrived, and the airport was quarantined, it was too late. It was already flying across the nation in planes, driving along interstates in cars, and spread by people on foot. With the information they had, all proper procedures were followed, and I cannot in good conscience blame any of those first responders for what is now happening."

"This was an airborne contagion of unnatural origin that exhibited no classic symptom of infection. Immediate quarantine procedures were initiated, and a sample was flown to the CDC for analysis. The potential threat was not immediately apparent as the biological agent lies dormant in a living human host. It does not interfere with normal bodily functions, does not attack living tissue. It acts like an additive to the bloodstream with no apparent behavior other than replication and attachment to the blood cells of its host. Our doctors worked through the night trying to uncover the threat it posed to those infected and found nothing of relevance. It wasn't until a person who contracted the virus died that we discovered the horror that had been unleashed upon the world."

"Now, let me stress this point. There was no sign of infection until brain death. From what the doctors at the CDC in Atlanta are telling me, the virus is not spread through bodily fluids; it is an airborne virus. By the time an infected person comes in close contact with an uninfected host, it's already spread. Estimates show that the majority of the nation has already contracted this virus and that any thoughts of quarantine would be a useless exercise. I have ordered the grounding of all civil air traffic and the Department of Transportation has been instructed to shut down interstate travel. However, it has already been flown beyond our borders and is even now spreading across the globe with no signs that containment is possible or would be effective."

"That does not mean that there is no hope of survival. Your government is throwing all its resources into developing a vaccine to fight this virus. It's important that you hear me on this and understand, you will be perfectly fine as long as you are alive. Simply getting bit is not enough to kill you unless the wound is left untreated. I cannot stress this enough. **Stop** killing people just because they have come into contact with the infected. The virus reanimates dead tissue; it does not convert the living. The top minds in the field assure me that as long as a person stays healthy and alive, they are not in danger of becoming one of these monsters the virus creates. If we are to survive this, we will need every living soul to help stave off the waves of undead and you are killing that by acting rashly, murdering those that could help ensure our survival."

"I have raised our threat level to red. Our military forces are on the highest alert and have been working throughout the day to fight outbreaks occurring in the largest population centers of our country. I have declared martial law to help differentiate the living from the undead and ask that all of you listening to this broadcast cooperate completely with this order. By nightfall, all citizens are to remain off the streets so that the military can easily tell friend from foe. This is for your safety, as the threat against our way of life is so severe that only drastic measures can be used to assure our continued existence. I have ordered all forces abroad to return home and the National Guard to be integrated with our other armed forces as we move to end this attack without further loss of life."

"I will not lie to you. Our nation is going through the darkest moment in our history and I need each of you to help me if we are going to see this through together. Stay within your homes, keep your televisions on, but keep them at a low volume to avoid drawing attention. Listen to the radio for updates. And most importantly, regardless of who it is, regardless of what they mean to you, you have to drive a sharp implement into the brain of anyone that dies. If you don't, you put yourself and everyone else around you at risk. I know that what I ask is a terrible thing, but I assure you that this is necessary. I promise you that your government is working hard at ending this threat. We will not spare any resource and we will take every measure possible to end this swiftly and return to our way of life."

"Keep those that are dying tonight in your thoughts and prayers. Preserve the lives of your family by fortifying your homes and staying indoors. Ration supplies and please use common sense when dealing with people trying to get into your home. One saved life is one less infected person trying to kill you. Let's help each other get through this and in the end, I promise you, we will prevail. Life will go on. May God be with us, goodnight," she finished, and the seal flashed on the screen for a second, before returning to its static state.

"She didn't say anything about the bomb," he muttered, still unable to believe it. There had been a lot of things unaddressed by her speech, like the communications black out. He had expected there to be some mention of the explosion, some warning for those downwind to get out of the path of radiation coming their way. But there had been nothing. Was it possible they didn't know about it? How could that be?

"Wait, what bomb?" Samantha asked with shock, and he realized that he had spoken out loud. They were all staring at him now; waiting for him to continue.

Well, there was no going back now. "A nuke went off at the Hoover Dam about an hour ago," he told them quietly, watching the horror spread across their faces. Monica got up and came over to him, where she knelt at his side and placed her hand over his, giving a reassuring squeeze.

"I'm sorry honey, Ros and Matt were there when it went off," he told her, loud enough for the others to hear. Michelle was standing there shaking her head and he put an arm out. She rushed forward into an embrace with her parents. Nick refused to move, his eyes dazed, stunned by what he was hearing. Lucy was crying in Rodger's arms, and Casey was looking at him with confusion. He would have to explain it to him when he was lucid; he wasn't going to make an effort now.

"This can't be happening," Sam whispered, shaking her head with horror. He put a hand on her shoulder and squeezed lightly, trying to convey as much sympathy as he could.

The phone he had liberated from Ben's desk went off, making most of them jump at the sudden noise intruding upon their grief. "Sorry," he told them as he put the Bluetooth into his ear and hit the answer button. He listened for a second and laughed, surprising them all. They gave him tearful confused glances, not understanding how he could laugh or who'd be calling to make him do so. "Well, holy shit Mark, welcome back to the land of the living!"

The sorrow they were all feeling was still there, but at the mention of Mark's name, it began to lift. One of their friends they had long thought dead was all right. If that was true for him, it had to be true for some of the others, didn't it?

The sudden news of Mark's resurrection even registered with Casey, who broke out in a big grin and told him he always loved a man in a fireman's uniform.

Sighing, he didn't repeat that over the phone and nodded at the others. He got to his feet and headed back to the communications room. Mark wanted to know where his family was, and he was going to do everything he could to help him find them. It was the one positive thing he could do, and he was determined to make it happen.

Chapter 34
Washed up

Rosilynn
Lake Mohave, AZ

Water, pain, bits of air, and arms clinging to her; that's all she could remember as she lay on the wet soil, her feet flowing with the water. Her lungs violently coughed up the river water in an effort to restore her airway. She could vaguely remember Matt finding her in that river, bringing her to the surface, and both of them clutching a piece of debris as the explosion sent the river violently south.

"Matt?" she croaked, her throat raw and slightly swollen. Her body was a storm of pain that raged on even after the river had deposited her here. Her limbs burned, her head was pounding, and she was still coughing up water as if she'd never get it all out. Her husband's arm was no longer around her and she tried to open her eyes as she realized that she was lying there alone.

The bright moon overhead seared her brain and she screamed, her hand flying to her head in an effort to somehow contain the daggers that were infiltrating her mind. She rolled away from the moon, her eyes squeezed shut and her scream cut off as she once again began to throw up onto the cold wet ground. "Matt?" she called again.

There was still no response.

Her hand reached out and struck something solid, making it scream in agony from the mixture of cold and the force of the impact. She withdrew her hand and held it under her mouth, her hot breath trying to soothe the cold, her fingers flexing in an effort to push back the pain. She cracked her eyelids and slowly let them widen, allowing them to adjust as they will to the world around her.

There was a concrete picnic table two feet in front of her and the entire thing was dripping water like it'd been recently submerged. Looking around carefully, she examined the manmade campsite that she had been washed up on. Debris littered the area and water was lapping at her legs. It was impossible to believe that the campsite had been built this close to the waterline and she could see that the metal box designated for campfires was underneath the surface of the water off to her right.

Her pack was still attached, and it pulled her onto her back. No matter how much she tried, she could not manage to get up the strength to turn on her side. She attempted to work her arms free and her shoulders flared where the straps had held onto her. She strained her neck to see if she could see her husband along the bank of the newly created shoreline, but there was no trace of him.

Something grasped her leg and she cried out. Pain shot up her hip and she nearly bit her tongue off with the agony it caused. There was a zombie crawling out of the water by her feet and the bloated body was desperately trying to puncture the rubber of her suit. It was wearing a white button-down and she knew that it had been one of the cult members that had leapt off the dam.

In fear and disgust, she clawed her way back, her feet kicking the monstrosity in the face, forcing it to momentarily pull back into the river. Her hands flung out in desperation and her fingers closed upon a large rock. Mustering all the strength she could, she brought it down on the head of the zombie that had clawed its way to her waist, the head crumpling under the blow and gunk spraying her in the face. Her stomach wrenched and she threw up again. It took the last bit of strength she had to break herself free of the waterlogged corpse and she kicked it away from her as she lay with her head next to the water. She didn't care what might be in it, she had to wash this taste out of her mouth and clean off as much as she could. Panic threatened to override her as she frantically worked on getting the infected gore off her skin as swiftly as possible.

After a few minutes, she had finally been able to turn herself over, temporarily relieved that she'd thoroughly cleaned herself off. Tentatively, she had tried to gain her feet. Using the picnic table for support, she lifted herself with her wobbly knees and sat down on the drenched bench. From this height, she was able to see that the geography of the land around her had been dramatically changed by the river as it rushed south. Broken trees were bent at odd angles and water occupied what once had been dry desert land. To the north an orange glow drew her eyes to the horizon. She shielded them as she gasped in horror at the sight of the mushroom cloud blossoming there.

How close had they been to it when it had gone off? How much radiation had she been exposed to as well? She recalled being in the water only a few minutes before the first wave pushed them downstream. Had it been a safe enough distance when the blast wave hit? Had the water pushed them ahead of the radiation generated by an explosion of that magnitude?

She didn't feel any immediate signs of radiation poisoning, and she cautiously checked her vitals for any irregularities. They were elevated but in a normal range. It didn't mean much, but it did a lot to ease her mind. The only measure of how bad it was, was going to be was time; how much did she have left?

A gunshot pierced her daze and her head jerked to the south. Her aching body refused to obey as she forced herself to her feet. She had to grip the tabletop firmly in an effort to steady herself and keep from pitching forward. Another shot rang out and a shout followed after. Someone was yelling her name.

"Matt!" she hollered back, hoping that he was in range of her voice. She felt at her waist and sighed with relief that the .45 was still on her left hip and her sword on her right. Somehow, they had stayed with her when her Rimfire was stripped away. Whether or not the .45 would be effective was the real question; how wet was the gunpowder after that journey downstream? She should've sealed their ammo in bags as well.

"Rosilynn?" she heard her name called again. It was enough to renew her strength as she began to stumble towards the sound of the voice.

Working her way through the broken carnage around her, she made steady progress, drawing her sword from its sheathe and holding it in an unsteady hand before her. After thirty feet, the moonlight distinguished two shambling figures; both heading away from her. Another gunshot penetrated the silence of the night. The head of the stumbling form on the right suddenly blew apart and fell to the ground, disappearing from sight. The one on the left was still limping onward, undisturbed by the loss of its companion. She heard a curse in the distance.

Trying to pick up her pace, she nearly fell forward again and was forced to slow down or end up face first in the wet ground she was trodding upon. Closing the distance as fast as she was able, she brought her sword up and swung it quickly. The blade embedded itself in the head of the white-shirted corpse and her hand refused to let go of the hilt as the body fell forward, dragging her along with it.

In a shriek of surprise, she found herself lying on top of the ruined corpse, her body shaking in revulsion. She jerked her head away from the ghastly ghoul, then turned over, landed on one knee, and gave the sword a yank. The wet sound the blade made when it left the corpse's head was sickening, but her stomach had nothing further to offer tonight. Her brain was numb from the violence afflicted on it during the day's events. Her breath came in quick rasps as she tried desperately to slow it down and regain her feet.

"Who's there?" she heard a voice call from just ahead.

"Matt?" she called, standing on her shaking knees and taking small steps forward.

"Rosilynn?" he asked, as she finally cleared the grass that had been hiding her husband. She found him lying on the ground with his gun raised and a smile upon his face. "Oh, thank God," he whispered.

She went to him then. The happiness that she felt at their survival was unrivaled by any she'd ever felt in the past. The sight of him lying there smiling up at her had been too much for her to handle in her current state.

As they embraced, she felt his lips on hers and welcomed the grip of his arms around her back. "I told you it wasn't goodbye," he croaked, and she laughed until her throat ached, then laughed some more.

Chapter 35
Make a Break for it

Saint
Tucson, AZ

"We're going to have to move quickly," she told Caesar. He had followed after her with Erik and Manny, the four of them leaving the others to search the fire station for supplies and weapons. She was in a large garage housing the two abandoned firetrucks. She hovered at the side door overlooking the employee parking lot and her heart lightened when she saw the fire-chief's truck still parked in its designated spot.

"What if there are more of them waiting out there?" Manny asked, making it quite known whose side he had chosen after that last confrontation with Robert. It had surprised her at first. She had thought the two men were friends and the young aspiring guitarist had been traveling with him long before their two groups met. But things had begun to change when Robert had gone after Erik, and his detachment since had been in a matter of degrees.

She shook her head. "Better to leave now while they are congregating at the front doors, than wait for them to find their way to this one. We're going to have to make a break for it."

Erik nodded in agreement, leaning against the wall to support his weary body. He knew what might happen if he stayed much longer and he would do anything if it meant getting away from Robert. "What about Him?" he asked, nodding back the way they had come in. He had been friends with Jeremy as well and she thought she saw fire kindling in his eyes.

"Fuck him," she growled, bringing a smile to their faces.

Caesar nodded and said, "I'll go check the Chief's office for the keys." He quickly dashed across the garage and disappeared from view.

"You up to this?" she asked Erik, seeing how pale he was. His arm had stopped bleeding, but the blood loss might make it hard on him to go much further on his own. He simply nodded. The slump of his shoulders told her how hard it was even for him to keep standing, but he was determined to push on. She could respect that. "If we make it to Caesar's place, we'll hold up so you can rest," she said, trying to sound confident, even if she didn't feel it herself.

What she wanted to do was to take her axe and bury it in Robert's skull. If they stayed here, she might not be able to stop herself from trying to do just that. No, it was best that they leave quickly before her anger returned and forced her along that path. She had other things to worry about and didn't want that monster's blood on her hands. He may think it was all right feeding her boyfriend to a bunch of ravenous corpses, but she wasn't ever going to believe so. She would never be like him. If refusing to sink to his level got her killed, then at least she'd die being true to herself and not some shadow of what she used to be.

Caesar ran back into the garage holding a set of keys. "Found them," he said needlessly, handing them over.

She simply nodded and glanced through the window. There was nothing moving out there, but she couldn't see what was lurking on the side of the door either. "We're going to make a run for it, stay right behind me. Try to move quietly, get in the truck, and then we're out of this freak show for good," she whispered, hoping not to draw the attention of those roaming the halls of the station. The sound would carry, and she didn't want them alerted to what they were doing until they were long gone from this place.

The three of them stood right beside her, each nodding that they were ready. Manny stroked his guitar case for luck, and she couldn't help but smile at that. Reaching out, she grasped the knob and opened the door cautiously, trying her best not to make a sound as she swung it slowly open. Sound was like a dinner bell to these things and her mind winced as she remembered that it had been her scream back at the store that had been responsible for David's death. And hours later, here she was, responsible for three others as she made another mad dash from a besieged building that harbored evil both within and out. The difference being, this time she was armed. The bad news? She was the only one of the four that was. None of them had found weapons outside the axe she was wielding, and she prepared herself as much as she could for what might come next. No one would die this time if she could help it.

She stepped out, checked both sides for signs of the undead, and let out her breath in a rush; relieved. So far so good. She motioned for the others to follow and they filed out after her. Moving silently towards the truck, her ears listened to the moans from the front of the building and she tried desperately not to make a sound as she slowly unlocked the doors. It had an extended cab and as she unlocked the passenger door, she lifted the handle slightly and slid it open. She opened the back door and Erik and Manny climbed in. Caesar hopped into the passenger seat and reached to unlock the driver door. She dashed around the front of the truck, eased the cracked door open; and hopped in quickly, clicking it shut behind her. She slid the keys into the ignition and paused; the instant she turned this engine over they would come. She closed her eyes and began to pray as she twisted the key.

The engine roared to life.

The two in the back were whispering and she looked in her rear-view mirror. Robert was staring out at them through the window on the door they had just exited. His eyes glared with hate as she rolled down the window to let in the night air.

Slamming the truck into reverse, she backed up quickly, then paused for a second to stare into those dark eyes, letting him see she hated him as much as he did her. Smiling, she threw it into drive, flipped him the bird, and hit the gas. The truck lunged forward and clipped a walker lunging around the corner. Flying into the road she veered left, leaving the pack of zombies in her wake. They must have realized part of their food supply was leaving as half raced after her. The others had stayed at the front door of the fire station and she hoped she hadn't drawn enough of them away to give Robert a quick way out.

She didn't see Jeremy in that herd of zombies, but if one of them were to take that fucker out, she prayed that it would be him. The poetic justice in that was not lost on her.

Robert would not give up now; he'd do whatever it'd take to find her again. Best to put as much distance between them as quickly as possible. As much as she hated it and didn't want to bring it up, he did know where they were going; after Caesar's wife and kid. The question was, did he know where Caesar lived?

She didn't want to spend the night there, it was too risky with that bastard following after her, but she didn't think there was a choice. Erik was done in, holding on by willpower alone. They needed a night to rest and regroup. She looked up at the moon and felt the rage in her body driving her on. She may not get any sleep this night.

Sighing, she turned the wheel and raced through the Diamond Shamrock's parking lot, avoiding the litter of bodies rotting in the intersection. Glancing behind her to make sure no one was following after, she floored it, fleeing through the darkness and trying desperately to get into the light.

Her phone buzzed and she jumped out of her skin. Handing the phone from her back pocket to Caesar, she continued on, wondering why it was suddenly working. She flipped on the radio and heard the President talking. Had something changed while they were in the firehouse? Was it possible they were going to survive this?

Caesar held up the phone and she saw she had two missed messages.

Todd: You still there?

That was a relief. Her heart lightened and some of the anger fled her. Her phone was working! Todd had made it and was still checking up on her. Thank God. They might have a chance after all. Then her heart froze as she read the second one. She had forgotten that she had given him her number and he must have found out the phones were working again. A coldness settled upon her as the hate in her heart blossomed into a white rage.

Robert: You're going to die bitch

Caesar's eyes said exactly what she was already thinking— *you've got to find us first.*

Chapter 36
Revenge

Robert
Tucson, AZ

Robert's rage was boiling over. While they were searching the fire station for supplies and weapons, that bitch had snuck out the side door and escaped him. While it had been part of his plan all along, the fact that she had gotten away without a single walker reaching her had deepened his hatred. Then the bitch actually had the gall to smile and flip him off?

His phone beeped in his hand and he grinned as he read the text floating on its screen.

(520) 555-3406: Good to go

Things might not have turned out the way he had planned, but he had still gotten exactly what he wanted. He needed her to believe that she was getting away, so she'd lead them where he wanted to go; to Todd. The fierce hate he held for the man was overloading his senses and he was willing to let the leash out for the little bitch to stretch her legs a bit if it meant that he'd get his hands on them both in the end.

The loss of his daughter had weighed heavily on him throughout the day, fueling his rage and changing his heart into this cold being that even he didn't recognize. It was all Todd's fault. If he had thought of the rest of them when he made his perfectly timed escape, then his daughter might still be alive. Oh yes, there was going to be a reckoning when he caught up to them, of that his heart was sure.

His smile grew as he pocketed the phone. Whistling, he toured the fire station, confident that they were safe for the time being and preparing in his head exactly what he'd do to each of them when he saw them next. Todd would die a slow death—but Sabrina? He fancied keeping her alive and making her live the rest of her life satisfying every dark fantasy his mind could construct. The human body could take a lot, and he slowly went over each and every little thing he could think of doing. His blood rushed south to his forgotten waist in response. Stiffening, his smile grew wider and those that saw it flinched. He laughed suddenly at the quickening blood singing through his veins; it felt like nothing he had ever experienced before, and he liked it—he really liked it.

He joined the others searching the building for supplies. He could afford to give her some lead time. With his spy planted, he had all the time in the world to catch up to her. Let her feel safe and protected. Then he'd show up, strip it all away, kill her friends in front of her, and take exactly what she had always denied him. The joy he felt at the power growing inside made him laugh harder. The pounding on the doors intensified, but he didn't care. He strode through the doorway and out of sight; the echoes of his laughter following him out of the garage, down the hall, and into the darkness beyond.

Chapter 37
Least likely scenario

Todd
Compound 2

He needed fresh air.

Ben was back at his post; the world ending hadn't let him stay in bed too long. He still looked exhausted. It had been a long, trying day and his body seemed sapped of all its energy. How he was able to keep going was a mystery. Maybe it was the boy's youth that helped him endure with only short periods of rest; something his own was long past capable of doing. As he had gotten older, he seemed to need more sleep than usual in order to recharge his batteries.

Midnight was drawing near and he realized that only fourteen hours had passed since his phone had gone off at work. What he wouldn't give to be back there complaining about his wife's annoying texts. He had a feeling that times like those were lost to him forever and as much as he hated it, he'd miss it.

He had tried to imagine what was going on in the world. The President had said that this was not only happening in America, but across the globe. How did that happen so fast? His mind refused his attempts at calculating the rate of infection, of how many airports or bus terminals had to have been infected, spreading ever outwards like some damn vine spiked on miracle grow.

He stroked his temple as his blood vessels throbbed and his head ached.

There was a nasty part of himself that resisted dwelling on how many people were out there dying, but rather on how much his own world was going to change. He hated it, but he couldn't seem to help it either. Would he ever find a Snickers bar, drink a frosty from Wendy's, or eat a roast beef sandwich from Arby's? These were the things he had taken for granted when they were readily available and now his mind kept fixating on the fact that he might never have them again. When they ran out of Coke, he'd be stuck with water. Maybe he should try to lower his caffeine intake now so that his withdrawals wouldn't be so bad later.

If the military lost this war on the undead, how would they survive? Sure, they had planned and trained for it, yet it didn't seem to be enough. His friends were out there dying, and all of the work had been for nothing. Even if they somehow got through, how many others would live through this extinction level event? There wouldn't be enough in the compounds to rebuild society. Would Mankind die out like the dinosaurs had? Would another species eventually take their place? He shook his head. A bunch of MMO nerds as the only hope for Mankind's survival? Yeah, they were doomed.

While he wasn't naïve enough to think that his group was the only one that had prepared for this, he couldn't be sure of how long it would take to establish contact with the others out there, if they ever. How long until they felt safe enough to leave their new home, to venture into the world and search them out? Mankind had become so dependent on their creature comforts that he wasn't sure they'd survive in the wild when thrown back into the trees from whence they came.

When the lantern ran out of fuel, what was he going to do? How did you get propane gas anyway? When the mantles were gone, who would make more? That was just one example of the life and comforts that the current age of Man had provided. Sure, he had gone camping, but was it really roughing it with all the gear and equipment that you could take with you? His mind insisted that those questions were just the tip of the iceberg on the list of *holy shit we're fucked*. He had joked about Twinkies no longer being around for the apocalypse when Hostess went belly up; now their return looked like a harbinger for things to come.

A pig's grunt brought him back to reality and he realized that none of them had fed the livestock that day; at least as far as he knew. Maybe Rodger had taken care of that before they had gotten there. He'd have to make a mental note to do it in the morning, his older friend wasn't in any shape to get up and do it himself.

The farming had been hard for them at first, even with the right equipment. None of them knew shit about that kind of work and what seemed like an easy job turned into a headache that none of them had anticipated. His respect for the agricultural world had increased after the initial failures they had suffered. They hadn't known about crop rotations, they were gamers. Studying had only gotten them so far and had cost them the second year of crops due to their inexperience.

Rodger had volunteered to live at the compound and with his family, they tended to the fields and maintained the livestock. But it still required the others to come and assist every fall during harvest. The gardens were simple when compared to the corn and wheat fields. He was just glad no one had dared suggest they plant cotton. Who would've picked it? Beyond creature comforts, what good would it serve in their quest to survive?

He walked towards the main building, letting the moonlight have its last look at him. He needed to try and sleep. His body was willing, but his mind wouldn't shut off. He looked at his new home and the moonlit building made him think of Jurassic Park. It was a large structure composed of concrete and steel. All the windows had steel shutters and exterior bars. It looked more like a building for death row inmates than a refuge, yet it was meant to keep people out not in. There was a tower on the third floor, barely visible over the wall and security bars above. They would eventually have to station people in the towers, but for tonight everyone just needed to get some rest. There would be time enough for that tomorrow.

As he entered the main building and walked to the stairway; he marveled at how much they had accomplished. He wondered if they had missed anything with their planning. There were redundancies everywhere. While there was a trauma room above, there was a better stocked and equipped one below. The training area was above ground, but he didn't think any of them would chance firing an unsuppressed round as long as the threat of being noticed was upon them.

There were multiple armories, both above and below the structure, and readily accessible to those defending their carefully designed fortress. He was now on the first basement floor. The exercise room was on his left, the stairs to the living quarters was at the other end of the hall on the right.

He was on his way to the dormitory below when he heard the pulsing bass of music emerging from their entertainment room. That was hard to do with the soundproofing and it was odd that any of them would be in the mood for it. He thought it ironic that Rob Zombie was pounding the walls and knew of only one of their group with the stomach to listen to a song like that after the day they had—Sean.

Approaching the door, he noticed that it was cracked open, explaining why he had heard the music through the soundproofed walls. He winced at how high it was cranked as he stepped through the doorway, instantly buffeted by the bass of the large speakers on either side of the room. There was a large TV and comfortable furniture arranged in the center; well used by the kids. They had made sure to have all the current game systems and had most of the new games shipped automatically to a post office box in Morenci. Rodger made regular pick-ups there each week. Their movie collection was just as impressive and their benefactor had insisted on a jukebox setup for most of the Blu-ray discs, to keep them maintained and protected from regular wear and tear.

Speaking of the devil, Sean was hovering at the bar on the right and was currently trying to drain a large bottle of scotch. Drunk did not cover the man's state. He was quite sure that even with the volume as loud as it was, he was barely hearing it. What kept the man on his feet was beyond him.

"Mind turning that down?" he roared, trying to get his friend's attention.

Sean looked up at him, his eyes bloodshot and barely comprehending what was going on. Yet, he reached over to a remote and the radio instantly dropped in volume. "What?" Sean yelled at him. Todd closed his eyes and jerked his head in response. Sean laughed. "Trouble sleeping?"

"What do you think?" he asked, a hand rising to rub the puffiness out of his eyes.

"Rum and Coke?" Sean asked, already reaching for the bottle before he had a chance to reply.

It would be so easy for him to give in, to let the alcohol drown the day away, but he couldn't bring himself to do it. His father-in-law had been a drunk and he had decided early on that he wouldn't do that to Monica. Still, after a day like this, how could he say no? Would his wife really be that cross with him for having a drink after all they had been through? He wouldn't be surprised to find a bottle of Cuervo in their room when he turned in for the night; that was her particular brand of poison. Hell, even Sam was three sheets to the wind when he had left her earlier, a large bottle of vodka lying on the floor next to her bed.

Giving in, he simply nodded and accepted the drink. "Bit loud in here."

Sean laughed again. "Oh, I know we don't like to make a ruckus, but I don't see how anything really matters anymore. I mean really, who were we kidding?"

His brows drew together. He was about to ask what Sean meant, but it was something that had been elusively crawling behind his consciousness throughout day. His words died in his throat when he tried to respond, not ready to be voiced. He took a moment to collect himself and decided to go at it from a different angle. "Are you saying you want to just give up? We don't know how this is going to turn out yet, do we? Isn't it early to just throw in the towel?"

The look he got chilled him to the bone. "Is it?"

"You're not serious," he responded, not believing what he was hearing. This was darker than any other conversation they had ever had, and there had been plenty of those before today. Things were depressing enough without ending his day with something as ugly as this.

Sean waved at the television. "Been shown for years what would happen when this shit goes down. They never have a happy ending." He grunted, "Well, except for that World War Z crap and their disease immunity. One of the worst endings to a rather good movie I've ever seen. Those were some of the most realistic looking zombies and to have the rest of the film blown by a bad script writer was a damn shame."

"You don't know that it's going to play out that way. Most of them were crap, never really looking at it realistically. The Walking Dead's about as good as they get and even that had its moments. I mean, if they were all already infected, then why did it matter if they got bit? What about the bite made the infection kill the already infected host?" This was a conversation they had all had more than once over the years and it felt like rehearsed lines at this point. "You think they're going to be making phone calls asking 911 operators to send out more paramedics? That they'll walk around crying for brains?"

His old friend laughed again. "I'm a writer buddy, believe me when I say that I've thought of it all. I don't see us coming back from this. Did you know that I had people research this particular scenario?" His eyebrows lifted in curiosity.

He hadn't, actually.

Sean simply nodded and continued. "Did you think I went into this just because some WoW nerds thought it was a good idea?" Upon seeing the look he was getting, the man grunted. "Sorry about that, I think I've had a bit too much to drink."

You think? He cleared his throat, trying to hide a smile.

Sean went on, waving off his retort. "I hired researchers to look into it, as well as every other doomsday scenario ever thought of. With all the crap in Korea, Al Qaida, Iran, ISIS, Syria, and Russia, how could one not take a serious look, to prepare for any eventuality? The will to survive and all."

Sean drained his scotch and poured himself another.

"So, all this time you had other people involved? After all that talk about keeping this place secret?" he asked, completely stunned by the secrets his older friend had been hiding. How had he not realized that Sean wouldn't have gone into this without some kind of research behind it? How had he been so naïve? If he had missed that, what else had he missed? He had this horrible feeling that there was more hidden and wondered if he could ever trust that he had been told the whole truth. Where there was one secret—

His friend took another long drink and wiped his goatee. "I've kept my money by not indulging my every whim. Do you think I would finance all of this if there was even a chance it'd be a total waste of my money? I'm mad, but I'm not insane. And don't worry, the researchers I employed thought it was all theoretical. They didn't know I actually acted on their information. Though, you might be happy to know that most of the ideas you all came up with were in line with what they suggested as well."

He drained his glass and Sean reached out to refill it; reluctantly he agreed. "Our plans were screened before we went forward, weren't they?"

"Of course. Like I said, mad not insane. What man in his right mind would spend a fortune planning for a zombie apocalypse?" Sean laughed as he said those last words, as if daring the world not to make it real. "No one even thought it was possible," he said in a lower voice, and stopped talking, holding his drink idly while staring off into space.

He waited patiently for Sean to go on. The man just shook his head, raised the glass to his lips, and downed another round of scotch.

He glanced at the TV, the uncomfortable silence weighing heavy upon him. Had that just been a glib remark or was there something else that his older friend was hiding? Turning his head, he began to wonder if the television stations had come back up yet. "All things considered," he finally said, making his friend laugh again.

Whatever dark moment the man was having seemed to pass as he poured himself another drink. "Obviously, now we look smart and not wasting our lives away. But all things being equal, you had to know inside that this had always been a fool's errand. Did you seriously think any of this would ever actually happen?" Sean threw back his head and let the scotch drain down his throat. His hand was already reaching for the bottle, but his shaking hands missed, pushing it off the bar instead. It clanked as it hit the ground and it was a miracle that it didn't break. "Did you know that the chances of a zombie apocalypse happening were the lowest in probable outcomes for a doomsday scenario? The greatest was a biological attack, the second being a nuclear holocaust. Yet, we prepared for those as well, didn't we?" Sean's voice was becoming heavily slurred and he looked like he'd pass out soon, yet the writer in him continued on. "No, the chance of this was like two percent. There was a greater chance of an Independence Day or Battlefield: Los Angeles scenario than fucking zombies. I mean, really? Night of the Living Dead? What kind of madman would let something like this loose upon the world?" he trailed off, that dark look returning once more.

What was going on? He had never seen Sean go off the deep end like this. Suddenly his drink wasn't going down so well. He put his glass down and concentrated on clearing his mind. None of what he was saying really mattered, yet he could see the irony in it. It was irrelevant what the chances were of something like this occurring; it was happening. Now they had to move beyond it, not reflect on how unrealistic it was.

His friend stumbled as he tried to move towards another bottle of scotch and he bolted around the bar, catching him before he fell. Grunting with the weight, he led him to a nearby couch. Sean was still trying to talk, but most of it was incoherent. He comforted him, telling him he understood. His older friend's face cleared for a second, like he had just confessed some dark secret and had been given absolution for it. He'd have to remind himself to talk to him again in the morning, hoping that Sean didn't hit the bottle right away and sweep any chances at a level-headed conversation with it.

He laid the man down on the couch and slid into the seat next to him. He wasn't surprised to hear a snore drifting up from his side. Sighing, he gave up and stood on his exhausted legs, the weariness of the day sweeping across him. With an overloaded mind, he began his long trek to his room and the bed eagerly awaiting him.

Monica was fast asleep when he entered their bedroom. He hadn't drunk enough for the alcohol to have any real effect and he smiled at the Jose Cuervo bottle on his wife's nightstand. There were a lot of questions raised by Sean tonight and though there were tons of things to be done the next day, a follow-up conversation was one of the highest priorities on that list.

He had a sinking feeling that there was more his older friend had been hiding. No matter how long it took, he swore to himself he'd get the rest of it in the morning. For now, he was content to let the matter go; they weren't going anywhere, were they? They had plenty of opportunity to hash this all out. What else were they going to do?

"Hey baby, come to bed," his wife moaned sleepily, tapping the mattress and motioning for him to join her. Slipping out of his clothes, he lowered himself onto his pillow. It wasn't the same as the one he had at home and no matter how he moved his head, he could not get comfortable. He felt his wife's arm slide over his shoulders, and he smiled. No matter what else had happened; they were all together and amongst the living. His eyes closed on their own and his mind drifted away, letting the worries of the day finally slip off of his shoulders.

To be continued…

In Book 2 of the Rotting Souls Series
Charon's Blight
Day Two

For more information on upcoming novels, visit:

https://www.facebook.com/TRayPublishing/
http://timothy-ray.com

or be added to the mailing list at:
ray.publishingaz@gmail.com

Timothy Ray

Timothy Ray was born in Tucson, AZ, where he resides with his wife and three children.

He graduated from Desert View High School and was part of the Writer's Club for three years.

He attended the Art Center Design College to work on a Bachelor's degree in Animation.

He wrote his first book, the Acquisition of Swords, his Sophomore year of High School.

*The Following is an excerpt from
My upcoming novel:*

Focal Point

A Slipstream Novel

CHAPTER 1

I

She stumbled out of the alleyway, her hand applying pressure to her abdomen in an attempt to stop the bleeding. Despite her efforts, she could feel the warm pulse of fluid escaping through her fingers. She couldn't tell how bad it was, but her limbs were already starting to feel weak, her head fuzzy.

She was short on time.

Of all the ways to go out, this was never even considered a possibility. They had been waiting for her to arrive, the ambush nearly killing her. Only her quick actions and honed reflexes spared her life, but now it looked like they'd get what they wanted anyhow. She was going to die, an echo of a future that no longer existed.

The device on her inner thigh throbbed, making her pulse quicken.

"Jennifer, your vitals are dropping. You require medical attention," a voice spoke up within her mind.

No shit, really? What do you want me to do? Not like I can just go to a hospital. I need options, dammit! There were items in her possession not easily explained, not to mention the nature of the wound. The questions would never be answered to anyone's liking and if she got separated from Weena—

She leaned against the brick wall, pausing briefly to try and catch her breath. Reaching into one of the many pockets in her black trench coat, she withdrew a bottle, fumbled at the top, then quickly slipped a couple of pills into her mouth. She tried to swallow them dry and could feel every inch of progress they made down her dry throat.

She closed her eyes and waited a minute, allowing the medicine time to kick in. It was fast acting and would help temporarily increase her stamina. If she was going to do something, this was the time; there may not be another.

"Weena, where the hell am I?" she asked, looking at the darkened world around her, unable to distinguish a period through the architecture; other than it was likely the 21st Century. They were still using halogens on the streetlamps.

She pushed herself forward and began heading for the street beyond. She could make an educated guess, but wanted confirmation first.

"Tucson, Arizona. Tuesday, May 24th, 2016. 11:06pm," Weena told her in a somewhat mechanical fashion. No matter how far artificial intelligence advanced, they still had problems reading a calendar without a slight pause in their voices.

"What am I doing here?" she thundered, more to herself than to anyone else. She didn't expect an immediate answer and doubted Weena knew any more than she did. Her escape was rather hasty and no planning had gone into her destination, but still—why here? Why now? "Any ideas on what to do next?"

She stopped at the edge of the alley and looked out upon the moonlit night. She was in a residential neighborhood and there was sparse lighting in the homes across from her. The one directly before her was white, a mesquite tree the lone vegetation in the rock covered lawn. A car was parked in the driveway, a white and very dirty VW Bug. There was a garage door and she wondered why it wasn't parked inside, did the person living there have a guest over? The living room light was on, but the porchlight was switched off, a common marker at the times that they weren't entertaining unexpected guest.

There weren't many choices, and it was the only real sign of activity. Weena did not answer and she ground her teeth against the pain as she slid a step forward. Maybe they would have some first aid supplies she could borrow until something more permanent could be found. She would have to chance it.

Crossing the street quickly, she approached the door, warily watching for moving shadows through the window; it was still as the night around her.

She rang the doorbell, feeling the strength of the pills beginning to wane. Glancing to the right, she saw a darkened home and wondered if she should have tried to break in there instead. It was too late to reconsider; her knees were beginning to wobble and she could pass out any second.

The door opened a crack and she saw a curious eye peer out at her. "I don't know you. What do you want?"

"Help me," she moaned as she pitched forward, her hand barely stopping her fall. Another pair of hands grasped her shoulders and for the briefest of seconds she felt relieved. "No hospitals," she managed, then blacked out.

II

She opened her eyes and was momentarily unaware of where she was. Her head felt foggy and she knew immediately that there were drugs being fed into her. Abruptly, she struggled to a sitting position and scanned her surroundings. There were no drapes, no bed rails, and there was the smell of coffee, not death, on the air. Her sudden relief was short lived, as she felt the absence of the device she always wore around her left thigh.

"Weena, what's your location?" she asked desperately, praying that she wasn't out of range. If they were separated, she'd be stranded with very little chance of ever going home.

"Hey, you're awake," came a voice from the open doorway across from her. She was in a bedroom, immaculate in appearance, a Phantom of the Opera poster the only decoration adorning the walls. It looked like a room that had been prepared for visitors, but rarely saw any.

"One meter to your left," Weena replied, her heart thudding with every word.

She glanced at the night stand next to the bed and felt a flood of contentment at the sight of the hexagonal device awaiting her immediate attention. It had a titanium-mixed alloy that made it nearly indestructible and other than the retractable band that was made to attach to her leg, was completely devoid of any sign to its purpose.

"Ah yes, I was worried it was for diabetes or something, and wasn't going to take it off, but the doctor insisted," came the male voice as a man hovered in the doorway with two steaming cups of coffee. "He says it doesn't look like an Insulin pump, but he had no clue what else it could be. Your sugar level was a bit low, so I hope you like sugar in your coffee," he said as he walked into the room and set one down by the device she had been anxiously worried about. He was of average height, with short brown hair, clean shaven, and a pair of humble brown eyes. He wore a gray t-shirt with Trust No1 blazoned across his chest. He also had on a pair of black jeans and by the shape of his hairline, probably wore a hat regularly.

"Doctor?" she managed. Her throat was feeling rough and she began to wonder how long she'd been out. Her hand automatically slid to her side and she felt the taped bandage beneath a white t-shirt she had been put in. It itched and made her grimace, but otherwise, whatever she had been given was working to keep the pain at bay.

The younger man nodded, gesturing for her to take the coffee.

Her hand was already in route and the smell was making her mouth water with anticipation. "Thank you for not taking me to the hospital," she offered as she took a sip and felt a smile creep across her face. God, how she missed coffee. It was a rare thing to have, especially since it'd been a restricted substance for at least a century, and happened to be one of the perks of her job. Feeling it swarm its way down on her throat, her body reacted instantly and her mind slowly started to become more alert.

Her host grabbed a nearby chair and brought it near her, where it looked to have rested for some time recently. "How could I resist? A beautiful woman shows up on my doorstep needing my help, didn't think it best to ruin it by calling the cops."

"Oh, a man that loves to live dangerously," she commented with a smirk and got a chuckle in response. There was an IV hanging from a podium on her right and her eyes fixated on the fluids being pushed into her right arm.

"Don't worry, you've been in good hands. A buddy of mine is pre-med at Banner University Medical Center. He was more than happy to get free practice working on you, and as a favor to me, promised to keep it quiet," he explained as he sipped his coffee, then set it down on the night stand. "We could both get in a lot of trouble if it gets out. I've taken quite the risk, was it worth it?"

"Do you mean, am I a criminal? Or was that a half-assed attempt at a sexual overture?" she asked and couldn't help but laugh. There was humor in his eyes, and he blushed a bit, but his mouth was firm; he really was worried. "Nothing like that. Trust me, no one even knows I exist, much less will come looking. And yes, I get it, trust no one, but I have no reason to lie to you."

He sighed with relief and nodded his head. "That wasn't a gunshot wound. Aaron says he's never seen anything like it. Almost like an industrial burn, but not quite. He got the bleeding under control and stitched you up. He says without knowing the nature of the injury, he can't make any promises, but that with your stabilized vitals you should be okay."

Her mind was racing the entire time he was talking. She couldn't tell him how she got hurt, and a reasonable explanation wasn't forthcoming. She was out or practice talking to people. She had been on her own for so long, she couldn't help but feel awkward under his intense gaze.

She reached up and pushed back her long black hair, a finger sliding her bangs behind her ears as she turned her ice blue eyes in his direction and met his. "I can't tell you how it happened. You wouldn't believe me if I tried," she finally offered, unable to formulate anything to explain the plasma burn she had suffered.

He was wrong, it had been a gunshot, just by a weapon that he would hardly understand. She set down her coffee cup and reached for Weena, intent on reattaching her to her thigh. She was wearing a thin pair of sweatpants, and she saw the younger man blush when it occurred to her that he must have changed her clothing.

He coughed. "They were covered in blood, I burned them in case they were evidence of anything," he told her, eyes flickering away. "Except for your coat that is. Must be murder wearing that in the Arizona desert. It's about to get hotter than shit soon enough, you could bake an egg on a car hood come mid-day."

She couldn't help but grin. "Hopefully not on the hood of that VW out there."

Coughing from a quick fit of laughter, he waved her off. "Not mine. Ex-girlfriend left it when we split, hasn't come back for it yet. Personally, I hate the things. Make me claustrophobic."

"Well, since you've seen me naked now, can I at least get your name? I mean, you haven't even bought me dinner yet."

The young man's cheeks flushed with so much blood, it was astonishing he had enough to keep his heart pumping. "Blake," he told her with a sheepish grin. "You know, we can fix that. I can take you out to dinner when you're up to going out again. And you weren't totally naked, I never touched your underwear, I promise."

"So chivalrous!" she laughed while sliding her pants down, then went to work reattaching Weena to her accustomed place on her thigh. She could see her trench coat hanging on a rack behind the door and wondered if he had tried to go through her pockets. He wouldn't have found anything, only her hands could retrieve the items she had hidden within.

"I don't know how long I'll be here, Blake," she returned, saddened when she realized just how true that was. Weena had been damaged during the fight and judging by where she ended up, wasn't functioning correctly. She felt tense at the thought of what that meant, but she pushed it away the best she could. Best not to think about it right now. "I'm Jennifer, by the way."

"You look like a Jenny," he grinned, the look of harsh disappointment not quite gone, but close enough.

She grimaced as she laid back, trying to get comfortable. The meds were still making her feel drowsy. She felt the war between them and the caffeine rage throughout her clouded mind. She wanted to forget everything that had happened over the last couple of days. Let it all go and take some time to rest and relax, but she knew it wouldn't happen. She might have to leave at a moment's notice; wishing otherwise was futile.

Her stomach grumbled and Blake leaned forward, patting his knees with his left hand. "That's my cue. I'll go fix us something to eat."

Something about the way he moved stirred a memory in her, and she couldn't quite figure out why. It was true she couldn't quite think straight, but still, one of the reasons she had been chosen to begin with was her clear recollection of everything she ever saw or experienced. She watched him exit the bedroom and after a brief pause, when she was sure he was out of earshot, she spoke as quietly as she could, "Weena, what's Blake's last name?"

"Marsh," she responded, and everything clicked into place.

She was not here by accident.

"Tell me you didn't do this on purpose?" she whispered harshly. Weena allowed the following silence do all the answering she needed. "Shit."

III

"How long was I out?" she asked anxiously, the date and place quickened her pulse as her memories flooded her. She silently cursed; she should have paid more attention during orientation.

"Three days. It is now May 27th, 7:06 p.m.."

"Oh hell," she groaned with the dawning realization that time was once again on short supply. Which was ironic, when you came to think about it. "I need to get up," she said more to herself than Weena, trying to will herself off the bed. Her fingers worked at removing the IV, the sting barely noticeable as she pushed everything away with only one clear intent, getting out of this bed before it was too late.

"Not advisable," Weena responded. *"You will tear your stitches if you're not careful."*

She grunted as she ignored her companion's advice and pushed back the covers, freeing her legs. "Not like I have a choice."

"You can't stop it. You know that," the A.I. reminded her.

Blake had taken her in during extreme circumstances, helped to save her life, and she had looked into his eyes and seen the soul of the man within. "There's no way I'm going to let this happen. He saved my life, I owe him the same."

"Jennifer," Weena began, but paused as it became apparent that the warning was useless. She could almost discern a sigh as the A.I. continued. *"You have fifty-three minutes."*

Slowly, she got to her feet, feeling unsteady with the remnants of the drugs coursing through her system. She needed to be clear-headed or she would end up just as dead as the man she was intent on saving. It would break a major commandment, but did it really matter anymore? The world she knew was gone.

Reaching into one of the pockets on her trench coat, she withdrew a pill bottle and quickly downed two more pills. Almost immediately her senses were fully restored and she exhaled a sigh of relief. She saw her shoes at the end of the bed and quickly pulled them on. Then she was back up, shrugging into her trench coat and walking out the door at a quick pace. Her right hand reached in a pocket and withdrew her MP-32. She set it to Pulse and carried it low within the folds of her coat, as she stepped into the kitchen and came upon the man fixated on making them dinner.

The smell was welcoming and it would be a shame they would never get to eat it.

He noticed the movement and turned to her with a smile. "Hey, what are you doing out of bed? Trying to ditch me?"

"Blake, we don't have time. There are two men on their way here right now. They've been paid to kill you," she stated bluntly and she saw him grin. He thought she was joking. "I'm completely serious. Sean Thompson didn't like losing his grant, felt you bribed your way into it. He hired a couple of gangbangers to take you out, make it look like a robbery gone bad."

The smile was slipping and for the briefest moment she saw the correct response, fear.

"What are you talking about? Who are you?" he turned, the spatula falling to the floor forgotten. "How do you know Sean?"

She shook her head in frustration. "Quit thinking of him as your best friend and move. Get what you absolutely cannot survive without, keep it light, and get ready to leave. Now. We have thirty-five minutes and counting."

He was going to argue further but the look she gave shut him up. He didn't look like he totally believed her, but he wasn't going to take that chance either. She watched him dodge down the hall as she stepped forward, grasped the pan, and removed it from the burner. She switched off the stove and moved towards the fridge.

Milk.

She missed milk almost as much as she did coffee.

"Do you understand the choice you're making?" Weena inquired.

She did. The gravity of it hadn't really set in. She was twitching with adrenaline and the lingering narcotics she had been on, but she knew from the instant she got out of bed how it would end. She was going to have to take him with her. Once this was in motion, there was no other way. She couldn't take the chance at making things worse; not yet, at least.

Five minutes later he was out of breath, but had a small gym bag on his shoulders and a laptop in his other hand.

"Leave it," she commanded, gesturing towards the computer.

He shook his head. "Not a chance."

"He can't—."

"I'm telling you, you have to leave it," she stated, moving towards him.

He finally noticed that she was holding something in her right hand and his eyes widened at the threat veiled within her tone. "You don't understand. This is my life's work."

"Leave it and you get a longer life. Or keep it and I walk, and you are on your own," she warned, leaving no doubt that she'd do just that. She knew exactly what was on that laptop and there was no way she could allow him to take it with them.

She slid the gun into her coat and reached out with her hand, gripping his free hand within hers. Taking a step closer, she looked him directly in the eyes and tried to soften her firm features. It probably looked comical, she wasn't good at this part of the job. "Blake. Trust me. Leave it. I promise you, your work will continue. But if you want to be alive to do so, then you have to put that down on the table and come with me. Right now. We are running out of time."

He looked like he was beginning to reconsider his decision, but before he could act on it, the lights went out.

"Too late."

IV

Two men, two exits. She knew there was no safe route no matter which way they went.

Fight or flight?

She would usually choose to fight, but now she was responsible for another life and she doubted he had even been in a fistfight as a kid. He had soft hands and a kind face, neither useful at the moment. She needed to make a decision. They would anticipate someone coming to check the electrical box for a blown fuse, which was at the back of the house.

So best bet? The front.

She turned towards the living room when she happened to catch another door by the pantry. The garage. That would work. She snatched the laptop out of his hand and grabbed his arm, forcing him forward. He was about to say something but she glared at him, making him gulp in response. Fear was rampant in his eyes and she felt for him.

It wasn't every day someone came to kill you.

Snatching the keys from the rack by the door, she silently slid the door open and pushed him through. There was a small tinkle of glass from the direction of the bedroom she had been in and knew they would quickly be in the house.

Closing the door, she turned to Blake. "Don't make a sound. No matter what happens, just keep your head down and stay by my side."

"They're really here to kill me," he stammered, eyes wide.

"Keep quiet. Open the driver's door, put the key in the ignition, do not start it. Then get in the passenger seat," she instructed in a rushed torrent. She backed away from the door, pistol raised, ready to respond the instant that door opened.

The device on her leg began to vibrate. It was a warning. Her eyes widened as she realized what was about to happen. There was very little time.

She reached into her right pocket and withdrew a device that looked a lot like Weena, only smaller. She sprinted towards the car, got in the driver seat and clicked the door shut. Blake was watching anxiously as she slammed the device into his hand.

"Put it on, like a watch," she commanded. When he hesitated she shook her head angrily. "Do it or die, your choice."

The door to the garage opened and she saw the tip of a gun appear through the crack. They were coming.

Weena began to vibrate once more, only more strongly this time. She glanced at Blake, her heart rate pounding in her chest. He was busy looking at his wrist and his vibrating new accessory; he hadn't seen the assassin stepping into view.

The glass shattered, the front windshield spidered, and she felt something whip by her head.

The vibration increased and her vision doubled.

"What's happening?" came Blake's trembling voice.

She brought her pistol around, intent on firing on the psychopath in blue baggy clothing, when all of a sudden, time stopped. A bullet had been fired and it was streaking their way, but now it was hanging suspended in mid-air. Her body grew cold, her chest tightened, and her brain fluctuated with the amount of input thrusting into it.

Everything doubled and as the world around her faded, another started coming into being. It was terrain of some kind, no buildings evident. Their shift through the Slipstream happened quickly and her body flooded with the after-effects of a time jump.

They were in a desert, the landscape lit by a warm rising sun. The air was clean and hot. It was going to be a scorcher, his warning about a blistering afternoon coming true.

He looked at her in surprise, then his eyes widened, his pupils rolled, and he passed out.

"That figures," she muttered in resignation.

"Death Valley, February 3rd, 1865 7:01 a.m.," Weena informed her.

"Oh, this is going to suck," she responded, looking at the desolate landscape and not seeing shade for miles. What was she going to do now?

Available now

Charon's Blight: Day One